"AN INSIDE JOB?" REMO ASKED

Smith frowned and shook his head. "The surviving marshal was given a polygraph examination and PSE first thing. They swear he is clean. However, you know as well as I do, polygraphs are wrong at least twenty-five percent of the time. That is why they are inadmissible in most state courts. The psychological stress evaluator is a little better, but it is still more art than science."

"Then it's all just a freaking waste of time," Remo said.

"I agree," Smith said, "but as it happens, that part of the problem is not our concern."

"What is?"

"The shooter."

"He's in custody?" asked Remo.

"You could say," Smith said dryly. "He is in the morgue."

Other titles in this series:

Created by
WARREN MURPHY
and RICHARD SAPIR

THE

Destroyer™

NEVER SAY DIE

A GOLD EAGLE BOOK FROM
WORLDWIDE®

TORONTO • NEW YORK • LONDON
AMSTERDAM • PARIS • SYDNEY • HAMBURG
STOCKHOLM • ATHENS • TOKYO • MILAN
MADRID • WARSAW • BUDAPEST • AUCKLAND

First edition February 1998
ISBN 0-373-63225-8

Special thanks and acknowledgment to
Mike Newton for his contribution to this work.

NEVER SAY DIE

For Mike Beckery, and for the
Glorious House of Sinanju.

1

"If I'da known about this in advance, I woulda kept my mouth shut," said the bookkeeper.

Vinnie Donatello wasn't buying it. "That's total bullshit, Ira. Balducci's people were about to let you take the fall for tax fraud, and you got pissed off. You knew exactly what would happen if you talked."

"I didn't know nothing about hiding out in the fuckin' house where Honest Abe was born," said Ira Goldblum, staring at the log walls with a pained expression on his doughy face.

Greg Brady laughed at that one, lowering himself into a chair directly opposite the bookkeeper. "Get over it," he said. "You know how long you'd last back in Detroit."

"We coulda gone down to Miami," Goldblum whined. "They got the ponies running now, at Hialeah. We could make a few bucks on the side. I got a system."

"And Balducci's people could make you," Blair Rooney said, returning from the kitchen with a sandwich on a paper plate. "They got a system, too."

"You guys." The witness scowled and shook his head. "I'm goin' nuts up here."

"Just two more weeks," Marsh Lockwood told him, staring out the window at the tree line, twenty yards away. "You lose your mind, we'll fly a shrink in from Milwaukee."

"Now you're talkin'," Goldblum said. "Nice little blond shrink, maybe. Watcha think?"

"I think you're dreaming, Ira."

"That's the problem, pal. I need a dream girl, help me get to sleep at night. This back-to-nature shit is killing me."

The safehouse was a one-time hunting lodge, upstate Wisconsin, east of Long Lake, in the Nicolet National Forest. It stood at the dead end of an unpaved logging track, five miles back from the nearest two-lane highway, in a clearing cut by hand from tamarack, dogwood, white oak, red maple, elm and sassafras. The single-story layout featured three bedrooms, a spacious kitchen, living room and bathroom, with detached two-car garage out back. The place was new to Lockwood and his team, but they had run the drill in other hideouts.

It would do.

They made an odd team, at a glance. Blair Rooney was a slender, red-haired Irishman. Greg Brady was a giant carved from ebony at six foot eight, the blackest great-great-grandson of the Congo you could ever want to meet. Vince Donatello was a stocky, olive-skinned Italian, constantly on edge about his weight. Marsh Lockwood was the senior member of their team, with sixteen years in service as a U.S. marshal. He was native white-bread all the way. Their mark had taken one look at the four of them and labeled them the Rainbow Coalition, after Jesse Jackson's late, lamented pressure group.

The mark was Ira Goldblum, forty-something, balding with a body like a roly-poly punching bag. Armani suits helped cover some of it, but Goldblum was nobody's dream boat. Ira had been the chief accountant for Local 137 of the National Waste Handlers' Union, in Detroit. The union represented garbagemen, and it was run by one Leonardo James Balducci, second-generation Mafia, with prior convictions that included statutory rape, assault with deadly weapons and attempted murder. Those had all been youthful indiscretions, though, and Leo B. had skated through the past two decades of his life without so much as an indictment or a traffic ticket.

Until now.

Their pigeon had been cooking Leo's books for eight years when the roof fell in. Local 137 was serving as a laundry for Balducci's secret income, which included weekly takes from prostitution, drugs, extortion, usury and an expanding line of child pornography he brokered out of Scandinavia. When one of Goldblum's flunkies was arrested with a teenage hooker of the male persuasion, he began to sing like Whitney Houston, spilling everything he knew about the union operation, plus a few things he dreamed up, for good measure. Enough of it proved true to put the squeeze on Ira, and it soon became apparent that Balducci was content to let his chubby Jewish accountant take the fall.

Which brought them to the former hunting lodge, where Ira would be chilling out until a federal grand jury opened hearings in Detroit in two weeks' time. He had already given statements running upward of two hundred pages, with supporting documents and copies of the "special" books he kept for Leo B. but justice runs on certain tracks and has to stop at every station on the route, or else it gets derailed. Once the grand jury handed down a list of federal indictments—which was guaranteed—then Leo B.'s attorneys would begin constructing paper road-blocks, putting off the trial as long as possible, while Leo's shooters beat the bushes for a certain book-keeper and tried to shut him up for good.

It could take months, or even years, Marsh Lockwood realized, and while the lodge wasn't intended as a long-term hideout, it would serve well enough while Ira waited for his first appearance on the witness stand.

But Goldblum had a point: the place was boring. They had television, with a VCR hooked up, but no one on the team had thought of bringing any videocassettes along. Lockwood started working on a mental list of titles, thinking he could phone it to Milwaukee and have a runner from the service bring some tapes out. And some deli food, to keep their pigeon quiet for a while.

"I'm going to the can," he said to no one in particular.

"Hey, thanks for sharing," Ira cracked. "At least the joint's got indoor plumbing, huh?"

"All the conveniences of home," Lockwood replied. He turned from the window, leaving Goldblum to amuse the others with his wit.

"Hope everything comes out all right," the pigeon told him, chuckling to himself. "Comes out all right! Ya get it?"

"That's one thing about you, Ira," Brady told him. "You're a card."

"You, too, big guy." The bookkeeper was grinning ear to ear. "I figure you must be the ace of spades."

THE CLEANER WORKED his way in from the north, no trail to guide him, but he had his compass and a hand-drawn map. He didn't know who drew the map, and didn't care, as long as it was accurate in all particulars.

The muddy access road off Highway 55 had been exactly where the map said it should be. Six miles due east, and he had left the stolen Chevy Blazer sitting in a turnout, with a set of new plates—also stolen—to confuse the police if any happened by.

The cleaner traveled light. He had a two-mile hike in front of him and was dressed for it, in denim jeans and jacket, with a black T-shirt beneath, and Doc Marten boots. No backpack, but he had a plastic Kroger shopping bag. Inside the bag, a matching set of Colt 191 A-1 semiautomatic pistols, each with an extended magazine accommodating twenty rounds. Four extra mags, in case the job took more than he expected from a simple hit.

Besides the rat, he was expecting several Feds. They wouldn't send an army to protect a piece of shit like Ira Goldblum, but they wouldn't leave him open, either, knowing that the Family was out for blood. Three agents minimum, he guessed, but no more than six. It was a high estimate, and he had enough hardware on hand to waste them fourteen times apiece.

The afternoon was cool, and that was fine. He didn't much like sweating, especially when the perspiration dribbled in his eyes and spoiled his aim. The ideal temperature for killing someone in the great outdoors was anywhere from sixty-five to seventy degrees. Above that, he would rather visit them at home and work where there was air-conditioning.

The safehouse wasn't bad, all things considered. It could easily have been some corporate jerk-off's weekend hideaway, someplace to bring the girl-friend while his wife thought he was out of town on business. Lay a little pipe and go home with the batteries recharged. Instead, the government had used taxpayers' money to acquire the property and use it as a roost for stool pigeons.

He circled once around the safehouse, staying well back in the trees and watching out for any movement of the curtains that would indicate a watch on the perimeter. Their vehicles must be in the garage, he thought. A passerby might think the place was vacant, perfect for a little B&E, unless guided to the spot by someone in the know.

The lodge had one door, in the front, with windows on three sides. Around in back, the blind side, storm doors opened on a cellar that would almost certainly grant access to the ground floor via stairs or a ladder. It was worth a try, and for sure a damn sight better than a stroll up to the porch. If he was forced to go in through the door or windows, he would have to wait for nightfall, six or seven hours yet.

He knelt behind a massive oak and took the pistols from the shopping bag, cocked each in turn, made sure they both had live rounds in the firing chamber. Then he tucked the extra magazines inside his waistband, the metal cool against his flesh. He left the bag where it was, to rot or blow away.

From the garage, he had to cross roughly twenty yards of open ground. No facing windows, but you could never tell when someone would come out to check the grounds, fetch something from the cars. He kept both pistols pointed at the lodge until he reached the storm doors, knelt before them. Only then did he reluctantly put down his weapons, setting one on either side of him, and take the lock picks from a pocket of his jeans.

The padlock was a good one, but he knew his business. Forty seconds saw it open, and he set it on the ground beside one of the .45s. Took time to check the hinges on the storm doors, ensure they wouldn't scream out in the quiet of the woods and give his act away. A flight of wooden steps led downward, into darkness, and he took the pistols with him, one tucked in his belt as he reached back to close the hatch.

It was pitch dark in the cellar, and he took a moment while his vision adjusted. Once he got used to it, thin shafts of light were visible between the storm doors, coming through the floor above his head in spots where there was no rug over wooden planking. He could see enough to find a second set of stairs, directly opposite, and navigate around some boxes stacked up in the middle of the floor.

The trapdoor opened in a narrow closet, with canned goods on the shelves behind him. Someone's notion of a nifty little secret, but they hadn't thought to bolt the latch shut the last time someone used it.

Once he had the trapdoor shut, the cleaner stood and listened to the house. A muffled sound of voices came from somewhere to his left, in the direction of what he supposed was the living room. He couldn't say how many voices—two or three, at least—but he wasn't intimidated by the numbers.

Feds were nothing special. When you shot them, they fell down like anybody else.

He held one pistol ready as he found the inner doorknob, cracked the door an inch or so and peered out through the slit. No one to challenge him that he could see. The next few seconds would be critical, because he was on the move, he had no fear of coming off as second best.

The cleaner stepped out of his closet, guns in hand, ready to crash the party.

One surprise for Ira Goldblum and his escorts, coming up.

THE BATHROOM FURNISHINGS were sparse but adequate. Someone had left a well-thumbed *Playboy* magazine behind, and Lockwood started going through it, killing time with Miss July. He was in no great hurry to rejoin the others, listen to another round of Ira's bullshit whining. Goldblum had been well versed in the risks and the requirements of the Federal Witness Program when he started talking to the FBI, and he could bitch from now till Doomsday without changing anything. As long as the Balduccis had an open contract on his head—in other words, as long as Goldblum lived—he would be running for his life, employing false identities and looking twice at every new acquaintance.

Either that or he would wind up in a sanitary landfill somewhere, maybe join the missing-persons list with Jimmy Hoffa and the rest of gangland's greatest hits.

In human terms, Marsh Lockwood didn't care what happened to the Mob accountant, once he did his part to ring the curtain down on Leo B. Conviction on a shopping list of RICO charges would eliminate Balducci as a force to reckon with inside the Mob, strike one more target off the federal hit list.

When Leo B. was safely locked away, then Ira Goldblum could be shuffled off to Phoenix, San Francisco, Newark—anywhere the Feds decided he would stand at least an even chance of living out his days. What happened after that was largely up to Ira—and considering his mouth, Lockwood thought he would be lucky to survive six months without a full-time bodyguard.

Tough luck.

The Playmate of the Month was honey blond and well endowed, fond of skiing, skydiving and "water sports." Her hot-tub layout made Lockwood feel a bit on the athletic side himself.

He had the gatefold open on his knees, examining a choice tattoo, when thunder rocked the lodge. The sound of small-arms fire vaulted Lockwood off the toilet, spilling Miss July at his feet. She held her enigmatic smile as he yanked up his trousers, grappled with the belt one-handed, reaching for his Smith & Wesson automatic on the run.

Two hours in the fucking safehouse, and it had

already blown up in his face. The best that he could do was try and save it now.

And maybe, in the process, save himself.

THE CLEANER WENT IN shooting, his eyes skimming over the four men spread around the living room, three with weapons showing. On his right was a massive black, first gaping at the unexpected new arrival, then exploding from his chair. The cleaner shot him in the face, one hollowpoint enough to blow his head apart as if it were a melon stuffed with fireworks.

That left three alive, but only two who counted at the moment. Over on his left, a skinny redhead and a guinea had been setting up a card game by the window, but they had to react in a hurry, reaching for their guns and cursing as the cleaner swung around to bring them under fire.

He gave them two rounds each. The redhead vaulted over backward, crimson spouting from his chest. His shoulders slammed against the wall and left a dark smear as he slithered to the floor.

His partner had some moves, despite his chunky build. Some kind of fast-draw artist with his stainless-steel Smith & Wesson, pulling from a high-ride pancake holster on his hip and squeezing off two rounds in rapid fire.

The cleaner heard them whisper past his face and smiled as he returned fire, nailing down the guinea with a one-two in the bull's-eye, opening his chest.

That left the rat.

He made a sorry spectacle, crouched down behind the sofa, crying and pleading for his life. What wasted effort. Any real man would have shrugged it off or made a last-ditch rush to grab the cleaner's gun, but this one was a pussy.

"Jesus Christ, I didn't wanna do this!" he blubbered. "They made me, don't you see that? I can take it all back, change my statement—anything!"

"Too late," the cleaner told him, stepping close enough to give the pussy one more chance. An easy grab from where he stood, one of his pistols almost touching Goldblum's forehead.

"Please!"

He didn't have to aim at that range, and he shot the whining bastard twice, to shut him up. Once more to grow on, as his body tumbled over backward, just because the cleaner hated cowards.

Done.

It had been all of sixty seconds since he stepped out of the closet, and he had twelve thousand dollars in the bag. How much was that per second?

Not too shabby.

He was turning toward the front door when a furtive scuffling sound behind him made him swivel, the twin Colts rising to confront another threat.

MARSH LOCKWOOD SMELLED the blood and cordite as he burst into the living room. He saw the stranger, guns in hand. He swung around to face Lockwood, firing as he came, and the reports of two big .45s were deafening.

Lockwood hit the floor, returning fire, the Smith & Wesson autoloader bucking in his hand. He had twelve rounds, couldn't afford to waste a single one of them if he was going to survive.

His first shot hit the stranger's thigh, an inch or so above his right knee, rocking him. The second was a miss, lost somewhere between the target's legs, but number three ripped through his groin and forced a gasp of startled pain. The bastard kept on firing, though, unloading with the .45s like there was no tomorrow.

And there wouldn't be, Lockwood realized, for one or both of them.

His fourth and fifth rounds qualified as belly shots. The hit man staggered, his bad leg folding under him. The .45s were way off target as he went down, both blasting at the vaulted ceiling. Lockwood squeezed off three more shots and saw two of them hit, one in the chest, one underneath the chin, before his adversary sprawled out on the floor near Ira Goldblum's headless corpse.

Lockwood kept the fallen shooter covered as he scrambled to his feet. The guy was dead, but Lockwood took time to disarm him, scooping up each .45 in turn and pitching it across the room.

That done, he made the rounds, confirming what he knew already from the silence of the charnel house. His friends were dead, clean hits in every instance, and Ira Goldblum's case had clearly been awarded to a higher jurisdiction than the federal courts.

Clean sweep. The bastards got it all, and only lost a shooter in the process.

Lockwood searched the dead man's body, turning out his pockets, coming up with lock picks and some lint. The real pros didn't carry ID on a hit, and this guy clearly knew his stuff, right up until the last.

"You should have checked the bathroom, asshole," Lockwood told the corpse.

It was the same mistake they made with Dutch Schultz at the Palace Chop House, back in '35. The more things changed, the more they stayed the same.

Next step was to get somebody on the horn, report this mess and pass it on to other hands. Two problems there: the lodge wasn't equipped with telephones, and while they had three walkie-talkies, to be used for walking circuits of the grounds, the radios wouldn't reach back to Long Lake, much less to the federal building in Milwaukee.

He swore.

It meant that he would have to drive the eleven miles back into town and use a public telephone to call the cavalry. No choice, but it was still embarrassing. He hated leaving three dead agents in the slaughterhouse while he went off to spread the word of abject failure, but he saw no other way to go.

Besides, his friends weren't going anywhere.

They would be safe enough while he was gone,

and he would scout the property before he left, make sure the shooter was alone.

He hoped the hit man hadn't touched their cars. Eleven miles was one thing driving, but a hike that long would take him three, four hours, easily.

The cars would be all right, Lockwood finally decided. This guy hadn't planned on anybody slipping past him, getting out alive and he'd seen no need for crippling their transportation.

Before he left the lodge, Marsh went around and picked up all the guns—five in addition to his own—and put them in a garbage bag he found beneath the kitchen sink. With his luck, he thought, some psycho hermit will come snooping while he was gone and grab the pieces, start some kind of rampage using service-issue weapons.

He would take the pistols with him, just in case.

It was a small precaution, far too little and too late, but Lockwood's options at the moment were distinctly limited.

They would want scapegoats back in Washington, and Lockwood was the sole survivor of a first-rate, triple-A snafu. Not only that, but he had been in charge, responsible for the security arrangements once the safehouse was selected and approved by someone higher up.

My ass is grass, he thought, despondent as he walked toward the garage.

And he could hear the mowers revving up already, getting closer all the time.

2

His name was Remo, and he was just killing time. The small city park in Compton, southeast of L.A., wasn't Sarajevo or Beirut, of course, but it almost could have passed. Even though he was minding his own business, he stood a decent chance of meeting some demented moron who would challenge him, attempt to take his wallet, maybe stick a knife between his ribs.

Some asshole who would make his day.

He wasn't really hunting. Not in the normal sense. That is to say, he never had a target picked out in advance when he went out to prowl. He did not follow scent or tracks to find his prey, but rather let the animals find him. They always seemed to. Even on nights like this one when he was, by and large, minding his own business.

So even though he had not come looking for a fight—at least not consciously—he resigned himself to the inevitable.

There could be no mistake when one or more of them approached him with the swagger he had learned to pick out from a distance, approaching

with scowls or mocking smiles that were supposed
to make the human predators look Bad. He almost
had to laugh, sometimes, as they played out the cut-
rate melodramas of their lives.

He didn't have a world of time tonight, but if
someone got in his way there would be enough. It
was Saturday, a party night, and every creep in the
greater Los Angeles area would be looking for an
easy score. Not all of them would try this park, of
course, but that was cool.

If push came to shove, he only needed one.

If he was riled to action, a group was better, but
he wouldn't quibble. Remo took what he could get
in these impromptu situations, and he never looked
a gift horse in the mouth.

Well, almost never.

In another life, before he "died" the first time,
he had been a cop in Newark. That was an entire
continent away, yet didn't seem too far removed
from the urban blight of Compton. Newark was another urban combat zone these days, but Remo seldom visited his old home town. His life had
changed, and there was nothing for him there.

It was already dark at 7:20, and his meeting
wasn't scheduled until eight o'clock. It was a short
drive up to Los Angeles and the hotel where Dr.
Harold W. Smith would doubtless occupy the cheap-
est room available. The mission must be something,
if it brought him clear across the country from his
Folcroft Sanitarium in Rye, New York, but Remo

didn't speculate. There was no profit in imagining, without the proper tools to make a logical deduction.

Remo entered the small park above the children's playground, the Alondra Boulevard entrance, moving southward, keeping to the smaller paths and off the drives where bikes and cars kept predators at bay. You didn't hunt for weasels in a shopping mall, and Remo knew his potential quarry would be hiding from the lights whenever possible, in search of joggers, helpless drunks or tourists crazy enough to venture down from the safer parts of L.A.

Stay out of any Compton park at night.

No signs had been posted, of course. Given the city's reputation the past three decades, no warning signs were necessary. Everybody was supposed to know that Compton was dangerous. The message came across on local news, Charles Bronson–type movies on the late show, romance novels, even stand-up comedy routines. The risks of going out at night in Los Angeles—much less in Compton— were legendary. They were also frequently exaggerated, Remo knew, but only to a point. It was a rare night when at least one rape or serious assault was not reported from the area, and homicides were far too common.

For the past two decades, the authorities had "closed" this particular park from midnight till sunrise, a futile effort at controlling the small patch of wooded acreage featuring a dozen public entrances, labyrinths of winding footpaths and thousands of places to hide. Policing the park had been a great success…if you considered Compton as a whole to be a safe and law-abiding place.

Which meant it was ideal for Remo's purpose.

He wasn't an urban vigilante, didn't even like the *Death Wish* movies after they went overboard and cast Charlie Bronson as a one-man army, toting .30-caliber machine guns through the ghetto unopposed and mowing down a hundred punk-rock psychos at a time. The violence didn't bother Remo, but he shied away from fairy tales that lost touch with reality.

If Bronson's character had been a Master of Sinanju, perhaps…

The very notion made him smile as he approached the center of the park. It was easy to get lost in here by daylight, much less after dark, but Remo had a keen sense of direction. He could chart a course by starlight, if it came to that, but there was no need to play Daniel Boone this evening. Alondra lay due east of the park's center, just an easy stroll. He still had half an hour left to kill.

His intentions had changed since coming in here. Now he *wanted* to be attacked. The desire increased as the time elapsed. There was an urgency now that had not been there before.

No luck so far in his attempt to make himself look easy. Two panhandlers had approached him near a rotted bench, but aside from cursing Remo when he failed to ante up, they let him be. It would require a more aggressive goon to offer him the workout he was suddenly craving. If he didn't find a likely subject soon...

The sudden, high-pitched scream was music to his ears. He smiled and homed in on the sound, a shadow merging with the darker shades of night.

"SOMEBODY COMIN'," Zero said, his pimply features broken by a crooked smile.

"Y'alls be ready," Monster told his crew. The others mumbled back at him, a silly giggle out of Squealer, showing they were set.

The past four years he had been Baby Monster, but the world turns sometimes and his luck had changed two months ago on Gage Avenue with a drive-by shooting in Florence that took out Monster Cody and a couple of his homies, thereby elevating Baby Monster to the status of a full-fledged, grown-up gangsta.

He was all of seventeen, and he was Bad. Eight felony arrests behind him, and the Man had never made one of them stick. No reason to believe he ever would.

Once a week, on average, Monster and his homies rode the bus from Florence into Compton, piled out in the middle of town, grabbed a bite to eat somewhere and then walked over to the park. That would be after dark, of course, when all the cops had gone home for the day, a little time for fun and games.

They used to call it "wilding," back when he was

still Baby Monster, till the press picked up the term and started using it like they knew shit about life on the streets. These days the homies called it "creeping," and Monster liked it better that way. Had a better ring to it, more sinister, like he was pulling off some kind of slick guerrilla raid against the Man.

They didn't hassle cops, of course. Not much. There was no profit in a game like that, and the risk of getting wasted for your trouble was extreme. The very least, some pig would go upside your head and drop you in the ER with your wrist cuffed to a bed rail—that's if he was feeling sociable. More likely he would come out shooting, since no grand jury and no one in the D.A.'s office would be too upset about another teenage gangsta going down. It was like open season nowadays, even in the hood. Old people packing heat and scribbling on petitions like they figured it would do some good, clean up the streets.

Dream on.

"Looks like a bitch," said Zero, putting on that crazy smile he always wore when he thought he was getting some.

With a man, they could have worked him over, stole his cash and plastic, maybe cut him up if he got lippy or resisted. With a bitch, though, you were talking entertainment of the finest kind.

A murmur rose from the homies, who were looking forward to a little action, and he pinned them with a glare. "Be cool," said Monster, glowering.

"Jus' do your part and don't be trippin', unnerstan'?"

They nodded like a bunch of little monkeys, all except for Squealer, who was giggling like a bitch himself. The boy had problems, absolutely, but he still held up his end when they were banging, whether it was on a drive-by or a straight-up rumble in the street.

They heard the jogger now, her sneakers slapping on the pavement. *Tip-tap, tip-tap, tip-tap.* Getting closer all the time. A few more seconds, Monster told himself, and she would have herself a sweet surprise.

"Suppose she be a pig?" asked Jumbo, out of nowhere.

"Hush yo' face, goddammit!"

It was something to consider, though. The pigs were not above impersonating joggers, lovers, old folks—anything at all, in fact, to try to sweep up riffraff in the park. They called it "stinging," and they liked to brag about it in the papers, come the morning after. Only if they pulled it off, though. When they blew it, they would keep it to themselves.

Most of the crew had been arrested—all but Fly, who had some kind of lucky streak in progress, going on sixteen years old and never busted. Two or three of them had gone away on charges that would mean a lot more to adults, but none were scared of going back. It was a part of living in the city with a gangsta rep and taking care of business every day. The juvey courts were overcrowded, predisposed to leniency, and you could almost always cut a deal—agree to bullshit therapy, community work, just to skate and get back to the hood.

But Monster didn't want to think about the Man right now. His mind was on the bitch and bumping uglies.

It was party time.

They had it set up so the bitch would pass them by, proceed a few yards down the path, before a whistle brought Godzilla out to intercept her. Probably she would try to turn and split, at which time she would find the path blocked off by Monster and his homies, closing in.

The one time it had failed, this Puerto Rican broad had come out with a .38 and started busting caps before they ever laid a hand on her. She got away, and Monster knew it was a miracle that no one stopped a slug.

You had to watch those fiery-tempered Latin types.

But this bitch was an Anglo, plain and simple, blond hair flying out behind her in a ponytail. She wore designer sweats, cut special so they wouldn't hide the goodies altogether when she went out jogging, just in case she might bump into Mr. Right.

Tonight she had a date with Mr. Wrong, times seven, but she didn't know it yet. Her own damn fault, if she had no more sense than running in

Compton after nightfall. Probably some college type whose do-gooder liberal tendencies refused to let her see the danger of the area.

Monster put two fingers in his mouth and whistled in the darkness, saw Godzilla jump out in the middle of the path and spread his arms like he was trying for a spot on big-time wrestling. He was six foot one, 220 pounds of malice on the hoof, and the very sight of him was enough to stop the bitch cold in her tracks and force a little squeak out of her throat.

"Le's go!"

They piled out of the bushes, twenty feet behind her, Monster in the lead, and formed a skirmish line across the path. To dodge them now, the bitch would have to go off-road, and that was bound to slow her down so much she wouldn't have a snowball's chance. Instead of running, though, she stood there panting, looking scared, her titties jiggling up and down with every breath.

"What do you want?" she asked, her voice all quavery.

Dumb bitch.

"We's gonna have a party, mama," Monster said, "an' you's the en'ertainment."

In a flash, she saw her future, understood that there was no use pleading with the likes of Monster and his homies. When she broke and ran, the thugs saw it coming, telegraphed beforehand by a nervous flicker of her eyes. Squealer got there first, a flying tackle from behind that sent her sprawling.

They mobbed the bitch, a rushing dog pile, pinning down her arms and legs before she had a chance to wriggle free of Squealer's grip. They had to get her off the path and well away, back in the trees, before they could have any fun, find out what she was made of.

"Move it!" Monster snapped.

And they were moving it, all seven hanging on, when she gave out a single piercing scream.

THE JOGGER CALLED herself Latoya. It was not her given name, of course—she wasn't black or even world-famous yet and not even distantly related to a certain famous family—but it was stylish, like a stage name ought to be.

She was a would-be actress who had run the gamut of employment since she came to L.A., all the way from topless clubs to serving veggie burgers in a joint in North Hollywood. A little modeling from time to time, and silent walk-ons in a couple of commercials that were cut before they aired. She had a twenty-three-year-old's inimitable faith in what tomorrow might bring. Her break was just around the corner, waiting for her—maybe in the two-line part she'd landed in a low-budget indie black comedy, with the rehearsal starting late next week.

A movie gig meant she had to stay in shape, in case there was somebody who saw it and liked her face and her personality. And with the waitress job from eight to five, no extra cash on hand for health clubs or aerobics classes, staying fit meant running after dark.

She knew about the park, but the streets were hardly any safer in Latoya's neighborhood these days, and she was still too young to jump at shadows, letting fear dictate the way she lived. The triple locks on her apartment door were one thing, but she would be damned if she was going to be driven off the streets by animals who ought to be in jail. Besides, no one was really safe these days—the President had bullets flying through his windows, airplanes crashing on the White House lawn—and there were some risks still worth taking for a sense of freedom in the world.

Latoya knew she had a problem when she heard the whistle, though. It wasn't like when the construction workers tried to get a rise out of her on the way to work. This was a signal, and she didn't have to guess about its meaning when the human hulk jumped out to block her path.

Her first instinct was to cut and run. The walking hulk was big enough to smother her, but she was betting he couldn't run that fast. If she could get a fair head start, Latoya reasoned, she could leave him in the dust.

About that whistle, though. The sound came from behind her, dammit, and she was expecting trouble even as she turned to run. Another would-be rapist, blocking her escape, but she would have to risk it.

What she got, instead, was six. That made it seven, with the hulk, and she could feel her stomach twist into a painful knot.

"What do you want?" The tremor in her voice embarrassed her to tears.

"We's gonna have a party, mama," one of them replied, "an' you's the en'ertainment."

That was all she had to hear. A swift glance toward the shadows on her right, and she took off, put everything she had into the sprint without a clear idea of where she meant to go or how she would get there.

Latoya made it halfway to the trees before one of them tackled her and brought her down. She skinned her palms on asphalt, had the wind knocked out of her, but she wasn't about to take it lying down. The little pricks would have to kill her first, and while she guessed they wouldn't mind, Latoya didn't plan to make it easy for them, either.

Kicking back, she missed her captor's genitals and connected with his thigh. The young man cursed her, wheezing, and his fist went home between her shoulder blades.

The others mobbed her then, a rush that flattened her against the pavement, pinned her arms and legs at painful, awkward angles. At least they couldn't rape her this way, lying in the middle of the path, facedown, with seven bodies piled on top of her.

Small favors.

"Move it!" someone snapped, and in another

heartbeat they were climbing off of her, hands clutching at Latoya's arms and legs, her waist, her breasts. They lifted her, propelled her toward the darkness as if they were off to storm a castle and her body had been chosen as a ram to smash the gates.

She saw one chance and took it, sucking in the cool night air and putting everything she had into the scream.

"Shut up, bitch!"

Someone clapped a hand across her mouth. She bit it, and a fist glanced off her skull, came back to strike a second time.

"No noise," a harsh voice cautioned, almost in her ear. "You yell again, I cut yer tits off, hear me?"

They were cloaked in darkness now. Latoya felt herself flipped over in midair, dropped on her back, with grass beneath her. Hands were clawing at her sweats, undressing her. She fought as best she could, with fists and feet, but there was always someone pinning down her limbs, while others cut and tore her clothes.

She felt her bra go, and her panties, and she struggled as a pair of wet mouths found her nipples. Clumsy fingers tried to worm their way inside her, hurting. Someone kissed her, and she bit down on his lower lip, hung on when he began to squeal and punch her, tasting blood, uncertain whether it was his or hers or both together.

AIDS, she thought, and then dismissed the fear. They were bound to kill her, anyway. She had seen faces. They couldn't afford to let her live.

Hands locked around her ankles, and her legs were wrenched apart.

Then one of the punks was kneeling in between her legs and fumbling with his belt, the pants so baggy that he seemed to have some difficulty with the snap and zipper.

She was winding up to scream once more, when a strange voice issued from the darkness, somewhere to her left, and froze her captors where they stood or knelt.

"Is this a private party," asked the stranger, sounding casual, "or can anybody play?"

JUST IN TIME, thought Remo as he stepped into the clearing, counting heads. Aloud, he said, "Is this a private party, or can anybody play?"

Two minutes, maximum, since he had heard the scream and homed in on the sound. A glimpse of pale flesh told him that the punks weren't wasting any time, but they were still on the preliminaries, maybe working up their nerve or simply savoring the moment for themselves.

The last thing they expected was an uninvited audience.

The would-be rapists scrambled to their feet when Remo spoke, except for one who hung back, kneeling by the lady's head and pinning down her arms.

That made it six-on-one to start, but Remo wasn't bothered. He surveyed the teenagers, two or three of them with switchblade knives in hand. No guns among them, which at least might help their chosen victim, with no threat of ricochet.

"You be smart," the leader of the rat pack told him, "you gwan run along now."

Remo put on his most engaging smile. "Let's try again," he said. "Does anybody here speak English?"

"Man, you fuck wid us, we be gwan fuck y'alls up, know what ahm sayin'?"

"Let me guess," said Remo. "You're a UN delegation from a new, emerging Third World nation, and you're looking for the embassy?"

"Yo, muddafuck, ah don't be playin' wid yo' ass. How's 'bout me an' da homies get to slice an' dice, dig it?"

Two more strides, and Remo said, "If you'll hang on a minute, I can send for an interpreter."

"Y'alls hang on dis, smart muddafuck!"

The leader rushed him, leading with a wicked-looking knife, two others circling left and right to cut off his expected flight. Remo stood his ground and let the pointman sacrifice himself. A sidestep to avoid the blade, and when his hand whipped up to crush the young man's face, it moved too swiftly for the eye to follow. Out and back again, a flat slap that connected with a solid crunch and threw the boy back out cold, and out of circulation for a long time.

The flankers came at Remo then, from the sides. He hesitated for a crucial instant, then stepped backward, watched them both slam on the brakes to keep from meeting like a couple of defensive linemen on the football field. That was enough for Remo, giving him the chance to drop both of them together at his feet for a truly prolonged break, like an extended convalescence if they got lucky.

That left four, and the guy detailed to hold the woman was already scrambling to his feet, the job forgotten as he fished around inside his pocket for a folding knife. The naked woman could have bolted but she made no attempt to rise. It could have been the shock, some kind of injury, or maybe she simply wanted to see how it turned out. Whatever, Remo had no time to chat with her just now.

The four survivors had begun to circle him, as if he were the maypole in a children's rite of spring. Three of them brandished knives or razors now, while number four had donned brass knuckles, trusting in his biceps and the moves he had picked up through brawling on the street.

"Next up," said Remo. "I don't have all night."

He heard the punk behind him gliding forward, trying to be subtle with the move, but making noise enough to wake the dead. A sharp blade whispered through the night, and Remo turned to meet it, gripped the young man's wrist and twisted, using the laws of physics as the Masters of Sinanju had for centuries on end. Momentum, torque, resistance, pressure.

There was a wrenching sound, and someone started screaming. But the teenage gangster lapsed into mindless silence. Remo dodged and closed the gap between himself and yet another adversary, using a floating strike to drive stunning blows to the heart and lungs.

Five down, and two remaining.

Neither one of the survivors was really up for fighting anymore, but they had stayed too long to have a choice. They were lucky because Remo suspected they could be patched up, and he didn't know if they deserved it. Experience told Remo that predators usually don't learn from the mistakes of others. He wasn't being careful, or pulling his punches, but something inside knew that for whatever reason, he was giving them a very narrow margin for survival.

The punks were backing off a little, toward the trees, and Remo followed. On his right, one of them tried to reach the woman, maybe use her as a hostage, but a straight-arm shot to the chest collapsed his lung and left him gasping on the grass, like a stranded trout.

He wasn't going anywhere, and Remo went for number seven, smiling at him as he closed the gap between them.

"Man, who is you?"

"Death," he told the punk. "It's your turn."

"Y'alls leave me alone!"

"Too late."

Too easy. Remo reached out to take the young man's knife away and pin his hand to the tree behind him.

All done.

The woman's clothes were a mess. Remo slipped a jacket off one of the punks and gave it to her, turned his back to offer her a modicum of privacy while she slipped into it. Her voice had come back, somewhere in the middle of the massacre, though it was strained from screaming, taut with fear.

"Who are you?"

"Just a Good Samaritan."

"I mean... how did... are they...?"

"You need some help," he said. "Let's walk back to the street and find a cop, okay?"

"Yes, please."

They walked in silence toward Alondra Boulevard. A squad car was idling just across the street. The lady turned to ask her savior something, and she found herself alone.

IT WAS NOT THAT COOL OUT so as Remo made his way south on Sunset Boulevard, no one paused to give the stranger dressed in a thin black T-shirt and chinos a second glance.

He was two minutes early, Remo saw as he stepped into the hotel and crossed the spacious lobby, headed for the bank of elevators opposite. His pulse was normal, respiration normal, nothing in his bearing to suggest that he had squared off against a gang of seven killers a half hour before.

Piece of cake, he thought.

A nice walk in the park.

3

He had the elevator to himself, a smooth ride to the fourteenth floor that took all of sixty seconds. It was actually the thirteenth floor, of course, but superstition dominated architecture even in the nineties in Los Angeles. The numbered buttons skipped from twelve to fourteen, just like that, and everyone pretended not to notice, willing to believe that clumsy sleight of hand could dazzle Fate.

An old man and a sexy blonde who could have been his granddaughter were waiting for the elevator when he disembarked, and Remo gave them both a smile.

More power to you, Grandpa. Smoke 'em if you've got 'em.

Number 1425 was on his left, around a corner from the bank of elevators. Signs directed Remo to his destination, and he moved swiftly down the hall, past numbered doors. He could pick out voices, television background noise, a toilet flushing. Not as bad as some motel out on the highway, but for total privacy you would need megabucks, the presidential penthouse suite.

He stopped outside the door to 1425, knocked twice and waited. On the far side of the door, a shadow blocked the peephole, lingered for a moment, finally moved away. The dead bolt snapped. The knob turned.

"Remo, right on time."

"We aim to please."

"Come in."

A psychoanalyst at Langley, working for the CIA, had once declared that Dr. Harold W. Smith had "no imagination whatsoever." He was wrong, but no one could have guessed it from examining the old man's outward life-style. He wore the same gray suit, white shirt and Dartmouth tie to work each day, ate the same lunch—a cup of prune-whip yogurt—and was never seen to smile. Ironically, Smith's personality—or lack thereof—had served him as the perfect cover for his true role as the head of CURE.

A supersecret agency designed specifically to deal with problems that were physically—or legally—beyond the normal government purview, CURE survived because successive Presidents had found they couldn't do without it in the crunch. They needed a lethal, ruthless instrument from time to time, in these days when *surveillance* was a dirty word and oversight from Congress handcuffed agents in the field. When a radical solution was needed, the President of the United States picked up a special phone hidden in the Lincoln Bedroom. Harold Smith was waiting on the other end.

The key to secrecy is limiting access to information. CURE met that requirement in spades. Only four men on the face of the planet knew of its existence. They was Smith, of course. Next was Remo, CURE'S one-man enforcement arm. The sitting President at any given time was fourth, although his knowledge was necessarily limited. Lastly was Chiun, Remo's trainer, the aged Master of Sinanju, although the old Korean was scarcely interested in the goings-on of the secret organization.

Smith's gray face puckered to resemble the look of a perpetual dyspeptic

"It is unusual for me to meet you this way, I know," the CURE director began. "However, there is a computer exposition in Los Angeles that I wished to attend. Please have a seat." He motioned to a nearby chair.

They settled into modernistic metal chairs and faced each other, with a small round table separating them. Though Smith's decrepit leather briefcase was on the table, he did not open it immediately.

"Have you seen the news within the last few days?"

"National or local?"

"Either."

"Nope," Remo said. "It's on against 'The Simpsons.'"

Smith frowned. "You didn't hear about what happened in Wisconsin Tuesday afternoon?"

"No, but my guess is it's either cheese or cow related."

"Neither," Smith said dryly. "The Justice Department lost a witness in a major racketeering trial."

"Did they check under the sofa cushions?"

"It is not a laughing matter," Smith informed him, looking pained. "They had a safehouse in the woods, upstate. Ten miles from nowhere. I am told that no more than a dozen people in the whole department knew where he was hiding out."

"That's ten too many."

"So it would appear. In any case, a shooter found the safehouse, killed three U.S. marshals and the witness. Marshal number four was, er, indisposed. But he got lucky with the shooter."

"Think he's part of it? An inside job?"

Smith frowned and shook his head, a somber negative. "He was given a polygraph examination and PSE first thing. They swear he is clean. However, you know as well as I do, polygraphs are wrong at least twenty-five percent of the time. That is why they are inadmissible in most state courts. The psychological-stress evaluator is a little better, but it's still more art than science."

"Then it's all just a freaking waste of time," Remo said.

"I agree," Smith said, "but as it happens, that part of the problem is not our concern."

"What is?"

"The shooter."

"He's in custody?" asked Remo.

"More or less," Smith said dryly. "He is in the morgue."

"It couldn't happen to a nicer guy."

"Again the difficulty is not his condition," Smith pressed. "It is a question of identity."

"You're losing me Smitty," Remo warned.

"Let me start at the beginning."

Smith paused to open his battered leather briefcase. Lifting out an inch-thick file, he closed the briefcase, pushing it to one side. He laid the file between them, on the tabletop.

"Two years ago," the CURE director began, "a minor left-wing politician with connections to the drug trade was assassinated in Palermo. Apparently he was strangled with piano wire and almost decapitated."

Smith opened the file; a photograph changed hands. A slender man of middle age lay stretched out on his back, head cocked at a peculiar angle, blood fanned out around him like a crimson halo.

"Four months later, in Toronto, two police detectives were machine-gunned in a brothel. Both were under scrutiny by their department, on suspicion of accepting bribes to help protect a major white-slavery ring."

Another photograph. One body draped across a chintzy couch, another on the floor. The wall behind them was pocked with bullet holes.

"Somebody took a shortcut. Probably saved taxpayers a bundle on another dipsy-doodle trial."

"Another twelve weeks after that," Smith continued, "a dignitary from South Africa was killed while visiting New Orleans."

"I remember that one," Remo said. "It was the first time that I ever heard of anybody famous falling down a flight of stairs by accident."

"There was no accident," Smith said seriously. "In fact, there were no stairs. That particular story was circulated for press consumption. In point of fact, someone slit his throat in bed. Likewise the prostitute who was with him. The State Department did a better job than usual on the cleanup, with co-operation from Johannesburg. They were concerned at what an interracial dalliance might do to the man's posthumous reputation. The truth was buried."

The crime-scene photo was a long shot, taken from the foot of what appeared to be a king-size bed. Nude bodies, ebony and ivory on scarlet sheets.

"No suspects?" Remo asked.

Smith's face was grim. "I am coming to that," he said. "Last June, in San Francisco, someone snatched the founding father of the National Gay Pride Alliance. He was gone three days before they found his body—tortured and mutilated—in the trunk of an abandoned car, near the Presidio."

The glossy eight-by-ten was taken from an angle, peering down into the trunk of a midsized sedan.

The victim's mother would not have been able to identify him, slashed and burned and bloody as he was. A rubber dildo had been tossed in with the body, also stained with blood.

"Sex crime?" asked Remo.

"Perhaps. Or perhaps it is only supposed to look that way. The victim had announced his plan to run for Congress in November. His supporters call the murder a political assassination."

"Are they right?"

"They could be," Smith admitted. He slid another photograph across the table.

"Geez, Smitty, can't you have vacation pictures from Florida like everyone else your age?"

Another car. This time with a corpse behind the wheel. Shot in the face, from all appearances, his head thrown back, mouth open, leaking crimson.

"This one is from Chicago," Smith explained. "The target was Jordanian. A legal immigrant and successful businessman. He owned a string of self-serve laundries and convenience stores."

"Somebody didn't like his Slurpee?"

"I have learned that on the side he handled money and munitions for Hamas, Abu Nidal and the like. The real hard-core resistance to a cease-fire in the Middle East."

"So, we've got chickens coming home to roost," said Remo. "Have you checked with Israel?"

"Mossad records indicate that it was not one of theirs."

"Hmm. There's more there," Remo said, nodding to the stack of photos.

"Miami," Smith replied, and passed another photograph to Remo. Bodies on a sidewalk, crumpled, still. "From April. These two were Colombians who were known to deal drugs on a heavy scale. The DEA was after them, but it would seem that someone else was quicker."

"That's life in the coke trade," Remo said.

"This time, however, we got lucky. Speeding from the scene, the shooter crashed his stolen car into a garbage truck and knocked himself out cold. He woke up in the ambulance and kept his mouth shut, right through booking. He did not ask for an attorney, and would not give his name."

"A pro."

"And then some. On his first night in the county lockup, he committed suicide by wedging his head through the bars of his cell and then breaking his neck."

"A determined pro," Remo amended. "But I still don't see—"

"Nine victims," said the CURE director, interrupting him. "Four states, two foreign countries. One might think that there was nothing much in common."

"I'm one of the ones."

"You would be mistaken, Remo. As it happens, all nine victims were apparently dispatched by the same killer."

Remo frowned. "Are you kidding me?"

"He did not take much care with fingerprints," said Smith. "In fact, according to the FBI and Interpol, he left clear prints at four of the five crime scenes. All except the double-murder in New Orleans."

"What's the link down there, then?"

"Blood and skin. It seems that the, er, lady scratched her killer. Residue beneath her fingernails was matched against the suspect in Miami. It came back positive—not only blood type, but a positive report on DNA analysis."

"No doubts?"

"One chance of error in a hundred thousand."

"Sounds like someone renting out his talent to the highest bidder. And the lucky winner is...?"

"That is one problem," Smith replied. "I mentioned that the subject in Miami carried no ID and would not speak to the authorities. Apparently he had no criminal or military record, either. The only record of his prints was from the unsolved cases prior to his arrest."

"And now he's dead."

"I am not so certain," Smith said worriedly.

"Meaning?"

"Here is the subject from Miami."

Remo took another photo from the CURE director's hand. It might have been a mug shot, but the subject's eyes were closed, his head cocked at a crazy angle, livid bruises showing on his neck and jawline. At a second glance, it was apparent he was lying down. Morgue table, Remo thought.

"Okay."

"And here is the assassin from Wisconsin," Smith informed him, handing off a five-by-seven from his stash.

Same face, without the bruises. Blood flecked at one nostril and the corners of his mouth. The eyes were open, fixed in death. It was impossible to tell if they were blue or gray. A dusty-looking film obscured the irises.

"Twin hit men," Remo mused. "I guess they like to keep it in the family."

"It is more than that," said Smith. "They are not just look-alikes. In fact, they seem to be, well, the same man."

Remo's gaze was level. "What do you mean?"

"The DNA and tissue types are problematical, of course. Identical twins can produce readings so similar as to be practically indistinguishable in that regard."

"So, what's the problem?"

"Fingerprints. No two sets are identical. However, for these two, they are."

"Identical? How?"

"I do not know," Smith admitted.

"All ten fingers, straight across with no deviation whatsoever. That is with the sole exception of a small scar on Miami's left ring finger."

"That's impossible."

"I felt the same way."

"Which means no ID from Wisconsin, either."

"It gets worse," Smith said. "An FBI technician was doing some recreational digging last night and tapped into data banks they had not checked before."

"Why not?"

"Because," Smith said somberly, "the subjects of those files are physically unable to participate in current crimes. They are dead."

Remo frowned. "Check me if I'm wrong, Smitty, but doesn't that usually slow them up a little?"

"I always thought so. Until the FBI man came up with a match."

"You're losing me again."

Smith took a final photo from the file. This one was black-and-white, a prison mug shot, numbers racked below a glaring face. The same face, once again, but appearing older than the first two. Lines around the mouth and eyes the others didn't have, even in death.

"This is Thomas Allen Hardy," Smith went on. "A freelance contract killer for the syndicate—or anybody else who could afford his price. Five thousand dollars was his base rate, I believe. The FBI suspected him of twenty-seven murders at the time of his arrest. He was convicted on two counts."

"Good. At least he's off the street," Remo said.

"Most definitely."

"What's he have to say about these other killings?"

"Not a word," Smith replied. "Hardy went to the Nevada gas chamber in 1965. I have reviewed his death certificate."

"That's thirty years ago."

"Correct."

"But these two—" Remo poked the photographs "—both had his face and fingerprints."

Smith seemed visibly shaken. "It is a baffling genetic impossibility. Basically we stand confronted with a physical anomaly. Three men identical in all respects—except, apparently, for age. One of them dead for more than thirty years, the other two…more recently."

"That's something, anyway. I mean, at least they're dead."

"Perhaps."

"You have some doubts?" Remo tossed the color photos of the two dead hit men back to Smith. "They both look pretty cold to me."

"Those two *are* dead," Smith said. "My concern is that there may be…others."

"Others? What is this, 'The Twilight Zone' meets 'Candid Camera'?"

"This is deadly serious," Smith answered. "Until we are certain where these two came from, we cannot rule out the possibility of others like them, still at large."

"Assume that's true," said Remo. "Where do we come in?"

"Agents for the FBI are already at their wits' end over this," said Smith.

"From the way those clowns have been running things lately, I'd say that's one mighty short trip."

"Be that as it may, the FBI director mentioned his agency's problem to the President during a White House briefing. We have been asked to sort it out," the head of CURE said.

"Exactly what does that mean?" Remo asked him.

"Do our best to find out what has gone on with Thomas Allen Hardy in the past three decades—"

"Gee whiz, Smitty, he's a corpse already," Remo interrupted. The guy isn't getting up at night to do the Monster Mash."

"—and find out how his fingerprints and DNA wound up in two dead hit men young enough to be the sons he never had," Smith concluded.

Remo sighed. "Is there any chance this Hardy wasn't really dead?" he asked.

"I have never heard of a survivor from the gas chamber," Smith said gravely.

"Maybe. But you are familiar with someone who managed to survive a date with the electric chair."

Smith frowned. "Yes. Let us hope we are not dealing with a similar situation."

In the ancient past, CURE had arranged for Remo—then a lowly Newark cop—to be arrested, framed, convicted and condemned on murder charges. The agency had staged an execution that effectively eliminated any risk that he would be identified on future missions for the government. Remo wondered if some other party might have had a similar idea.

"If Hardy is still alive," Smith continued, "he would be nearly seventy today. It is obvious that neither of the dead shooters is the man executed in Nevada in 1965. Even given the latest breakthroughs with those sheep in Scotland, we are still light-years away from duplicating fingerprints and bodies."

"Plastic surgery?" suggested Remo.

"On the faces it's feasible. But not on fingerprints. You know as well as I that erasing prints— or changing them—has been a top priority with criminals for close to eighty years. Some have experimented with acid, others even whittle down their fingertips like pencils, but the prints grow back. It is the same thing with skin grafts, Remo. While it is possible to transplant fingerprints, when the epidermis sheds, the old prints resurface."

Besides, thought Remo, what would be the point? A Thomas Allen Hardy fan club? It was laughable.

"Okay," said Remo, "let's assume we have a problem here. It doesn't tell me where to start or what I should be looking for."

"The first part is relatively simple," Smith replied. "Start with Thomas Hardy."

"So I guess I should pack a shovel with my clean underwear," Remo said dryly.

"Obviously I am not referring to the man himself," Smith replied aridly.

"He had no relatives that anyone could find, between the time of his arrest and execution. However, Hardy had at least one friend. A woman cared enough to claim his body from the state for burial. Her name was...let me see..." Smith checked the file. "Devona Price."

"You've checked her out?"

Smith nodded. "A quick preliminary. Ex-nurse, retired, age sixty-two. She is a registered Democrat but hasn't voted since the Vietnam era. Apolitical these days, from all appearances."

"Whereabouts?"

"She lives on Greenbriar Drive, in Burbank."

"Sunny California." Remo cracked a smile.

"Illinois, actually. It is a Chicago suburb."

"Oh, *that* Burbank."

"This is not a vacation, Remo," Smith said, annoyed.

"Not in Chicago it ain't," Remo replied.

"Please." Smith brought the conversation back to business. "I have not found a connection between Devona Price and Hardy. It is another point you will need to clarify."

"Nobody checked it out back then?"

"The man was dead. When Ms. Price appeared, she saved the state the cost of his cremation. There is no reason to believe the FBI at the time was even told. Their interest in the case expired with Hardy's arrest.''

"Smith spoke as he gathered up the photos. Now that Remo had seen them, they were due for shredding.

"You understand why this has taken everybody by surprise, Remo," the CURE director said. "No one wants to touch a case that involves walking corpses. Since it clearly must be handled, we are elected."

"Meaning me," Remo said, perturbed.

"Correct."

"I'll pay a visit to this Devona Price," he sighed. "But I promise I won't enjoy it."

"She may have no idea what is going on," Smith admitted, "but she remains the last link in the chain concerning what became of Hardy after he was executed. At the very least, she must have some idea what happened to the body. Whether he was buried or cremated. We need to know this for a start."

"Squeeze the old lady," Remo said, standing. "Got it."

"I would have preferred 'debriefed.'"

"I'm sure you would have. How far do I go?"

"As far as necessary," Smith said, snapping his briefcase shut. "Whether we like it or not, the President's interest makes this a priority."

"I would have thought his top priority would be

deciding if he wanted fries with that subpoena,"
Remo said.

"Yes," said Smith evenly. "Be that as it may,
you have all the information you need."

"I'd say about fifteen pages more than that."

Zombie hit men, Remo thought as he turned to
go. He shook his head in wonder.

Behind him, Smith was standing, as well.

"Be careful," the CURE director said. Again, the
disquiet was evident in his sere voice.

"I didn't know you cared." Remo smiled, paus-
ing near the door.

Smith ignored the jibe. "Please keep me up-to-
date."

"Of course. Anything else Henny Penny?"

"Yes. If you should encounter any opposition—"

"Relax, Smitty. I'll handle it," said Remo.

"Seriously, Remo," Smith said. "It is important
that we find out what is behind this business. Everyone is worried, from the top on down."

"Geez, repeat it another twenty times so I don't
forget," Remo griped. "I'll take along my garlic
necklace and some wooden stakes if that'll make
you happy."

"How is Chiun these days?"

"Is that a broad hint for me to take him along on
this? He's the same as ever. Some things never
change."

"If that were only true," said Smith, "both our

jobs would be a great deal easier.'' His gray face
was gathered into a concerned frown.

"Don't sweat it, Smitty, okay? I'm on the case."

Remo got out of the room quickly so that Smith
could not prolong the meeting any further.

It was a short walk to the elevators, but it gave
him time to think about the new assignment. Carbon-copy killers who, apparently, had found some
way to come back from the grave. Garlic and
wooden stakes.

I'd better take along some holy water, too,
thought Remo. Just in case.

4

"We look for dead men?" asked the Master of Sinanju.

"That's about the size of it," said Remo.

"You are certain they are not *gyonshi?*"

Remo glanced at Chiun and saw the way his eyes had narrowed, thinking of another mission that had pitted them against an ancient Chinese vampire and a close encounter with the proverbial fate worse than death.

"The Leader is dead," Remo said. "This is more like twins who don't know when to quit."

It wasn't in Chiun's nature to display confusion. At the moment, he was seated in the middle of the living-room carpet in their Massachusetts condominium in a perfect lotus posture, with his green kimono almost wrinkle free. If he was curious about the last comment from Remo, he concealed it well.

"Smith would now squander the talents of the Master of Sinanju on crazed forays into the cemeteries and mausoleums of this land? What is next? Goblin chasing? Leprechaun assassination? The man is an imbecile."

"No one asked you to come," Remo pointed out.

"I am bored," Chiun sniffed. "Therefore, I will come."

"Lucky me," Remo grumbled.

"I suppose Smith wants you to slay the dead men?"

"Something like that. Along with whoever is behind the operation—whatever that is."

Chiun pressed the back of one bony hand to the parchment skin of his forehead. "Please let it not be the fiendish Booger Man. Or that wicket harlot, the Tooth Fairy."

Remo sighed. "Can you save this for after we get to Burbank?"

In spite of himself, Chiun's eyes suddenly lit up. "Not the home of Jay Leno?" he asked.

"Sorry, Little Father, we're going to Burbank, Illinois," said Remo, stifling a grin. "It's near Chicago."

"Chiun hid his disappointment." There is a paucity of imagination in this land," said Chiun, annoyed.

"Were you aware that there are seven Nashvilles in America, including one in Indiana?"

"That's probably so the Hoosier All Jug Band knows where to meet."

"No imagination," Chiun repeated. "There is only one Sinanju. Only one Calcutta. One Beijing. One Tokyo. The Asian mind abhors confusion and redundancy."

"It's just a shame you guys don't rule the world."

"Indeed," said Chiun, ignoring Remo's note of sarcasm. "You will be going to this bogus, Lenoless Burbank, then?"

"To see the woman," Remo told him.

"'Adam-12'," Chiun said. "A mediocre substitute for 'Dragnet'. All filmed in California. The place we will not be visiting." The last was intended to sound like an accusation.

"You can't blame me for that one," Remo said. "You're the one who jumped to conclusions."

"And you are the one who is now a Ghostbuster. I will accompany you, but do not expect me to arouse any enthusiasm."

"That'll make two of us," said Remo, getting up to pack. "The next flight to Chicago is the red-eye, but I thought we'd wait till morning. That is, if you're sure you're coming with me. Don't feel you have to."

Chiun considered it for several moments, hazel eyes closed. "I will see this imitation Burbank," he declared at last, "though it will doubtless be a disappointment without Leno," he quickly added.

"I liked Johnny better," Remo said.

"Of course, but even Jay is preferable to Letterman."

"I thought your favorite was Arsenio."

As he left the room, he felt Chiun's glare at his back and smiled.

Chiun muttered something as he gathered up the

television remote from where it rested near his knees. As the TV blared to life, Remo stuck his head back in the room. He carried a pink toothbrush—his sole piece of luggage—in one hand.

"Aren't you turning in?" asked Remo.

"I will be watching Leno on television," Chiun informed him, "since you refuse me a pilgrimage to the one true Burbank."

"Take it up with Smith, Little Father."

"I would, but he is probably deep in planning a strategy of attack against the dreaded Loch Ness Monster," Chiun replied.

With that he settled his robes neatly around his knees. Using his thumb on the remote control, he turned the TV up so loudly, the whole house shook.

THEIR FLIGHT TOOK OFF from Logan International Airport ten minutes late, but made it up somehow—a tail wind, Remo guessed—and landed at O'Hare three minutes early.

Magic.

They were objects of attention on the plane and in the terminal, but that was nothing new. While Remo's face and form were perfectly forgettable, it was unusual to see a white man, average height and weight, accompanied by an elderly Korean who was barely five feet tall. When the Korean dressed in silk kimonos day and night, the double-take potential was increased a hundredfold. They didn't quite stop traffic on their trek from the arrivals gate to baggage claim, but it was close.

So much for being inconspicuous.

The good news was that Remo could sense the difference between your average rubbernecker's stare and the furtive, glances that were standard in surveillance. Checking out the crowd this morning, he saw nothing to suggest that anyone was waiting for them in the Windy City.

At least they weren't starting with a handicap.

They had a Plymouth Sundance waiting at the Avis counter. Remo signed the forms, including overpriced insurance. The credit cards and driver's license in his wallet bore the name of Remo Walker. It was not a whopping change from "Williams", but it didn't have to be, since Remo Williams shared one trait with Thomas Allen Hardy.

He was officially dead and buried.

They had reservations at a modern chain motel in Ashburn, a Chicago subdivision two miles east of Burbank. Remo took Chiun's lone steamer trunk upstairs and checked the local telephone directory while the Master of Sinanju staked out his place in front of the TV.

Devona Price was listed, but Remo didn't call ahead. There was no point in giving her a chance to run when he could simply show up on her doorstep and surprise her.

Sixty-two years old. That made her five years Hardy's junior, thirty-one or thirty-two when he was put to sleep. She had been living in Nevada at the time, turned up in various directories for Reno and Las Vegas, which was no surprise. The Silver State was big on transients, chasing jobs in the casinos, restaurants and cocktail lounges, strip joints, service stations, brothels—whatever would serve to cut the mustard in a modern Wild West atmosphere complete with instant marriage, legal prostitution, no state income taxes and the infamous six-week divorce.

But she was now quite a bit older, and almost certainly retired. The twilight years were unforgiving this close to Lake Michigan, and Remo wondered what had made her leave the desert warmth behind.

Another question he would have to ask her, if he got the chance.

"I'm going now."

"Give my best to Big Foot," Chiun answered. He was already engrossed in a program-length commercial for something called the Psychic Pals Web. Remo left him to his educational programs.

It was twenty minutes from the motel parking lot to Burbank, driving west through morning traffic. The boundary line was marked with tasteful signs—Welcome To Burbank—but the markers were unnecessary. Anyone with eyes to see could spot the change: more trees and grass, tract houses giving way to styles with just a little more imagination. Nothing fancy, mind you—this was strictly middle-class...but tasteful. If Devona Price owned land here, she had done all right. If she was renting, Remo figured she was still two steps ahead of most unmarried women in her age bracket.

CURE's background search had turned up nothing useful on the woman who was Remo's first— perhaps his only—handle on the mystery of Thomas Hardy and his killer look-alikes. They had a birth certificate from Oakland, California, along with evidence that she had lived in L.A., San Diego, Phoenix, Denver, Reno and Las Vegas, once she got out on her own.

From all appearances, the long road ended here.

The house on Greenbriar Drive was blue-painted stucco, on the small side—Remo guessed two bedrooms—with grass and well-kept roses out in front and an attached garage. There was a shaded porch of sorts, with ivy climbing on a trellis to the left. The storm door was constructed out of metal trim and glass, a normal wooden door behind it. Both were closed when Remo parked his Plymouth at the curb and walked up to the house. He rang the bell.

It was a wait, and a salesman might well have given up before Devona Price responded to the bell, but Remo had all day. He heard the dead bolt turn at last, and a short, round, gray-haired woman filled the doorway, staring at him through the storm door.

"Who're you?"

He read her lips, but frowned and pointed to his ear, pretending that he couldn't hear her.

She cracked the storm door to repeat the question. "Who're you?"

"Name's Remo Walker. Agent Walker. FBI."

The badge and ID card he showed her would have passed inspection at the Bureau's headquarters in Washington.

"You have a warrant?" asked Devona Price.

He smiled and shook his head. "Just questions, ma'am, for now. I'd rather handle this the easy way. It's best for all concerned."

"What kind of questions?"

"It's a matter of some delicacy," Remo told her. "We can talk about it on the porch, if you insist, but privacy might be a good idea…for your sake."

"Lemme have another look at that ID."

Remo obliged her, waiting patiently.

"You won't mind if I call the federal building and check you out?"

"I recommend it, ma'am," he said, and rattled off a number. "You'll want to ask for Special Agent Smith. He's my supervisor."

"Humph." She thought a moment. Shrugged. "I guess I'll let it go. You may as well come in."

She closed the door behind him, leaving it unlocked, and steered him toward a parlor on the right. There was a smell of citrus-scented cleanser to the house, and every inch of woodwork he could see was polished to a glossy shine. The furniture was aging well, and while the carpet had seen better days, she kept it clean. The coffee table hosted a display of blown-glass figurines: three unicorns, a smiling frog, a poodle and a wriggly shape that could have been a worm or chubby snake.

"Want coffee?" asked Devona Price.

"No, ma'am. I'm fine."

"Stop 'ma'aming' me, for heaven's sake. I know how old I am. No need to rub it in."

"No, ma— I mean, all right."

They sat, Devona on the couch, and Remo in an easy chair that faced her from an angle, to her left. She wore a shapeless housedress, and the hem kept both knees covered, even when she crossed her legs.

"Let's hear the questions, then," she said. "You figure I've been up to something federal in my golden years?"

"Not quite. I'm looking into something that went on a while ago. Some thirty years ago, in fact."

Devona Price was pale already, like a woman who preferred to spend her time indoors, rose garden to the contrary, but Remo saw her face lose color as he spoke.

For all that, though, her voice was firm as she replied, "I'm listening."

"It has to do with Thomas Hardy," Remo told her.

"Tom?" She covered fairly well, but there could be no doubt that she was shaken now. "He's dead."

"I'm well aware of that."

"You figuring to dig him up and file a few more

charges, Agent Man? He paid the biggest price he could. Why can't you just let well enough alone?''

The last thing Remo planned to do was fill her in on details of the recent murders and the mystery of Thomas Hardy's deadly doppelgängers. If she didn't know the story yet, there was no reason why she ever should. Conversely, if she was a part of the conspiracy, it would not help to tip his hand.

"We're tying up some loose ends in the files," he told her. "There were more than twenty murder charges pending on your friend when he was executed in Nevada, back in '65. Some of them still aren't technically resolved."

"My friend?" She spoke the word as if it left a bad taste in her mouth.

"You claimed his body," Remo said. "I can't imagine that was charity extended to a total stranger."

"Can't you? No, I suppose you couldn't. Ask your questions and be done with it."

"How well did you know Thomas Hardy?"

She considered that one for a full two minutes, chewing on her lower lip with yellowed dentures. When she finally answered, it was like a woman talking to herself, debating some concern that has been preying on her mind.

"It's past thirty years," she said, eyes focused on a point across the room, ignoring Remo. "Don't suppose it matters now, though some folks have long memories. Indeed they do."

She blinked twice, turned to face him, leaning forward with arms folded in her lap. "What kind of trouble am I looking at if I refuse to answer you?" she asked.

"There's no statute of limitations on a homicide," he told her truthfully. "You're well beyond the prosecution deadline now, on any crime except for murder. Trouble is, if I don't wrap this up the easy way, somebody may decide it's worth grand-jury hearings. You'd be called to testify, and since you have immunity from prosecution, there's no Fifth Amendment you can hide behind. Refuse to answer on the witness stand, and they can jail you for contempt until you change your mind or the grand jury issues its report."

"How long is that, you think?"

"I've seen investigations drag on for a year or more."

"Shit-fire! A year for clamming up?"

"And if they catch you lying, that's a brand-new charge of perjury. It doesn't matter when the actual events took place. We're talking three to five on that one. Figure eighteen months inside, with good behavior, while the lawyers spend whatever money you've been saving for that rainy day."

"Goddamn leeches!"

"Up to you, of course, but knowing that you can't be charged for anything but murder—"

"Hey, I never pulled no triggers. That's a pure-D fact."

"Well, then?"

"Go on, then, Agent Man."

"How well did you know Thomas Hardy?" Remo asked again.

"I never laid eyes on the man," Devona Price informed him, putting on a tight-lipped smile.

"Excuse me?"

"You heard me right. I never met him in my life."

"You did claim Hardy's body after he was executed, though?"

"I did."

"And why would you do that if he was a perfect stranger?"

"No one's perfect, Agent Man. I was a working girl in those days. Working on the streets, I mean to say. You get my drift?"

He nodded. Waited. Listening.

"I've no apologies to make for what I done. It wasn't such a bad life, all around. I took my share of lumps—who doesn't? But I saw a lot of country, too, and not just on my back in some motel room, either. I was never wired on dope and never served no time. I'm proud of that."

"Okay."

"Go on and judge me all you want. The fact is, I had no one lookin' out for me but me, and I got on all right. You can believe that if you want, or blow it out your butt."

"And Hardy?"

"I was working Reno, back in 1964 and '65. Come winter, I'd run down to Vegas, miss the snow, then go back north in spring if I felt like it. Free and easy. Easy, anyhow. You follow me?"

"I'm listening."

"I had my regulars, like any other girl who gives good value for the money. Some of them were wise guys, some were businessmen. I even had some politicians on the line. State capital's just down the road, there. Carson City. It's a scrubby little town, compared to Reno or Lost Wages, but they do have cash to throw around. State prison's five, six minutes from the heart of town."

"Go on."

"I'm goin', in my own good time," she told him, chewing on her lip again. "It was in May of '65, one of my regulars come askin' me if I would like to make an extraspecial score. I ask him what he's got in mind, and he says nothin' special. There's a guy about to buy it at the joint, he says. Some people want to claim the body for a decent funeral, but they can't afford to have their names on paper. I assume he's talkin' wise guys, but it's all the same to me. I ask how much. He tells me seven grand. I ask him does he want it gift wrapped, and he tells me never mind. That's all."

"You signed for Hardy's body."

"Right. What I was told, he had no next of kin. The state'll cremate if nobody claims a stiff, but they prefer to let it go and save the fee."

"And after you received the body—"

"Nope." She stopped him cold. "I told you once, I never saw the man. That means alive or dead. I never saw him on the street, nor in a cell, nor in a box. Fact is, I never even saw the box."

"How's that?"

"I had instructions, Agent Man. I told the prison where to send him, and they did the rest. Somebody else picked up the tab, though I expect you'll find my name writ on the check—if you can dig it up, that is. Won't be my signature, of course, but close enough."

"Where did they send him?" Remo asked.

She barked at that, a laugh of sorts. "Went to a funeral home, of course! What would you think?"

"I don't suppose..."

"That I recall the name? Sure do. I'm not that old."

"And it was...?"

"Cristobal," she told him, with a smug expression on her face. "That's Basque, in case you didn't know. They got a lot of Basques up Carson City way. Sheepherders when they first come over to the States, but now they're big in restaurants, casinos, anything you want to name. One of 'em was a senator, back there a while, in tight with Ronnie Reagan. I expect you heard of him."

"So, the mortician's name was Cristobal."

"That's what I said." She sounded huffy now, as if expecting him to contradict her. "Don't recall his first name, and I sure as hell can't guarantee he's still in business. Thirty years go by, and folks move on, you know?''

"And you received the seven grand?"

"I did. The statute's run on tax evasion, too, I do believe.''

"I'm sure it has."

"Damn right. You know, it's funny, now I think of it.''

"What's that?"

"My client paid me right on time and no complaints, but looking back, I don't believe he ever came to visit me again.''

"Was that unusual?"

"Not really. People come and go, especially in Nevada. Hell, it's not like we were friends to keep in touch or anything.''

"Do you recall his name?"

"You won't believe me if I tell you."

"Try me."

"I just called him John."

"No last name?"

She smiled at that. "I understood he was a married man who liked variety. You follow me? Last names don't pay the rent—they just get in the way.''

"Can you describe him?"

"Let me think about it. He was probably forty then, or getting close. A little gray upstairs, but he still kept himself in shape. Hung like a horse, I can remember that. Show me that prick, and I can make a positive ID.''

He smiled. "I don't imagine it will come to that."

"I'm off the hook, then?"

"You've been very helpful," Remo said, "and that's how it will read in my report. We're done."

"All right, then. Sure you wouldn't like some coffee for the road?"

"No, thanks. It keeps me awake while I'm working."

"You're a pisser, Agent Man. I'm glad to meet a Fed who's got a sense of humor."

"Well, the day's still young."

"It is, and that's a fact."

DEVONA WATCHED HIM GO, no longer smiling as the Plymouth pulled away. No good had ever come from digging up the past, and if there was a rare exception to the rule, Tom Hardy wouldn't fit the bill.

Bad news, that bastard, and she didn't have to meet him in this life to know that much. His case had been in all the papers, back in '64 and '65. The law had nailed him for a double contract murder, and they reckoned there were twenty-five or thirty more he pulled, before they ran him down. Tom Hardy wasn't talking, though, and in the end it made no difference.

Dead was dead.

They couldn't gas him twenty times, so what the hell?

The problem wasn't Tom, though. He was history, and while Devona had no reason to believe the men who anteed up to have him taken care of were alive today, much less concerned about a decades-old funeral, you never really knew. Those wise guys had long memories, some of them, handed down through Families like every scrap of information was a frigging heirloom. If they found out she was talking, even after all this time...

A sudden chill raised goose bumps on her arms and made her tremble, standing at the window, staring out into the empty street.

It was the Feds, for Christ's sake, but she knew how those things worked. There were all kinds of leaks these days. She couldn't turn the TV on without some story jumping out at her about an agent from the FBI or CIA who got arrested spying for the Russians, the Chinese, the syndicate.

Trust no one, and you won't get burned.

It had been stupid, talking to the G-man, but she damn sure didn't want to go the other route, with public hearings and the press involved. This way, at least she bought some time and gave herself a running start.

Provided that she started running soon.

Right now, for instance.

There was Sheila in Kentucky, just a cousin, but they kept in touch and got along all right. Devona could stop off down there, a few days, while she thought about her next move, got things straight inside her head.

She needed time to think, and something told her time was running out.

The house was paid for, ditto on the furniture, and she could take a while to sell it off if that was necessary. Or if things were still cool in six months or so, she might come back, pretend that nothing ever happened. Settle down again and let the good times roll.

Not many good times rolling in the golden years, though, when she thought about it. Teeth gone, thinning hair, arthritis coming on.

Why run and stretch it out? she asked herself.

Because I don't know how to quit.

It wouldn't take her long to pack a suitcase, and the banks were open. She would leave enough in the account to make it seem like she was coming back, in case somebody thought to check. And later, if she needed what was left, the cash could be retrieved by wire. It wasn't like the old days, when you had to do it all yourself, right on the spot.

Some things were better now, she realized.

But death was still a stone-cold drag.

With a last glance out the window, she retreated toward her bedroom, anxious to be out of there and on the open road.

5

Another westbound flight, departing from O'Hare at half-past seven in the evening, bound for Reno. They could just as easily have flown direct to Carson City, but the choice had been a conscious one on Remo's part. Nevada's capital was small enough that new arrivals could be watched with ease, and he was not entirely sure Devona Price would keep her mouth shut. If she reached out to someone from her past and blew the whistle, Remo stood a better chance of slipping through the net in Reno, with its larger airport, larger crowds. And if the enemy was looking for a G-man, he would have another edge.

For once, the presence of Chiun would qualify as cover.

How many federal agents traveled with an old Korean dressed in native garb?

Reno's Cannon International Airport is named for a man, not a weapon. Howard Cannon was once a big gun in the U.S. Senate, though, scrutinized for his connections to casinos and the Teamsters, once a central figure—unindicted—in the trial that sent a union president to federal prison for attempted bribery. His was the kind of reputation that sits well with voters in Nevada, proud defiance in the face of condemnation from outside.

Remo had another rental car on hold, a Mazda Protegé LX from Hertz. He also had a room booked at a "family" hotel downtown, a block from City Hall. The "family" part of it included clowns who hung around in the casino, goosing cocktail waitresses, together with a claustrophobic video arcade where loving parents could deposit Little Johnny with a roll of quarters while they slipped away to drink and lose their hard-earned money.

Life was good.

The desk clerk barely noticed Chiun as they were checking in, and no one in the hotel lobby paid him any mind. The elevators were strategically positioned so that new arrivals had to walk through the casino, passing banks of slot machines, crap tables and roulette wheels if they planned to go upstairs and find their rooms. Chiun might have been invisible, for the attention he attracted in that setting. Everyone around them was distracted, mesmerized, by the pursuit of easy cash.

We ought to work Nevada more, thought Remo as they reached the elevators, riding up to nine. Those suckers wouldn't notice if I took somebody out right there, in the casino.

It was true. Some years ago, in one of the Nevada "carpet joints," it was reported that a gambler had collapsed and died while betting on a crap game.

Heart attack. The guy was dead before he hit the floor—and just as well, because his fellow players left him where he fell, and went on with their game. Some of them literally stepped across his prostrate body, moving in to place their bets.

Chiun crinkled his nose disdainfully on entering their room. "A lavatory stall would be larger than this," the Master of Sinanju complained.

"They're calling it a suite."

"One bedroom with a tiny bath is a hostel, not a suite," the Master of Sinanju said. "You should refuse to pay."

"I think that curtain is supposed to close an alcove off, for privacy."

"Curtains are made for windows and showers," said Chiun. "And look. There are marks from burned tobacco products on this filthy plastic furniture."

"That's fiberboard," said Remo. "I think."

"Fake is fake."

"They've got TV."

Chiun switched it on. "Poor color," he declared, and started channel surfing with the small remote control. A Jackie Chan movie caught his eye, the hero throwing high kicks at a gang of greasy-looking hooligans.

"Impostor!" Chiun accused the screen, and kept on searching for a program he could stomach.

"Try not to break the set while I'm gone," said Remo.

"I make no promises," replied Chiun. He had found yet another psychic-hotline infomercial.

As Remo headed out the door, the Master of Sinanju called to him. "If you find one of Smith's walking dead men, do not bring him back here. It is enough that my delicate nose should have to sniff you in such close quarters. With two of you, I fear my nostrils would drop off."

"Har-de-har-har," Remo said as he closed the door.

A PHONE CALL from Chicago had confirmed that the morticians known as Cristobal and Son were still in business, planting stiffs from Carson City and surrounding, smaller towns. Remo had the address when they left O'Hare, confirmed it from another telephone directory upon arrival, plus the home address and number for a Yuli Cristobal—in fact, the only Cristobal in town whose name was listed in the book.

It was a toss-up: make a house call or sit tight until tomorrow rolled around and catch the guy at work. Remo was curious enough to push it, and the house call won. He aimed the Mazda south along Virginia Street toward Carson City, twenty miles away in Ormsby County.

If Las Vegas is a painted whore, then Reno is her older, smaller sister. Once upon a time, it was the largest city in the Silver State, a few miles from Lake Tahoe and the California border, boasting trees and elevations where the heat was bearable in summertime. *Nevada* means "snow clad" in Spanish, but you'd never know it from the sunbaked desert that comprises eighty-five percent of the state.

. In Reno you could breathe and gamble all at once. Throw in the great six-week divorce, and it was perfect. After World War II, however, things began to change. The Mob discovered Vegas; air conditioners and airplanes made it practical to plant a new oasis in the middle of a wasteland. Movie stars from Hollywood could cut their travel time in half, get married in a flash. Strangely enough, although the same laws held throughout Nevada, Reno held the edge on broken marriages, while Vegas rang with wedding bells. Go figure. By the 1970s, Las Vegas housed three-quarters of Nevada's population, putting Reno squarely in the shade.

The big fade was more obvious in daylight, when the neon wasn't glaring in your eyes, but Remo recognized the signs by day or night. The town's main drag was small, perhaps one-sixth the size of that in Vegas, and you didn't need a tank to force your way through tourist traffic. Near the edge of town, he found the most convincing evidence of all: a failed casino, dark and vacant.

Any time a gambler couldn't make a living in Nevada, there was definitely something wrong.

There was twenty miles of nothing on the drive from Reno down to Carson City. This was the real Nevada, empty space that seemed to stretch forever, with the city lights no more than a reflected glow on the horizon. You could almost close your eyes and picture wagon trains, all hot and dusty, weary scouts in search of water fit to drink.

He pushed the Mazda, holding it at seventy until a highway sign announced that he was rolling into Carson City. If Las Vegas had diminished Reno, the state capital was nothing but a fly speck by comparison. Aside from the casinos jammed together on a few short blocks downtown, the view reminded him of something lifted from the dry plains of Wyoming, maybe Kansas or Nebraska.

It was cow town all the way. Or maybe sheep.

He drove through town on Carson Street, paused in the parking lot of a convenience store to double-check his street map, then proceeded south until he hit Kings Canyon Road. A right turn there, and Remo drove another few blocks, till he found the address he was looking for. There was a Lincoln Town Car in the driveway, pale light spilling through thin curtains from the living room's broad picture window.

Remo killed his lights, pulled in and parked behind the Lincoln. Took it easy when he closed the driver's door behind him, then circled around the Mazda's nose and moved toward the front door of the house. The curtains weren't designed with privacy in mind, but he saw no one in the living room. More lights were burning in what Remo took to be a dining room and kitchen area beyond, but he was not prepared to scramble through the flower bed to peer inside.

He rang the bell instead, and waited half a minute before a stocky man with thinning hair and wire-rimmed glasses answered. Charcoal slacks and white dress shirt, the collar button fastened, but no tie in evidence, as if the doorbell had distracted him midway through taking off his business suit.

"Good evening. Mr. Cristobal?"

"What do you want?"

"That's Yuli Cristobal?"

"And who are you?"

The man had a knack for answering one question with another. Remo palmed the bogus federal ID and gave him time to read the fine print.

"FBI?"

"Yes, sir."

"What do you want?" he asked again.

"Your name, for starters. Are you Yuli Cristobal?"

"I am."

"In that case, I have several questions for you. May I step inside?"

"What? I mean, yes, of course."

The house revealed a woman's touch, but from the dust and scattered magazines in evidence, the touch had not been all that recent.

"We're alone?" asked Remo.

"Yes. My wife is visiting her parents, down in

Beaver,'' Cristobal informed him, adding "Utah" almost as an afterthought.

"Can we sit down?"

"Yes, please. I'm sorry."

He was nervous, this one. Remo wondered how much of it was the natural result of being startled by an unexpected—and unwelcome—visit from the FBI. Was there a guilty conscience underneath the soft exterior, complete with oily sheen of perspiration?

"Mr. Cristobal, are you the owner of the local mortuary known as Cristobal and Son?"

"I am."

"Which one are you?"

"Excuse me?"

"I mean, are you 'Cristobal' or 'Son.'"

"Both, I suppose. My father died in 1986. I never got around to changing names."

"How long have you been working in the family business?"

"May I ask what this is all about? I mean, if there's some kind of problem, why not come directly to the point?"

"That's what I'm doing, Mr. Cristobal, if you'll allow me to proceed."

"Of course." He slumped back in his La-Z-Boy, thick fingers drumming on the padded arms. "What was the question, please?"

"How long have you—"

"Oh, right. Since I was born, in one way or another.'' Yuli Cristobal displayed a fleeting smile that could have been mistaken for a grimace. "Dad was always talking shop, you know? I started working holidays and summers at the home when I was nine or ten. Two years of junior college on the technical procedures, just to satisfy the state. I went full-time in 1970...no, make that '69.''

"I'm looking into something that occurred before that time," said Remo.

"As I said—"

"Specifically in 1965."

The undertaker shut his mouth so quickly, it reminded Remo of a snapping turtle. He could almost hear the teeth snap, and it took a moment for his grudging host to speak again.

"In '65, you said?"

"That's right."

"And it's about a client?"

"Yes."

"My father would have handled any business details," Cristobal informed him.

"Still, you might recall the case. It was...unusual."

More perspiration beaded on the undertaker's forehead. Trying to be casual, he took a swipe with his right hand, and must have smeared some in his eyes. It left him blinking for a moment, blushing with embarrassment.

"Unusual?"

"An inmate from the prison who was executed. Thomas Allen Hardy."

"Executed? Hardy? No...well, hmm, perhaps I do remember that one." Cristobal was jamming mental gears, a vain attempt to get his story straight without appearing foolish. "Yes, in fact. The name would have escaped me, but I do recall we got a client from the prison, back around that time."

"Your father would have done the paperwork on that?"

"Or Mom. She kept the books in those days."

"And is she...?"

"Passed on in '81," Cristobal answered.

"My sympathies."

"I'm curious," said Cristobal. "This gentleman—well, maybe not—this fellow has been gone for thirty years. Are you investigating him?"

"It's technical," said Remo, judging that the time had come for some selective bullshit, seasoned with a dash of truth. "He was a contract killer in the sixties, with a number of suspected cases still unsolved. New evidence suggests we may be able to indict a couple of his past employers, but we have to start at the beginning."

"With his funeral?"

"I've spoken to the individual who claimed his body from the prison," Remo said. "It turns out she was paid to make arrangements for the funeral, specifically instructed that the body should be sent to Cristobal and Son."

"Instructed by...?" The undertaker cocked one eyebrow, looking rather like a sweaty barn owl.

"I was hoping you could tell me that," said Remo.

"After all these years?"

"Mr. Cristobal, please believe me when I say this is a very serious investigation. We have reason to believe the men who paid for Hardy's funeral are involved in large-scale racketeering and a list of other crimes, including several very recent homicides. It is most important that you cooperate with our investigation."

"Yes, well, there's confidentiality to think about."

"Are you a doctor?"

"No."

"A lawyer?"

"No."

"A priest?"

"Well, hardly."

"Then you have no privilege of confidentiality. Of course, if you insist on a subpoena, we can always treat you as a hostile witness, Mr. Cristobal. The average penalty for an obstruction charge, if it's your first offense, should come down in the neighborhood of eighteen months."

"In jail?"

"No, sir. Jail's where they book you, prior to trial. You serve your time in prison. It's another world, entirely."

"Good God! You can't be serious!"

"I'm deadly serious." The smile on Remo's face would have unsettled Norman Bates.

Cristobal thought about it for another moment, then said, "All right. What do you want?"

"I'll need to see the paperwork on Hardy's funeral."

"Impossible."

"Now, Mr. Cristobal—"

"I'm telling you, there is no paperwork. My father saw to that, all right?"

"I'm listening."

"I was sixteen years old in 1965, already working weekends, nights and most of my vacations at the home. As I explained, my father liked to talk about his clients—how he fixed them up, the damage he restored, which relatives were cheapskates, who he talked into a more expensive casket, all that sort of thing. You understand?"

"Go on."

"With Hardy, it was something else. It was the only time he ever got a client from the prison. Most were sent to Tolson's for cremation at a discount rate, or relatives came in from out of state and took them home. This time, though, I remember Dad explaining that the client's people were avoiding Tolson. Someone didn't trust him, all that business he was doing with the state."

"I see."

"Not yet, you don't. My father agonized about

that deal. A hundred times, at least, I heard him say he should have turned the offer down, but it was twenty thousand dollars for a funeral that would otherwise have cost about eight hundred, tops, in those days.''

"Why so much?'' asked Remo.

"Less is more, you might say.'' Cristobal released a kind of wheezing sound that could have been a sigh or throttled laughter at his own expense. "They bought the casket and a plot, but that was all, you understand?''

"Not quite.''

"I'm telling you, the client wasn't buried.''

"What? You mean he wasn't dead?''

"Oh, he was dead, all right. My dad was clear on that. He wasn't going to involve himself in breaking someone out of prison, even for that kind of money. No, the buyers wanted Thomas Hardy's corpse, dead on delivery, no embalming. Nada. Zip.''

"For twenty grand.''

"In cash, it was. My parents kept it off the books, of course. You did say FBI? Not IRS?''

"Forget about the taxes,'' Remo said. "That's ancient history. I need to know who bought the stiff.''

From the expression on the undertaker's face, he might as well have defecated on the coffee table. Cristobal sat back and gaped at Remo for a moment, finally found his voice.

"You mean the client.''

"Right. Whatever.''

"I'm afraid I can't supply the name of any individuals," said Cristobal.

"You can't, or won't?"

"I'm trying to cooperate. My father never mentioned any names, and as I told you, there was nothing written down."

"You must have something," Remo insisted.

"I do recall a corporation. There was a business card, I think, before my father threw it out. I know the name intrigued me, at the time."

"Which was...?"

"Eugenix."

"Spell it."

Cristobal obliged, seemed pleased and nervous all at once. "That's really all I know about the matter," he continued. "Dad would talk about it sometimes afterward, but always in the context of an easy profit. He was quite the businessman."

"I gathered that."

"He had mixed feelings, though. That still came through. It was another eighteen months before he even touched the money. Latent guilt, I think, to some degree."

Or careful planning, Remo thought. A twenty-thousand-dollar windfall, back in 1965, would certainly have made the tax man curious.

"And that was all you ever heard from this Eugenix Corporation. Just the one transaction?"

"Yes. There was a moratorium on executions in the state, a short while later. By the time they started up again, my mom was gone and Dad was getting on in years. The bottom line is, no one from the corporation ever came around. Got what they wanted, I suppose, and that was that.''

THE UNDERTAKER STOOD and watched as his unwelcome visitor climbed into a sedan, switched on the engine, backed out of the driveway, disappeared from view. He didn't make it obvious, like standing at the window with his nose pressed up against the glass, but he made sure the man was gone.

FBI, for Christ's sake, after all these years. His father's chickens coming home to roost when Yuli needed one more headache like he needed cancer.

Shit!

His wife was leaving him—had left him—for another man, and business wasn't all that hot, besides. You could forget those half-assed jokes about the mortuary business—everybody's dying to get in, and all that crap. It might be true, more people dying all the time, but fewer of them came to Cristobal and Son for processing these days, and that meant cutting back on certain luxuries around the homestead. No bright, shiny Lincoln when the new year rolled around. Less money to impress the girls down at the Crazy Horse Saloon.

But he had more-important problems now.

The Hardy deal had been his father's contract; that much of his story to the FBI man had been true. There was a catch, of course: the clause demanding secrecy forever. He had blown it, frightened by the talk of prison and obstructing justice, giving up more than he should have to a total stranger.

He couldn't take the words back now, but he could try to mitigate the damage. Make a call. Spread the alarm.

The desk had been his father's, but the old man hardly would have recognized it, sanded and refinished to a satin shine. The lower right-hand drawer was locked. Inside it, to the back, a smallish metal strongbox, also locked. Two separate keys were required to access the ancient address book.

It was a weird sensation, thumbing through those pages, reading names of people long since dead and gone. His father's friends, a handful of the relatives he seldom heard from anymore.

And business contacts.

Near the back, a name. The phone number beside it had been scratched out and corrected half a dozen times.

They made a point of checking in, every five or six years. The voices varied, and the number changed with every call, but letting Cristobal keep track of them was not the point. He understood that they were keeping track of him. It had been more than thirty years, for God's sake, and the bastards never let it go. They weren't forgetting anything.

Not ever.

Yuli's hand was on the telephone receiver when he caught himself. The FBI was in it now, and that meant someone could have tapped his phone. He couldn't place the call from home.

But what if they were watching him, as well? Departure from the house just now would look suspicious. They might follow him, perhaps observe him if he used a public telephone.

They couldn't hear him, though, he told himself.

Yuli decided he would wait one hour, then go out and make his call. There was a convenience store three blocks away, with indoor pay phones. He could duck in, make the call, then buy some beer and stuff, come out with the goods and look like he was shopping, if he had an audience.

No sweat.

Now all he had to do was fabricate a logical excuse for spilling everything he knew about his father's dealings with Eugenix Corporation. Maybe claim the federal man knew all about it, going in, and simply pressured Yuli to confirm the details. It was weak, but he could sell it from the heart.

And in the process, maybe he could save himself.

6

Brandenburg, Kentucky, is a peaceful town on the Ohio River, twenty miles southwest of Louisville. Two thousand residents call Brandenburg their home, and most of them are law-abiding citizens who work or go to school five days a week, reserving Saturdays for sport or chores around the house, and Sundays for the Lord. The children tend to leave home after high school—college or the military, jobs or travel, anything to glimpse the world outside Meade County. Later, if they come back home to stay, at least they know what they are giving up.

Few residents of Brandenburg knew Dr. Quentin Radcliff. Possibly a hundred would have recognized him, passing on the street, but less than half that number could have put a name together with the face. Of those, perhaps two dozen could lay claim to having spoken with the man. No more than six or seven would have said they knew him well.

And they would all be wrong.

How could they hope to recognize his genius?

Small towns enforce a kind of intimacy that the natives take for granted. Everyone knows everybody

else's business. It is neither good nor bad, a simple
fact of life. Tongues wag, and in the finest Biblical
tradition, every secret thing is finally revealed.

In Dr. Radcliff's case, however, no one knew
enough to talk with any kind of credibility. His few
employees were outsiders, and they were good at
keeping quiet. Dr. Radcliff and his daughter mostly
shopped in Louisville, or had their things delivered
from away. No one in town had ever called them
rude, exactly, but they loved their privacy, and no
mistake.

Back in the good old days, a nosy operator might
have eavesdropped on their calls and spread the
word that way, like on ''Green Acres'' or ''The
Andy Griffith Show'', but that was ancient history.
There was no one to listen in when Dr. Radcliff took
a call at half-past midnight, no one to remark on
whom the doctor called five minutes later.

It was 1:05 a.m. before a jet black Buick Skylark
pulled into the broad circular driveway of Radcliff's
home. The new arrival had a stunning, moonlit river
view as he stepped from his car, but he paid no
attention. He had seen it all before, and there were
chestnuts to be rescued from the fire.

Radcliff observed the new arrival's progress on
closed-circuit television in his den. Six compact
monitors were mounted in a cabinet on Radcliff's
left, against the wall, allowing him to swivel in his
high-backed chair for a fragmented view of house
and grounds.

Security was critical. The doctor had too much at stake to let his guard down now.

A trusted servant brought the visitor to Radcliff's study, showed him in and closed the door behind him, leaving them alone. The doctor didn't rise or offer to shake hands. No social visit, this. They had important business to discuss.

"What's so important, Quentin?" Warren Oxley sounded curious, a bit concerned but light-years away from panic.

"I received an unexpected call this evening," Radcliff told his second-in-command.

"You told me that much on the telephone," said Oxley.

"It was relayed from Nevada. Carson City."

Oxley blinked at that. "I don't believe it. After all this time?"

"Indeed. It seems he had a visitor, some kind of federal agent asking questions."

"Jesus, Quentin!"

He had Oxley's full attention now. Radcliff felt better, seeing the fear behind the sky blue contact lenses Oxley wore. The nonchalant facade was breaking down before his very eyes.

"We always knew that it might happen some-time."

"Sometime, right. But after thirty-plus years? The Feds are asking about Hardy?"

"Why else would they be in Carson City?"

"Well…"

"It has to be the fingerprints," said Radcliff. "Someone's checked the older files. I was afraid they might."

"We're screwed," said Oxley.

"I'm inclined to disagree. The prints create more problems than they solve," said Radcliff. "Think about it for a moment. If they get an exhumation order, all they'll have to show for it will be an empty casket. There's no paper trail of any kind. The slug in Carson City has no names to pass along."

"The contact number—"

"Has been canceled," Radcliff said. "He's on his own."

"Still dangerous," Oxley argued.

Radcliff sighed. His chief lieutenant would not be mistaken for a man of vision. "We can deal with that, don't you suppose?"

"Of course. But if the FBI—"

"Let's take a look at the worst-case scenario," said Radcliff, interrupting him. "Suppose they manage some connection on a thirty-year-old body-snatching case. The subject had no family—he had been executed by the state. We could have dumped his body on the street, and it would only be a misdemeanor. After thirty years, they have no case at all."

"But, Quentin—"

"They can only get to us through us. If you believe that, Warren, then we're covered."

"Right. Okay."

"It wouldn't hurt, however, to dispose of some deadwood as expeditiously as possible."

"I understand."

"You'll get right on it, then?"

"Of course."

"Let our associate cope with the details. He has specialists on staff."

"I will."

"You have the necessary information?"

"Certainly."

"I'll leave you to it, then."

"It's done."

Not yet, the doctor thought, but soon. And when the deadwood was eliminated, any chance of drawing an indictable connection would be gone forever. Let the FBI match fingerprints from now till Judgment Day, for all the good that it would do them. What fools they were, to think they could match wits with genius and emerge with anything but absolute frustration and humiliation as their just deserts.

Radcliff poured himself a double Scotch and drained half of it in a single swallow, feeling liquid heat spread through his body, calming him.

Another crisis narrowly averted. Such is life, he thought.

And life goes on.

For some.

IT WAS a thirty-minute drive across the river, back to southern Indiana and his home, but Warren Oxley shaved ten minutes off the normal time by speeding, watching out for cops and taking full advantage of the empty roads. There was no on the highways at this hour, and the raw demands of driving at top speed distracted Oxley from his larger worries.

Christ! The fucking FBI!

The risk had been there from Day One, of course, but he had slowly come to think of it as ancient history. Each passing year had seemed to make the prospect of exposure more remote. Two losses in the past twelve months were troublesome, of course. They gave the Feds more raw material to work with, but you had to know the secret, starting out from scratch, before it all made any sense. If they were onto Hardy now...

Radcliff was right, actually: there was no Hardy anymore. His pitiful remains had been consumed, the dregs cremated, decades earlier. The undertaker in Nevada didn't know enough to really hurt them, even if he lost his nerve and started talking to the Feds.

Had he already talked?

No matter. He had been a child when it began, and even knowing the preliminary steps still left him miles away from any logical conclusion—much less the astounding truth.

If the investigation should proceed, and it came down to an interrogation, Oxley was prepared to lie his ass off for the cause. To save himself. He had been on the job too long to even think of working out a deal, betraying Radcliff or the project that had been his life.

He still believed, in spite of everything. The doctor was a genius, and a man of vision. He was working miracles.

I'm getting old, he thought. Ten years ago, I would have shrugged this off like it was nothing.

But he wasn't forty-five today, and never would be. He was coming up on sixty in a few more years, and it was all downhill from there. Before he knew it, in the twinkling of an eye, there would be nurses, rest homes, maybe a dialysis machine.

Unless he kept the faith, hung tight with Radcliff and was born again. The ultimate reward for faithful service to the cause.

The house was dark when Oxley pulled into the driveway, parked the Buick, killed the engine. There was no one home to greet him. He had never married, never learned to nurture a relationship beyond the "fuck 'em and forget 'em stage," had never been much good with pets. A moody type might have called the empty house symbolic of his life, but there were many different ways to live.

Right now, for instance, Oxley had a chance to save himself some grief, refer his problem to an expert who could make it go away—or minimize its repercussions, at the very least. This time tomorrow—or the next day, at the latest—they would have it made.

He made a point of checking out the house before

he went inside. A simple thing, but he felt better having done it, knowing that the Feds were out there somewhere, sniffing inch by inch along his trail. They couldn't be this close, not yet, but Oxley had a flair for anticipating and taking care of details.

Once inside, he poured himself a drink and took it with him to the bedroom, shed his jacket and the tie that he had worn to Radcliff's house from force of habit. Always put your best face forward, even in a crisis.

Oxley didn't have to look the number up. He had it memorized. Long distance, with the prefix for Miami, even later there than where he was.

Tough shit.

With so much riding on the line, he didn't give a damn if Lasser got pissed off about the loss of sleep. He could catch up on sack time later, when the job was done, and take a couple of his pricey bimbos with him.

Thinking of the women, with their year-round tans and supple bodies, Oxley wondered if it wasn't time for him to take a short vacation of his own. There was a little village south of Manzanilla, on the coast of Mexico, where he was well received. At least his money was, and it came down to the same thing. The women there were most accommodating. Sometimes, he could hear them laughing in his dreams.

But it would have to wait. Before he started planning any getaways, he had to deal with business,

wait and see it through. When they were home and
dry, there would be ample time for Oxley to con-
gratulate himself and take his just reward for one
more job well done.

Eleven digits. Oxley waited while the distant telephone rang once, twice, three times. Lasser picked
it up at last, his voice a groggy snarl.

"Hello!"

"It's me. No names."

"Do you have any fucking clue what time it is?"

"We have a problem."

"Oh?"

"It could be serious. I'll call you back in fifteen
minutes, at the other number."

"Make it twenty, will you? Give me time to put
some clothes on."

"Hurry!"

Twenty minutes later, Oxley tapped another number out from memory and waited for his man in
Florida to pick up on the secure phone.

"I'm here. Get to it."

Oxley spelled the details out, told Lasser what he
had to do. He got no argument.

"The three of them. Is that all?"

"For the moment," Oxley said. "Take care of
that, and I'll get back in touch."

"Okay. Will do."

He felt immeasurably better as he cradled the receiver, slumped back on the bed and heaved a weary

sigh. He had done all that he could do, for now. It would be Lasser's job to take care of the dirty work.

And if he failed?

Forget it.

Lasser's specialty was solving problems. It was what he did, and it had made him rich. He wouldn't fail this time, because his own head was among those on the chopping block, if anything went wrong.

He would not let them down.

IT WOULD BE all his life was worth to drop the ball. The chairman of Security Unlimited was thirty-eight years old. It was ironic, he supposed, that the events that shaped his adult life had their beginning in the days when he was still a third-grade student, but the normal course of any life was filled with ironies. It took a sense of humor to survive, much less succeed and prosper in this crazy world.

For Morgan Lasser, laughing at the world had never been a problem. He enjoyed life's little challenges, the rush that came with ironing out a sticky problem, whether it involved some piece of new technology or human obstacles just waiting to be forcibly removed.

Security Unlimited was Lasser's brainchild, one of several companies he had created out of piss and vinegar, with other people's money, using sheer audacity in place of ready capital from time to time. The other companies had folded, but they always left him better off than when he started. This time, Lasser was convinced, he had it right.

The call from Indiana was a problem, no doubt about it. Feds meant trouble, and he didn't relish dealing with the FBI, but there were ways around that difficulty if he only kept his head. The plan that Warren Oxley had suggested to him sounded feasible, though Lasser had some private doubts about whether it went far enough.

Three names, and that was all. There had to be more loose ends somewhere out there in the ozone, waiting to snap back and sting his two esteemed associates—sting *him*—if he wasn't prepared to deal with trouble as it came. The good news was that he could try to sniff around, elicit more details from Oxley and initiate the necessary corrective measures.

No sweat.

But he would take the three names first, and deal with them. They were the obvious weak links, and two of them should have been dealt with years before, in Lasser's judgment. It was not his call, of course...until tonight.

There was a saying, source unknown—though many gave the credit to Hell's Angels—that three men can keep a secret, provided two of them are dead. A corporation obviously couldn't run on strict enforcement of that rule, or there would be no corporation, but the sentiment was sound enough. The best way Lasser knew to eliminate the weak links in a chain was to remove those links, forge new ones, or maybe settle for a shorter, stronger chain.

He rose and padded naked from the bedroom, hearing Debbie mutter something on the edge of sleep, ignored her in his concentration on the problem.

There was only one man Lasser trusted to coordinate a job like this. As for the hands-on labor…well, his business partners could help out in that regard.

It was, in fact, what they did best.

He would consider it a gesture of good faith.

Security Unlimited had bankrolled Dr. Radcliff's labors for the past eight years, the latest in a string of sponsors who had recognized his genius and pursued it with a profit motive. There was nothing wrong with making money, after all. In fact, it made the world go round…or was that love?

No, it was money. Absolutely.

You could always purchase love, or its facsimile, if you had ready cash on hand.

In Lasser's private study, on the spacious teakwood desk, there were two telephones. One was the businessman's special, with a dozen buttons for the different lines; its mate was something else entirely, boxlike in appearance, mounted with a row of colored lights.

He used the second telephone to dial a local number, frowning as he stood there, naked, waiting for his party to respond. Four rings and counting. Damn it all, if he was out—

"Who's this?" said the gruff, familiar voice.

"Turn on the scrambler."

"Right."

As Lasser spoke, he reached down with his free hand, pressed a button on the flat face of the chunky telephone. At once, a green light glowed to tell him that the scrambling device was functional, no defects in the hardware, no third party tapped into the line. A winking red would tell him they had company, while steady amber pointed to a technical malfunction jeopardizing the integrity of conversation on the unit.

Green was cool.

The static whisper in his ear dissolved as Tilton switched the second scanner on and closed the circuit. They could both speak freely now, assuming there were no bugs in the room itself—and Lasser swept the whole house daily to ensure precisely that.

"You there?" asked Tilton.

"Yes."

"It's early."

"We've got trouble."

"Tell me."

Lasser spelled it out in simple terms, no frills. His strong right arm was less concerned with motives than with method. *How* was always more important than the abstract *why*.

"It should be simple," Lasser said when he had

finished ticking off the list of names, addresses and descriptions for his chief of physical security. "The undertaker's sitting tight, scared shitless, waiting for instructions."

"Good."

"As for the others...well, just do the best you can, but get it done.

"No problem," Tilton said. "I'm clear to use the drones?"

"Nobody's given me instructions to the contrary," said Lasser. "Hell, it's what they're meant for."

"Right. Okay."

"I'll talk to you again when you have something to report."

"Affirmative," said Tilton, breaking the connection.

Lasser switched his scrambler off, then cradled the receiver. It was done—his part, at any rate. The delegation of authority presumed a modicum of trust, and Tilton had not failed him yet.

He felt a stirring in his loins and knew it was the warm excitement of a brand-new hunt. He missed the trigger-pulling days sometimes, but it was safer this way. He could have his cake and eat it, too.

The thought of sweets brought Debbie back to mind, and Lasser walked back to the bedroom, smiling in the darkness as he pulled the covers back, exposing her.

"Hey, babe, wake up. I brought you something."

GARRICK TILTON READ the list of names once more, as if he might learn something of his quarry from the letters scratched on paper. He gave up the exercise when nothing happened.

So he wasn't psychic. Screw it.

Illinois, Nevada, Florida.

Ideally Tilton would have liked to catch them all together, but solutions seldom came that easily in life. At least the targets weren't professionals. An undertaker, an old woman and a fat cat who believed his worry days were over.

Guess again.

The one thing Tilton knew for sure was that a mess you left behind would catch up with you some-day, when you least expected it, and fuck you up. He took great pains to clean up as he went along, no loose ends dangling that could mutate into snares and trap him somewhere down the line. Even if that meant burying a one-time business partner or a for-mer friend. Garrick Tilton's loyalty was restricted to himself and those who paid his salary right now, this minute. If he got a better offer, and the risks were not extreme, he had no problem switching sides, ex-changing masters. Anyone who didn't like it could be dealt with swiftly and decisively.

The best thing, he decided, was to deal with the most-distant targets first. That meant the undertaker, then the woman, shooting for the fat cat last of all. Surveillance would be simple, making sure he didn't bolt or spill his guts before the drones caught up with him. They could be finished with the whole list in a day, if Tilton got a move on, sending out his troops.

Okay.

The drones were testy sometimes, when they had to take a briefing at peculiar hours, but they always came around. It was the breeding, Tilton thought, and smiled.

Sometimes it helped to keep things in the family.

He wondered idly if the Feds were making any progress, and the question made him think, in turn, of the escape fund he had started building up the day he took his present job. A true professional was never taken absolutely by surprise. He always had some kind of fallback option waiting, just in case the game unraveled on him and his sponsors started bailing out.

The one thing Garrick Tilton wouldn't do for money was play scapegoat for a bunch of self-important bastards who regarded him as nothing but a button man. He had experienced enough shit back in school, then in the military, finally on the streets, to know that only suckers went down with a sinking ship.

Things hadn't come to that point yet, weren't even close, if he believed what Lasser had to say, but Tilton wasn't taking any chances, either. He could always sniff the wind himself, see which way it was blowing, smell the pigs before they moved in close enough to bag him.

What could Lasser and the others do if he bailed out one day and let them take the heat? Complain to the authorities that their chief executioner had left no forwarding address?

Get real.

They couldn't say a fucking thing about the work he'd done for them, without admitting guilt themselves. Plea bargains would be risky, since the Feds were more inclined to deal with trigger men to nab their sponsors than the other way around.

And if the day came when he thought that someone on the team had sold him out...well, Garrick Tilton always paid his debts, with interest.

In the meantime, though, he had a job to do. Nevada, Illinois, then Florida. He was excited, thinking of it.

It was time to call the drones.

7

Dr. Smith had handled Remo's urgent query from his office at Folcroft Sanitarium. It was a relatively simple matter to pursue Eugenix Corporation through computer records, with his access to the IRS and other federal databases paying off. Unfortunately there was only so much to report about a company that had dissolved in 1984.

Eugenix had its roots in Delaware, a state renowned for incorporation statutes that allowed residents of other states and nations to employ a local lawyer, rent a post box to fulfill the residency guidelines and cash in on tax breaks they might otherwise have been unable to achieve. All strictly legal, and it brought the Diamond State sufficient revenue to make the laws worthwhile. In fact, an estimated seventy percent of corporations "based" in Delaware did little or no business there, aside from filing annual reports and keeping up on legal fees.

Eugenix Corporation had been chartered in July of 1961, four years before the scam with Thomas Hardy in Nevada. Under "Goals and Purposes," the officers in charge had listed "education" and "genetic research," in that order.

Could mean anything, Remo had said when he spoke to the CURE director. It could also mean nothing.

Smith had explained to Remo something about one law that governed corporations: they could claim most anything when making application for a charter, and it made no difference in the long run. Fine points like an argument for tax exemption would be argued elsewhere, with the state and federal agencies in charge of revenue. The Ku Klux Klan was chartered as a "benevolent fraternal order," and for those who bought that nonsense, there were still some hefty pieces of the Brooklyn Bridge available for purchase any time they chose to lay their money down.

The charter officers who launched Eugenix Corporation had included Jasper Frayne as president, his wife, Lucille, was vice president, and Roscoe Giddings was secretary/treasurer. The Fraynes had lived in New York City at the time, while Giddings was a cut-rate lawyer chasing ambulances in Wyoming, Delaware, a few miles from the capital at Dover. Giddings on the board made everything legitimate, at least on paper, and the state was satisfied once it received the stipulated fees.

None of the named Eugenix officers had any background whatsoever in the fields of education, medicine, biology or any other discipline that would have helped the corporation to attain its stated goals. A background check on Jasper Frayne described him as a Wall Street stockbroker, cashiered from the exchange in 1958 on allegations of insider trading. He had paid a fine of twenty-seven thousand dollars to the SEC, avoided any jail time and resurfaced six months later as a ''corporate analyst'' with several major clients on his string. Three of the client corporations, incidentally, were said to be front groups for syndicate investments, while a fourth—Laredo Chemical, in Texas—specialized in flooding Third World markets with substandard medicines and drugs.

The medical connection, Remo thought... Or was it?

Mrs. Frayne had been a high-school cheerleader and home-economics major who dropped out of college, married well and afterward confined her interests to the New York social scene. The only ''genes'' she understood were the designer kind, with fancy labels on the ass. Her listing as vice president of the Eugenix Corporation was almost certainly a sham to keep the lion's share of stock in her husband's hands, but such shenanigans were hardly criminal—in fact, they ranked as standard operating procedures in the corporate jungle. As for Roscoe Giddings, he had been the local front required by law, and nothing more. His office satisfied the mandate for a Delaware address, and almost certainly provided him with extra tax breaks for a minimal investment of his time.

Where were they now?

The record showed Eugenix posting heavy losses for the last five years of its existence, finally going belly-up and filing for bankruptcy in February 1984. The corporation's creditors were left without a prayer of making up their losses, and they couldn't even slap a lien on lab equipment, since the previous December a fire of undetermined origin had razed the corporation's sole research facility in Belding, Michigan. Arson experts declared the blaze suspicious, but they never proved complicity by anyone on the Eugenix payroll, and the corporate insurance finally paid off around Thanksgiving.

The Fraynes dropped out of sight for eighteen months, then surfaced with a hefty wad of cash in Coral Springs, Florida, where they apparently retired. Lucille made the mistake of purchasing a new Mercedes-Benz, which tempted her to drive a bit too fast. On June 4, 1987, driving south from Stuart, she misjudged her own ability to pass three semitrailers on the turnpike, met a fourth truck heading north and she was history. Closed casket, R.I.P. Since then, her husband was reputed to enjoy the company of younger women who disrobed for tips at nightclubs in Fort Lauderdale.

The lawyer, Giddings, had no luck to speak of, either. Six months after Eugenix Corporation folded, he went on retainer with the Alvarado brothers, late of Medellín, to help them organize a trucking company, ostensibly involved in hauling citrus fruit from Florida to New York and New England. The brothers seemingly grew paranoid when federal agents picked off several truckloads of cocaine in transit through the wilds of Georgia and Virginia. Suspicion fell on Giddings, and the lawyer disappeared. He had been missing thirteen days, when hunters found his vintage Caddy in the woods near Jacksonville, with Roscoe's headless body in the trunk. His head was never found, but rumor had it that the eldest Alvarado brother, Rico, had it shrunk as a dashboard ornament.

So much for traveling in style.

The Belding fire had wiped out all Eugenix personnel and payroll records, scuttled the computer data banks, reduced the work of two decades to ashes. A covert scan of records at the FDA and U.S. Patent Office turned up nothing to suggest the company had broken any new ground in the area of drugs or medical procedures—no new products whatsoever, for that matter. There had likewise been no applications for a research grant of any kind, a circumstance that, while peculiar in the world of medical experiments, was hardly grounds for an investigation. Federal auditors would surely have been grateful for a corporation that eschewed the public trough, assuming they were conscious of Eugenix in the first place.

What exactly had Eugenix Corporation done for

something like a quarter of a century? Was it connected to Laredo Chemicals in some way, picking up the slack when that esteemed conglomerate dissolved in 1970? If it was all one great, extended scam to swindle Third World customers, what use would the Eugenix team have for the body of a hit man executed in Nevada?

The only person still on record who could answer Remo's questions would be Jasper Frayne, in Coral Springs, Florida. He might be hesitant to talk, but there were ways around that problem. Remo could be damn persuasive when he set his mind to it, and getting nowhere fast on an assignment always put him in the mood.

He booked the next flight out of Reno, for Miami, and advised Chiun to pack his steamer trunk.

ALL THINGS CONSIDERED, life hadn't been hard on Jasper Frayne. He had experienced his share of setbacks and embarrassment like anybody else, but you took the bitter with the sweet and kept on rolling, or you gave it up and pulled the plug.

If there was one thing Jasper Frayne could never tolerate, it was a quitter.

Like Lucille, for instance.

Despite the fact that she was drinking on the afternoon she totaled the Benz, Frayne would never buy it as an accident. She had been going through the Change and giving everybody hell about it, trying quacks for size like they were some new Paris fashions, taking pills that made her alternately loopy and depressed. Frayne always figured that she meant to slam that semi rig head-on, though he would never say that to the pricks from the insurance company. Hell, no. They would have screwed him altogether, and why should he do anything to cost himself a quarter million?

Check the dictionary under *stupid*, and you would not find his picture, no damn way at all.

It was too bad about Lucille, of course, but things were getting stale between them anyway. Frayne was cultivating an enthusiasm for the game of jai alai, which let him slip out two, three times a week to nudie bars in Lauderdale, and he suspected that Lucille had found diversions of her own. So what? She was entitled, after all, and jealousy had long since faded in the stretch, along with love.

Frayne missed his wife of twenty-seven years, in the abstract, but not for long. It was a new, wild world out there, and never mind the crap you heard on television, how the sex was hard to find with everybody scared to death of AIDS. In Jasper Frayne's world, money talked and bullshit walked. The past eight years, if anyone had asked him, Frayne would have to say that he was living, bet your ass.

He hardly thought about Eugenix anymore, at all, except when there was something in the paper to remind him. Like the bullshit in Miami, back in April, with the two Colombians. He would have shrugged it off, another case of scum eliminating scum, except the shooter had been captured and refused to give his name, then offed himself in jail. The dicks at Metro-Dade had put his mug shot on the tube for three nights running, asking anyone with information to call in, and Frayne had nearly shit himself the first time he had seen the photographs.

That face.

He wasn't likely to forget it, even after all this time. The old crowd had no hold on him these days, at least in theory, since they knew he was a man who could be trusted taking secrets to his grave. It looked like they were getting careless, though—or cocky. Convinced that no one in the world could crack their secret, they let their guard down just enough to start the Feds asking questions.

On the other hand, he told himself, there could have been a problem with the drone—or plain bad luck. They had gone twenty years without a glitch, before they lost the first one. Any other company with products on the market, they were making recalls every time you turned around. Bad tuna, flammable pajamas, cars that went off like a fucking atom bomb if they got love-tapped from behind, airliners crashing when some idiot forgot to double-check the nuts and bolts.

Frayne lounged beside his pool, eyes covered with those little plastic cups that looked like something from a 1950s horror movie, flaccid body slathered with enough sunblock to protect him from a napalm strike, and waited for Justine to put in her appearance. He had met her dancing at the Lucky Strike, in Lauderdale—that is to say, she did the dancing, while he sat and tried to keep his pulse from going through the roof. His second time to visit, she had joined him at his table, stalled a little bit before she finally agreed to private sessions at an hourly rate that should have qualified her as a lawyer or psychiatrist—perhaps even a plumber.

Frayne had to smile at that, his capped teeth glinting in the sun. Justine had cleaned his pipes, all right, and she was well worth every cent she charged. It wasn't like a man his age could drop into a singles' bar and find some sweet young thing to love him for his personality, much less the body that would surely fail him one fine day before too long.

They did not go to dinner or the movies, were not dating or engaged. It was a straight-up pay-for-play arrangement, and Frayne liked it that way, everybody knowing where they stood. When Justine tired of him, or found somebody with a bigger bankroll to entice her, Frayne could always shop around for a replacement. Maybe something Latin next time. Get a little piece of NAFTA working for himself.

Lately, though, he had trouble maintaining interest in the game. He still looked forward to the visits with Justine, of course, and went out trolling in the clubs at least three nights a week, but it was getting stale. Frayne had begun to wonder if maybe there was something more to life than lying in the sun and chasing someone else's tail.

It could be worse, he told himself. He could be like that asshole Giddings, stone-cold dead. Or like that crazy fucker Radcliff, hooked on some great cause that made the rest of life seem like a fever dream.

No, thank you very much.

If Frayne got a vote, he would prefer his current life-style over the alternatives—no life at all, or a crusade that ate up every waking moment of his time. Wall Street was bad enough, while it had lasted, with the damn margin calls and everybody screaming in the pits all day. It almost came as a relief when they had caught him with his fingers in the cookie jar, especially since he had already socked away enough cold cash to send him on his way in style.

Good times, he thought. And then, there was Eugenix.

Fuck it.

Frayne heard the side gate creaking on its hinges, and he smiled at the image in his mind. He felt himself begin to stiffen in anticipation. Should they start out with a little skinny-dip this afternoon, or maybe a massage? He had two hours booked, and if he needed more—

A shadow fell across Frayne's face and stayed there, blocking out the sun. He waited for a moment, psyched up for the phony compliments she always threw in free of charge, then became a bit confused when she said nothing.

Finally he raised a hand and slipped the sci-fi goggles up onto his forehead, blinking at the man who stood above him, where Justine should be. The sun was at the stranger's back, and yet—

That face.

"Aw, shit," he muttered, bolting upright, angling for the house and the guns inside.

A set of steely fingers gripped his throat like talons, stopped him dead and slammed him backward to the deck.

REMO DROVE WEST from Lauderdale on Highway 84, picked up 817 northbound, the final thirteen miles to Coral Springs. He had an address memorized for Jasper Frayne's retirement, directions from another street map, but his mind was busy with a replay of his latest conversation with Chiun.

"I take it from our flittering hither and yon that you have not yet located one of Smith's walking dead men," the Master of Sinanju had blandly inquired as they were settling into yet another motel room.

"Not yet," said Remo.

"Nor will you," Chiun sniffed. "The man has obviously taken complete leave of his senses. How does he expect you to kill a man who is already dead?"

"We never really got that far," Remo admitted.

"Pah! He is a fool and you are on a fool's errand."

"Is that why you keep barricading yourself in these hotel rooms and refusing to help with the legwork?"

"Legwork is for dancers, not Masters of Sinanju. If you want to be a Rockette, that is your business."

"Thanks a heap, Little Father."

Chiun tipped his birdlike head to one side. "I am somewhat curious," he said. "Your targets simply wear a dead man's face?"

"And fingerprints. Maybe the same DNA, for all I know. The new technology didn't exist in '65, and no one bothered saving Hardy's blood."

"But someone saved the body," Chiun reminded him. "The act required some risk. You should assume it has significance."

"I sort of had already."

"Are they religious?" Chiun asked suddenly.

"Who?"

"Your adversaries."

"From the nature of their crimes, I tend to doubt it."

"Perhaps they are politically motivated," Chiun ventured.

"Their choice of victims doesn't indicate that, either."

"So they are hired killers."

"Almost certainly."

"Then you must understand that everything they do is done for money or to save themselves."

As the preeminent assassin from a village known for expertise in that regard, Chiun knew whereof he spoke, and Remo didn't argue with his personal assessment.

How long before his unseen, unknown adversaries started working overtime to save themselves? Within the past few months, they had lost two of their peculiar carbon-copy killers, and they had to realize that the authorities would be investigating the bizarre phenomenon. It was a time for plugging leaks, and Remo wondered if Devona Price would be all right. Or Yuli Cristobal, in Carson City. Both of them had spilled their guts, and while they only pointed him toward nameless shadows, toward a corporation long defunct, that breach alone would be considered a betrayal in the big leagues, justifying punishment.

But they had taken a risk a long time ago, and now they were on their own. And he had more-important fish to fry. If anyone could tell him what was cooking with Eugenix Corporation, that someone was Jasper Frayne, the former CEO and founding father. Remo meant to keep his FBI facade in place as long as possible, but he would use whatever pressure might be necessary if he met resistance from the one-time leader of Eugenix.

There was nothing in the book that said Frayne

had to come out of their interview alive, much less intact.

He found the address, parked his rented compact at the curb and walked up to the house. No answer to the bell, but Remo heard a muffled sound, like someone coughing, that appeared to issue from the yard in back. He circled to the left and found a gate half-open, beckoning him to proceed. The scuffling, thrashing sounds were louder now, and Remo knew exactly what they meant.

Someone was fighting for his life.

He came around the corner in a burst of speed, found two men grappling in a grim, uneven contest. The older, softer of the two, was sprawled across a chaise longue, clad only in a black bikini bathing suit, his brown skin slick with oil and blood. The man who stood above him, bending at the waist, wore linen trousers and a garish flowered shirt that gave him the appearance of a tourist gone astray. He held down his victim with one hand, while his other made repeated, choppy jabbing motions from the waist.

A knife, thought Remo, closing in.

He spoke because he wasn't quite there yet, and he wanted to distract the killer now, while there was still at least some chance of saving Jasper Frayne.

"Back off!" he snapped, still moving toward the executioner, his legs almost a blur.

The killer turned to face him, and the sight made Remo hesitate for something like a quarter of a second. He had seen that face before, in photographs displayed by Dr. Smith. It was Tom Hardy, minus thirty years or so, the same face worn by hit men lately buried in Miami and upstate Wisconsin.

"Want some?"

It was strange to hear the voice. To him, Hardy was a photograph. A man long dead. Somehow the killer's voice—so normal it was almost pleasant— was more worrisome to Remo than the bloody knife he held in front of him or the too familiar face he wore.

Behind him, Jasper Frayne was thrashing weakly on the chaise, blood streaming from the stab wounds in his chest and abdomen. A slash across the throat would have been quicker, more efficient. Maybe the killer liked his work enough to drag it out by torturing his victims.

"What's your name?" he asked the killer, circling to his right, toward Jasper Frayne.

"Fuck you!"

"That's funny, you don't look Chinese."

The killer blinked, uncertain what to make of that, and sneered in lieu of a rejoinder.

"Well, Fuck, I have to tell you that the best thing you can do right now is drop the knife and give it up. No reason you should die, if you cooperate."

"Fuck you!"

"I see. Name, rank and number, is it? Fair enough. We'll play it your way."

Remo feinted to the right, saw the hit man shift

his weight to meet the charge, and went straight up the middle in a rush that left his enemy with no time to correct or compensate. The blade flashed red and silver, Remo blocking with his left hand, striking with his right, a straight jab to the chest that slammed his adversary over backward.

Remo planned to take the guy alive, for questioning. But down and out appeared to be two very different things. The assassin's shoulders barely hit the turf before he rolled over, grimacing in pain, and scrambled to his feet once more, the knife still in his hand. His first few steps were shaky, but he came back, straight at Remo, cursing underneath his breath.

A roundhouse kick disarmed him and set him up for Remo's backhand punch. The killer staggered backward, bleeding from the nose and mouth, but still not beaten. Remo saw his free hand rummage underneath the baggy shirt and come out with a shiny automatic pistol, muzzle-heavy with a silencer.

Remo kept his eyes fixed on the weapon, saw his adversary's finger tighten on the trigger, heard his flexor tendons creak as he prepared to make the killing shot. The trick to dodging bullets was anticipation, readiness, and Remo sidestepped as the first round whispered past his face, bare inches to his right. The shooter tried correcting but overdid it, and the next round went to Remo's left, his forward motion barely interrupted by the revolution of his torso as he turned to let another round zip by.

The hitter used up four of his nine shots before a hand shot out and took the gun away from him with such force that he spun about, then slammed his temple into the unforgiving corner of a square standing flower urn. When he landed on the grass, he didn't rise again.

Three steps to the chaise longue, and Remo knelt beside the dying man who must be Jasper Frayne. The quantity of blood around his nose and mouth told Remo that at least one lung was punctured, maybe both. The heart was beating, but it would soon be running out of blood to pump. No ambulance could get there fast enough to make a difference, and the time he wasted on a phone call would remove whatever hope remained of getting any information from the dying man.

Frayne's lips were moving, blowing slow crimson bubbles. Remo bent down low enough to try to hear what Frayne was saying.

One word, repeated in a weak whisper, twice.

Radcliff.

Remo was about to try a question, when the light went out behind Frayne's eyes, his muscles going slack in death.

Too late. He'd have to fit the name, be it a person, place or institution.

He spent another twenty seconds with the killer, turning empty pockets inside out. Besides the knife and gun, his adversary carried nothing on his person. No ID, no money, credit cards, no Kleenex—nothing.

A professional, thought Remo, who just happened to have someone else's face. The fingerprints and DNA analysis would fall to someone else.

A twenty-something fox was just emerging from a taxi when he hit the driveway, reaching in her purse to pay the driver. Glancing up at Remo with green eyes that had seen an awful lot of living, she hesitated.

"You for Jasper Frayne?" he asked.

"So what?"

"He's indisposed. You'd better go on home."

"Did he say that?"

"He isn't saying much of anything."

She got the drift then, wise enough to know that life was cheap in southern Florida. She muttered something to the cabbie, closed her door and glared at Remo as the taxi pulled away.

He watched it out of sight, then followed in his rental, heading back toward Lauderdale. The name, two syllables, kept playing through his mind.

It wasn't much, but he would have to check it out. And if he came up empty, then presumably the game was over. He would be the loser, no place left to turn.

But Remo wasn't ready to concede defeat.

Not yet.

The game still had at least one inning left to play, and he was hanging in until the bitter end.

8

"It may take some time," the head of CURE had warned him. "Even if you are sure of what you heard—"

"I'm sure," said Remo, interrupting.

"Yes. Well, you will agree it is not the most uncommon name. With spelling variants—Ratcliff, and so on—it could run to several hundred thousand names, you understand. Town-wise, my atlas shows two Radcliff's at a glance—one in Kentucky, and the other up in Iowa, the latter with an *e*. I would venture there must be schools, libraries, hospitals...."

"Just do the best you can, Smitty."

"Of course. You are staying in Fort Lauderdale?"

"Until I hear from you."

"Do you think that its wise?"

"The cops have got their man. I'm clear here."

"Very well. I will be in touch."

May take some time, he thought, disgustedly, as he replaced the phone. Smith had been right on that score, anyway. Two wasted days in Lauderdale, at the motel. Chiun didn't seem to mind. To the Master of Sinanju, this was just the logical continuation of Smith's lunacy. But it was making Remo nervous.

He already had the bad news, a return call from the CURE director no more than thirty minutes after he had hung up. Devona Price was missing from her home in Illinois, the house ransacked, though nothing on the surface indicated she was dead. The word from Carson City had been more decisive—Yuli Cristobal shot twice and stuffed into a casket at his place of business. No apparent witnesses, no clues.

Leak-plugging time.

Someone had been concerned enough by Remo's questions to react with violence. Who had spilled the beans? Not Frayne, since Remo didn't have a chance to question him before his killer paid a call. That narrowed it to Price or Cristobal, but Remo knew it made no difference. Both of them were gone, beyond his reach. It might have helped to grill the squealer, find out whom he called, but there would be no hope of that now. If Price was still among the living, it could only mean that she had found herself a hidey-hole, and chasing her would be a waste of energy.

Instead, he swam by day—innumerable laps around the motel's swimming pool—and worked the beach at night. No showing off in front of tourists during daylight hours. Remo backed off the Sinanju dives that he had learned from Chiun and simply swam to work off nervous energy.

The nights were something else.

He went out late, allowing youthful drunks and lovers ample time to finish up their business on the beach. A brooding fear of crime helped clear the water's edge, and Remo rarely saw another living soul. If there were muggers lurking in the shadows, watching him, they had enough sense left in wasted brains to let him be.

Too bad. He would have welcomed company, if they came armed and looking for an easy touch.

Instead, he worked the sand. Ran miles along the beach without a footprint to betray his passing, up the coast from Lauderdale as far as Pompano, or south to Hollywood. It felt like floating when he ran, barefoot, left nothing for the naked eye to follow. Hunting dogs could have picked up his scent, perhaps, but he was not concerned with hounds just now.

His enemies were human beings.

Once each night, when he was sure he had the beach all to himself, he stripped his clothes off, dashed into the surf and swam as Chiun had taught him, the Sinanju way. He didn't struggle with the current, but rather used it, let it help him as he swam for a protracted distance underwater. An observer could have been forgiven for assuming he had drowned, his body carried out to sea or maybe savaged by a shark. When Remo surfaced, better than a hundred yards from shore, he felt no weariness or pain. Instead, it was as if the worries of the day had sloughed off, like a reptile's skin, to leave him fresh, renewed.

He carried no towel with him, but the warm air dried him as he ran back toward the motel. A mile or so before he reached his destination, Remo stopped again, this time to dress. He wondered what the police would make of the reports if someone saw him running naked on the beach, and finally decided it would not make news in Florida—unless, of course, he was a politician, televangelist or host of some insipid children's TV show.

Chiun was sleeping when he left the room at night and made no sound when he returned, but Remo knew the old Korean was aware of every move he made.

The Master of Sinanju didn't sleep with one eye open, but he very likely could have if he wanted to. Instead, he was so perfectly attuned to his environment—wherever and whatever it might be—that he could sense a change, regardless of his waking state.

He was Chiun. That said it all.

On Day Three, when they came back from a long walk, the message light was flashing on the bedside telephone. Remo's Aunt Mildred had called, the operator told him, asking Remo to return the call as soon as possible. Smith's code.

The blue contact telephone rang only once before Smith picked it up.

"I have some information for you, Remo." No amenities or salutations. The CURE director ran true to form, got straight to business, as if every wasted moment was a personal affront.

"I love to talk to you first thing in the morning, Smitty. You're like a sparkling ray of sunshine. What have you got?"

"First I should tell you the bad news—or I suppose I should say the non-news. The police and FBI came up with nothing on the killer in Coral Springs except his fingerprints. Another perfect match with Thomas Allen Hardy. DNA analysis will take a while, but my guess is that it will be another match."

"So, now it's triplets," Remo said, seriously.

"He drove a rented car," Smith said. "They found it two doors up the street. Hardy's fingerprints all over it. He had to show a driver's license for the rental, but it was bogus. A patrolman found it in the glove compartment along with a street map. Maybe we can trace the artist, maybe not. It is doubtful he or she would know our Mr. X, in any case."

"That's it? No airline tickets? Nothing that will help us backtrack?"

"Nothing," Smith replied. "Right now I could not even prove he flew to Florida. I am going to check airline registers against the driver's license, but I have a hunch he would not use the same name twice. If there is a round-trip ticket sitting in a locker or a motel room somewhere, it is likely we will never hear about it."

"Damn! These guys drop out of nowhere, like

they beamed down from the freaking starship *Enterprise* or something."

"Perhaps not," said Smith. "I began with the bad, but there is some good news."

"I could use some," Remo told him.

"I got lucky with a hit on Radcliff. Working from the logical assumption that the move on Jasper Frayne was probably related to Eugenix Corporation, I made cross-checks on the personnel my first priority."

"I thought you said the records were destroyed."

"Correct." Smith sounded smug, and Remo wondered if his lemon face would be showing just the bare hint of a smile. "I had to do it backward, which was no small task, I can assure you."

"Backward?"

"You recall the stated goals on the Eugenix corporate charter?"

"Education and genetic research," Remo said.

"Correct. I think it is safe to say the education part of it was fraudulent, but I pursued both angles just in case."

"I still don't follow you."

"Education calls for teachers, and genetic research calls for scientists—geneticists and biochemists at the helm, with all kinds of supporting staff."

"Makes sense."

"With that in mind," Smith said, "I programmed the computer to select all secondary-level educators, medical researchers and physicians by the name of

Radcliff who were practicing from 1961 to 1984, inclusive.''

"You can do that?'' Remo never ceased to marvel at the ways in which advanced technology invaded private lives.

"It is not foolproof,'' Smith admitted. "Someone always tumbles through the cracks, of course, but the computer threw up nineteen thousand names. Approximately half of those were teachers, anywhere from junior-high-school English to the dean of girls at a Midwestern university, but none of them had any visible connection to Eugenix.''

"Wow. Surprise.''

"The medics were a different story, but it still took time. Of the 8,295 subjects, I scored a hit on number—let me see—3,014. Naturally I finished off the run, but this is it. The one and only.''

"Do I have to guess, or what?''

"His name is Dr. Quentin Bishop Radcliff— He is an M.D., not a Ph.D. He specializes in—''

"Genetics?''

"Correct. Anyway, he did.''

"And now?''

"Let me begin at the beginning. Quentin Bishop Radcliff, born in Cambridge, Massachusetts, on March 7, 1931. His father was a Harvard-educated surgeon. The son followed the father into the medical field. However, his preoccupation was with research. Interned at Boston Memorial and passed his boards in 1961. Apparently, he went directly into theoretical research.''

"The same year Jasper Frayne set up Eugenix Corporation.''

"That is correct. It would seem that Radcliff made Eugenix his career for almost twenty years. He left in 1981, three years before it finally collapsed, and opened up a private practice in Raytown, Missouri, east of Kansas City.''

Remo frowned. "What kind of private practice?''

"Obstetrics and gynecology,'' said Smith.

"A baby-delivery doctor?''

"So it would appear.''

"How long was he in Raytown?''

"Five or six years,'' Smith replied. "It is hazy. There is a gap of several months before his name turns up again, affiliated with an institution in the southern part of Indiana. A small town called Dogwood.''

"What kind of institution?'' Remo prodded.

It looks like a tie-in with his late-life redirection of careers,'' Smith said. "Some kind of live-in clinic Radcliff calls the Ideal Maternity Home.''

"A maternity home? You mean for unwed mothers? I thought those kind of homes went out with free love and the pill a hundred years ago.''

"You would be surprised,'' Smith said. "I grant you, illegitimacy does not have the stigma that it carried thirty years ago but for some it is still a deep concern. Some families do not like the reminder staring them in their face. These will oftentimes go the adoption route. A maternity home is not so unusual in the latter stages of pregnancy.''

The conversation struck a chord in Remo. He had been abandoned as an infant on the steps of a Newark orphanage and tried off and on for years to track his parents down. He had found his father at last, Sunny Joe on the reservation, but saw his mother only in dreams of the beyond. But he had made a kind of peace, and now Sunny Joe helped him maintain his own generational connections.

Old business, Remo thought, and concentrated on the mystery at hand.

''So, Radcliff starts out with Eugenix, fresh from internship. He puts his twenty in, presumably genetic research, then he sees the writing on the wall and takes a hike before the creditors move in. Do we know anything about his rank within the corporation?''

''The notation on his c.v. says he was chief researcher, which could mean anything. It does not say a word about what he was working on.''

''Okay. And when he bails out from Eugenix in—where was it?''

''Belding, Michigan,'' said Dr. Smith.

''In Michigan, right, he moves to Raytown. Wasn't there a TV show about that place?''

''I would not know,'' Smith answered rather stiffly.

''Never mind, I'll ask Chiun.''

"He moves to Raytown, close by Kansas City, and hangs out his shingle as an OB-GYN."

"Correct."

"A baby doctor," Remo said again, still grappling with the concept.

"We have established that," said Smith.

"Another six or seven years go by, he moves to Indiana and sets up a home for unwed mothers."

"Right again. What are you getting at?"

"I'm not sure yet," said Remo. "He was absolutely with Eugenix when they picked up Hardy's stiff in Carson City?"

"On the payroll, yes. There is nothing so far to connect Radcliff directly with the buy."

"He was their chief of research," Remo said, "unless you think he doctored up his credentials to make himself look more important, giving Pap smears out in Raytown."

"What is your point?" A subtle undercurrent of suspicion was apparent in the CURE director's tone. "Are you suggesting—?"

"Where do babies come from, Smitty?"

Smith's delivery became more formal. "If you need a refresher course on sex education, perhaps Chiun can fill you in. Right now, we have a more important—"

"Sperm and eggs," said Remo, interrupting him. "They come from sperm and eggs."

"Yes," Smith told him, "that is correct."

"And what's inside the sperm? Inside the eggs?

DNA," said Remo, answering himself. "Genetic building blocks."

"You are suggesting—"

"I don't know what I'm suggesting," said Remo. "At the moment, I'm just talking to myself."

"Please do so on your time. What you have in mind is physically impossible with present-day technology."

"Tell that to Dolly the sheep. We still don't have a clue what the Eugenix crowd was working on from 1961 through '84, correct?"

"That is true, but—"

"They were using private funds exclusively, no federal grants, no applications to the FDA or Patent Office, nothing in the media or scientific journals. Someone strikes a match in Michigan, and there's no paper trail at all. Is that about the size of it, so far?"

"Even given the current advances in this field, remember we are talking about the 1960s. Back then it was science fiction, Remo."

"Maybe, but it's all we have. Ideal Maternity, in Dogwood, Indiana, correct?"

"Yes." Smith's voice had taken on a note of caution. "Dr. Radcliff lives across the river, in Kentucky—Brandenburg, to be precise. He also runs a clinic there. It specializes in fertility research and treatment."

"Getting better all the time," Remo commented.

"Be advised, Remo," Smith said, "small-town

Indiana and Kentucky might not be what you are used to. Ideas and customs that went out of vogue in mainstream culture years ago still thrive there.''

"Maybe you should FedEx my zoot suit."

"I am serious," Smith said, his voice turning lemony.

"No kidding," Remo replied. "I don't know why you're so worried about such a stupid nothing assignment."

Smith sighed. "Will Chiun be going with you?" he asked.

"Are you kidding? And miss out on an opportunity to fly halfway across the country and sit in yet another hotel doing nothing? He wouldn't miss it."

Smith was silent for a long, reflective moment. "Maybe I should hand this over to the FBI," he said at last, "and let them carry it from here."

"Your call." said Remo. "But lately that's a virtual guarantee of a screwup."

"Yes." The CURE director was still thinking.

"Is there something wrong with bringing Chiun? Other than the fact that he's done virtually nothing on this assignment so far."

"It is known that in the hinterlands sixty years ago, the KKK ran politics in Indiana. Kentucky was not far behind."

"Are you trying to tell me to bring along some clean sheets just in case?"

"I am trying to be delicate about this, Remo."

"You're telling me an old Korean may look out of place?"

"Precisely." Smith sounded relieved that it was Remo who said it.

Remo felt Chiun's venomous glare from across the room. "I'll fill him in on your concerns," he told the CURE director, "but I think the Asian Anti-Defamation League is already in business."

"My point is that you need to be discreet. There are times when Chiun is not up to that particular challenge."

"If there's been a time when he was, I haven't been around to see it."

Remo cradled the receiver, turning to face Chiun. "We've got a lead," he said.

"I heard," Chiun said flatly. "The baby doctor."

Despite his age and seeming frailty, Chiun still had a falcon's eyesight and the hearing of a bat. Combine that with a cheetah's speed, the striking power of a Bengal tiger, plus a cobra's lethal bite, thought Remo, and you could have based a wildlife video around the aging Oriental.

"We traipse off now to this Indiana," said Chiun, not asking.

"Smith's given us the green light."

"Yes, Smith," Chiun said. "Chaser of hobgoblins. This doctor he mentioned is engaged in something evil?"

"Maybe," said Remo. "Guess we'll know when we get there."

"Then kill him and let us be done with this fool mission."

"I'm going to investigate him," Remo said. "It's no good dropping him before I find out what he's up to."

"Wonderful. Now you are not content to just be a Ghostbuster. You are Remo Williams, P.I. Do you believe this doctor brings assassins back to life?" Chiun inquired.

The question made him hesitate. As an assassin who had "died" and then been resurrected with a new identity, he of all people could not automatically dismiss the notion as preposterous. Still...

"No, it's not that simple," Remo answered, almost smiling at the notion of reanimating corpses as a simple project. "Bringing Hardy back somehow would give him one assassin maybe, but it wouldn't give him three. On top of that, they're so much younger. Hardy would be pushing seventy by now."

"Age does not preclude a man from living an active life," the ancient Master of Sinanju said.

"It does if he was pumped full of cyanide in '65."

"So the answer to this riddle is something else. Something to which you know the answer already," said Chiun. "I see it written on your face."

Remo smiled. "Let's say I have a hunch, okay? If it proves out, we've got a major problem on our hands."

"*You* have a problem. I am merely a tagger-along.

You admitted as much to Smith. I will sit by and wait for your shrewd detective's brain to solve this fiendish puzzle.''

"Your confidence is overwhelming," Remo said aridly.

"I am confident only in your ability to make a nincompoop of yourself when you indulge Smith's idiotic whims. He even expressed worry over me. *Me*. Do not deny it."

"Smith was concerned...." Remo began.

"About everything and anything." Chiun filled in the blanks. "He is a nitwit. What is this cluck-cluck clan?"

"It's like a social club for the discriminating psychopath. They dress up like refugees from a linen closet and run around terrorizing people who don't pass their color test. We've met their kind a couple of times before."

"I tend to forget the most distasteful elements of this land," Chiun said.

"Selective amnesia," Remo said. "Anyway, I think Smith would appreciate it if you kept a low profile."

"I will eliminate no more of them than absolutely necessary," Chiun assured him with a frosty smile.

"Seems fair." Remo could almost find it in his heart to pity any skinhead, redneck, Ku Klux clown who tried to push the wizened old Korean around.

Almost.

"We'd better pack," he said.

"I am done already," Chiun informed him, marching for the door. "Take care not to scratch my trunk or I will remand you to the custody of the backward cluck-clucks."

"Maybe I should have just left him home," Remo sighed to the empty room.

9

Harrison County, Indiana, is named for the president Hoosiers sent to Washington in 1889. His term in office was mostly distinguished by the admission of six new states, but he remains a local hero in the state that still congratulates itself on giving birth to one John Herbert Dillinger. The county seat is Corydon, on Highway 62. Ten miles to the south is Dogwood, a tiny town of fewer than one thousand year-round residents.

The nearest airport, Remo had discovered, was in Louisville, Kentucky, on the wrong side of the river. Flying to the closest strip in Indiana proper would have meant a stop in Evansville, some eighty miles due west, and spending two more hours on the road to reach their destination. Coming out of Louisville, the trip was more like thirty miles.

No contest.

Chiun got all the normal looks, and then some, in the terminal at Louisville. He spoke to no one, let Remo do all the talking at the Avis counter, and it was a challenge trying to decipher his impression of the rubberneckers who kept gawking at him. Sometimes Remo thought the old Korean took it as his due, assuming they were awestruck by the Master of Sinanju; other times he caught Chiun glaring back and was convinced that shortly some gaping fool would find himself on the receiving end of an uncomfortable lesson in respect.

A Chrysler Concorde waited for them in the Avis parking lot, and Highway 64 took them across the river to New Albany, best known in recent years for the sadistic murder of a junior-high-school student by a gang of teenage girls whose motive was a curious amalgam of black magic, homosexuality and simple boredom.

The world is collapsing around all our ears, thought Remo as he picked up Highway 62.

The highway branched off nine miles east of Corydon, a narrow strip of two-lane blacktop veering south. New Middleton was there and gone almost before he knew it, catching State Road 337 for the short run into Dogwood.

The town lived up to its name, the nearby woods ablaze with flowers, pink and white. A fair percentage of the homes they passed along the way were built from logs, some obviously new, while others looked as if they could have been around when Daniel Boone was fighting Indians and redcoats in the neighborhood.

Chiun absorbed the rustic atmosphere without commenting on it, watching as they passed a horse-drawn carriage, followed closely by a pair of shaggy thugs on Harley-Davidsons. Most of the vehicles Remo saw were pickups and four-wheelers, with a visible minority of old sedans, the bodies rusting out from long exposure to the salt laid down on snowy winter roads.

The Dogwood Inn reminded Remo of the Bates Motel, except there was no mansion looming on a hill behind the simple L-shaped structure with its twenty rooms all facing toward the highway. If the motel parking lot was any indicator, they had twenty vacancies to choose from. Tourist business in the tiny town was obviously no great shakes, despite the painted sign out front that promised free TV and telephones in every room.

Predictably it was the one and only place in town with rooms to rent. Remo considered getting straight to business, and to hell with staying overnight, but he would still need someplace for Chiun to stay while he was checking out the target. There were two restaurants in town—a drive-in that reminded him of something from *American Graffiti,* plus a little mom-and-pop that specialized in family dining—but he couldn't see the Master of Sinanju killing time in either one. It could have been amusing, Remo thought, to watch Chiun order rice, and then demolish the establishment if someone gave him any lip, but this was not a pleasure cruise.

He had to scope the target out, and something told him that it would be wise to wait for nightfall. That meant moving in and sitting tight until the proper moment, insulating Chiun from any contact with the local yokels that could spark a minor riot.

Although in a small place like this they were more noticeable, there was one advantage: Chiun looked too "irregular" for anyone to consider them as investigators of anything—especially a home for unwed mothers owned and operated by a doctor who was bound to rank among the wealthiest and most respected men in town.

It could be worse, he told himself. I could've brought the circus with me, maybe rode an elephant down Main Street, with a marching band and fireworks. Get some acrobats and clowns in funny little cars.

Step one was leaving Chiun outside when he went in to register. The motel manager was five foot six or seven, skinny as a rail, with ancient pockmarks from a killer case of acne on his sunken cheeks. His hair was almost gone on top, and he attempted to conceal the fact by combing what he had across the barren wasteland of his scalp, from left to right. His wife wore hot-pink curlers and at least two hundred pounds of excess flab that dangled from her arms like the voluminous sleeves of a choir robe.

Jack Spratt, thought Remo, swallowing a smile as he signed in and paid for two nights in advance, a double room.

"Wife with you?" asked the missus, wobbling dangerously on tiptoes for a glimpse of Remo's car outside.

"No, ma'am."

"Your girlfriend?" Scarface asked.

"Just passing through on business."

"Hmph. An' what would that be?"

Remo left the question hanging, finished filling out the registration card and slid it back across the counter with a ballpoint pen that advertised a nearby funeral home. He thought of Norman Bates again, decided Scarface couldn't pull it off, and wondered for a moment if the Dogwood Inn was so depressing that its guests were prone to thoughts of suicide.

He reckoned it was time to put the ball in play.

"I'm looking for Ideal Maternity," he said.

"Ideal?" the woman echoed.

"Some directions would be helpful," Remo told her. "I could save a bit of time."

"Ideal Maternity, you say." Her husband wore the look of someone trying to do calculus by counting on his toes and fingers. "I don't rightly know—"

The woman jabbed him with an elbow in the ribs to shut him up. "Keep on through town," she said, "until you meet Highway 11, 'bout a mile or so from where we're standing. Left's the only way it goes from there—that's east to you and me. Another mile and something, there's a private road off to your left. They got a sign."

"Appreciate it," Remo said. He palmed his key and turned to leave the office.

"Selling something, I expect," Scarface chimed in.

"You never know," said Remo, and he let the door swing shut behind him as he walked back to the car.

"YOU DIDN'T HAVE to tell him, for God's sake!"

"What was I supposed to do, then, Raynard? Maybe stand around and make believe we haven't lived here thirty years? Like we're so blasted dumb we couldn't find our way across the street without a map?"

"We don't know who he is, Matilda!" Sweat had beaded up on Raynard's forehead as he paced the tiny office. "Why, he could be anybody!"

"So? What's that to us?" she challenged him.

"Dammit, woman, you know as well as I do! Talk about how much you know, and then play stupid like a little child!"

"Nobody's paying us to send some stranger on a wild-goose chase," she said. "And if they are, I damn sure haven't heard about it."

"Strangers asking questions lead to trouble," Raynard Bisbee told his wife. "It don't take no rocket scientist to figure that one out. This Mr. What's-his-name starts raisin' hell, who do you think them folks out there are gonna blame? The ones what told him where to go, that's who!"

"Think straight for once," Matilda snapped. "The home ain't like some kinda secret military base. They got a sign out on the road. They're licensed with the state, got people goin' in and out there all the time. They must be on a hunnerd lists for people sellin' everything from pills to sheets and toilet paper. Jumpin' Jesus, Raynard, you beat all!''

"So why'd he have to ask directions, then?"

"Well, lemme think about that puzzle for a second. Could it be because he's never been here in his life, before? You figure that could have something to do with it?"

"Don't mock me, woman!"

"No one's mockin' you, for Lord's sake. I'm suggestin' that you use your head for once, and don't go makin' mountains out of mole hills."

"I don't plan on windin' up like Winthrop's boy, awright?"

She flashed him a look that didn't thank him for being reminded. "That was an accident, for all you know." But Matilda Bisbee didn't sound convinced somehow. "Besides, the doctor settled out of court on that. Good money, what I hear down at the Clip 'n' Curl."

"You'd like that, I expect. Found money, you could just forget about me, easy as you please, and find yourself somebody else."

"You're talkin' foolish, Raynard."

"Accident, my ass. Boy gets electrocuted, fried like catfish on the griddle, and they claim he did it messin' with some kinda fuse box."

"Can you prove he didn't?"

"Can't prove nothin', 'cept he's dead as hell, and I'm in no great rush to join him."

"Jimmy Winthrop was a troublemaker, Raynard. You know that as well as I do. He was trespassin' the night he had his accident, most likely hopin' he could catch one of them girlies with her britches down. Can't say I miss him all that much, you wanna know the truth."

"You got a cold streak, woman."

"Maybe so," she said, "and maybe not. One thing I am sure of, the doctor and his people haven't hurt this town one little bit. Spend money here, they do, and never make no fuss. They pay their bills on time, but otherwise keep outa sight and outa mind. Good neighbors all around, the way I see it, even if they haven't been here fifty years, like some who think they're so damn special."

Raynard Bisbee couldn't argue with her logic, even if it gave him chills sometimes to think about the Winthrop boy. The Dogwood Inn was not a major beneficiary of the financial benefits from Ideal Maternity, although a family had been known to spend the night from time to time, when they were dropping off a pregnant daughter, waiting to be sure she settled in just right.

And then, there was the little something extra Raynard got each month as an incentive to keep both eyes open and alert for strangers in the neighborhood. He had a hard time working out exactly why a home for unwed mothers would be so concerned about security, but it was certainly a crazy world these days. You had all kinds of pressure groups around—pro-life, pro-choice, whatever—butting into other people's business, telling them what they should read or watch on television, whether they should keep a kid or get it farmed out at the clinic. Hell, for all he knew, they could be hiding Russian agents at the home. No skin off Raynard Bisbee, either way.

He got a hundred dollars on the first of every month—in cash, with no reports to Uncle Sammy—just to keep a watch for anybody who came snooping thereabouts.

"Why me? he'd asked, suspicious, when the matron from the home had first approached him.

"You're a man of substance, with his roots in the community," she said, so sweet and flattering that Raynard didn't even mind if it was soap before the bar. Besides, with the motel, you have a decent chance of meeting any strangers stopping off in town.

It made good sense, and so what if he found out later they were also paying someone at the two restaurants? Fool and his money, Raynard thought. It didn't shave his profits any if they chose to throw more cash around. His curiosity was piqued, given the way they seemed so paranoid, but Jimmy Winthrop's fate was a reminder of the risks that came with snooping into other people's business.

It pissed him off, the way Matilda took it on herself to point the stranger on his way, but there was only so much he could say about it. Going on five years, he hadn't told her yet about his monthly stipend from the home, and Raynard didn't plan on sharing with her now.

Too late to throw the stranger off, but that had never been a part of Raynard's job, in any case. He was supposed to watch, report and mind his own damn business after that.

"I'm goin' out awhile," he said.

There was suspicion in her whiny voice. "Where to?"

"To have a brewskie at the Pine Room, if you must know," Raynard told her. "Arguin' with you's done made my throat sore."

"Brung it on yourself, at that."

"I'll see you later on."

They had a pay phone at the Pine Room, with a good old-fashioned wooden booth where you could close the door and not be overheard by every jackass in the place. First time in all these years that Raynard had to earn his monthly C-note, and he didn't want an audience. Whatever happened after he made his call was someone else's headache, he decided.

INDIANA'S COUNTY ROADS showed signs of neglect and infrequent repairs. Baked in summer, frozen in winter, they displayed the scars to prove it—potholes disguised as harmless puddles when it rained, but were still deep enough to jolt a vehicle off course and sometimes blow a tire. "Repairs" consisted, in large part, of sporadic asphalt drops to fill the more impressive craters, but the patchwork never seemed to last. Throw in a few steep hills, blind corners, one-lane bridges, season it with roadkill, and they were a proper driving challenge for the inexperienced.

The scenery was something else. As Remo motored south from Dogwood, past the handful of small businesses that were the town, he understood why tourists might be drawn from other states. It wasn't Yellowstone, but there was simple beauty here, perhaps a fond reminder to the city-bound that life wasn't confined to steel and concrete, traffic noise and air pollution.

Maybe—for a few of them, at least—it felt like coming home.

Highway 11 branched off to his left, a small sign making sure he didn't miss it. Remo signaled for the turn, although he had the highway to himself, and kept within the posted limit as he headed east. Based on the directions he was given, he was almost there.

Chiun had taken one look at their motel room and grunted in disgust. The television was an ancient black-and-white with rabbit ears, which seemed to get four channels and a lot of static. There were two small beds, with bedspreads that resembled terry cloth, and other bits of furniture that would have made a swap meet seem like shopping on Rodeo Drive. The bathroom was an afterthought. Any sudden moves while sitting on the toilet, and you risked collision of your elbows with the sink and the adjacent wall.

Chiun was mollified, to some degree, when he located a new infomercial on Channel 4. It was for something called a Fat Blaster. He settled on the floor, legs folded in the lotus posture, frail hands resting on his knees. His recent, inexplicable passion for football seemed to have died off, Remo thought. Or had it been a pretense, a front, for some other preoccupation at the time?

"Beware of any and all who would say you have a 'purdy' mouth," the Master of Sinanju had warned, eyes locked upon the television screen.

"Will do."

He saw the sign now, coming at him on the left, nailed between two upright posts set back a few yards from the road. The overhanging trees almost obscured it, and it would have been no trick at all to miss the sign if Remo hadn't known what he was looking for. Ideal Maternity Home. He wondered what prompted Dr. Quentin Radcliff, with two decades of his life invested in genetic research, to bail out and spend his golden years providing care for unwed mothers. It was a most unusual step in the man's career path.

And what did any of it have to do with Thomas Allen Hardy, much less carbon-copy killers with his face and fingerprints?

"There were no answers yet, but now he had a

likely starting point. If Dr. Radcliff's name still troubled Jasper Frayne, more than a decade after they had parted company and the Eugenix Corporation was dissolved—more to the point, if Jasper, with his dying breath, blamed Radcliff for his own assassination—then the doctor must be worth a closer look.

Remo had never been a great believer in coincidence, especially where murder was involved.

Beyond the sign, a one-lane gravel track wound out of sight among the trees. Another pair of upright posts had been erected at the entrance to the driveway. These were steel and painted black, a chain stretched out between them, decorated with a smaller sign that cautioned Private Drive—No Entry.

Remo drove on past, another mile or so, until he found a handy place to turn around. His second pass confirmed that there was no chance of observing Dr. Radcliff's operation from the highway. He would have to penetrate the grounds on foot, and that was something he preferred to do by night.

He didn't know what to expect in terms of security. After all, what kind of risk could pregnant women pose to anyone except themselves, or possibly their unborn children? Remo understood the urge for privacy, especially if Dr. Radcliff drew his clients from among the semi-rich and famous, but there was a world of difference between discretion and defense.

Still, the early indications were that something was different here.

Correct or otherwise, the late, lamented Jasper Frayne had seemed to think his executioner was sent by Dr. Radcliff. The killer had been somehow linked to Thomas Allen Hardy and the late Eugenix Corporation. Radcliff, by his own admission was once the top dog in genetic research at Eugenix. And if Jasper Frayne still feared him, after almost fifteen years...

Then, what?

A vague suspicion loitered in the back of Remo's mind, reached out to nudge him every now and then, but he resisted the suggestion, unwilling to follow where it led.

His mind rebelled at driving back to the motel so soon and sitting in the squalid little room for hours, waiting for the sun to disappear. A drive would do him good, check out the local scenery and get a feeling for the back roads, just in case he had to beat a swift retreat.

The Chrysler handled well enough, if Remo took it easy on the speed and watched for potholes in the road. Squirrels dodged across the road in front of him, defying him to run them down, oblivious to the repeated evidence of others who lost the game. At one point, Remo stopped to let a turtle cross the highway, keeping one eye on his rearview mirror while the brightly colored reptile took its time.

He had to give the doctor credit, if there was some

kind of plot in progress at the home for unwed mothers. Dogwood was the last place anyone would think to look for something sinister. It was the perfect cover, tucked away in Nowhere, USA.

And it could still be nothing, Remo thought.

But told himself, Don't bet your life on it.

There were certain hallmarks about the operation, sight unseen. Remo recognized them from a distance, long exposure having sensitized him to the nuances.

He was picking up a pattern that spelled death.

There are no Asian restaurants in Dogwood, Indiana, and the closest—in New Albany—would probably have been Chinese, so Chiun was out of luck on native fare. The local diner managed rice to go, although it was not to the Master of Sinanju's liking.

"This is vile," Chiun complained.

"You don't have to eat it," Remo told him while the Master of Sinanju grumbled, poking into the foam container with his long fingernails.

"You would have me starve?" Chiun retorted between mouthfuls of rice.

"You'll survive."

"Fish would have been nice. Did they not have duck?"

"Hey, you asked for rice, I got you rice."

"White rice. There is no nourishment in these bleached grains." Chiun scarfed another mouthful.

"When I get back," said Remo, "I'll see if I can scrounge up some brown rice."

Chiun made a disgusted face. "Do me no more favors. This tea is like water," he added.

"Little Father, tea *is* water."

"Tea is tea. And this is noxious."

"Best I could do," Remo told him, moving toward the door.

He hesitated on the threshold, glancing back at Chiun. The ancient Asian sat and muttered to himself while eating, watching the evening news. Despite the signs of age, there was a spry, an almost muscular air about him.

"I should be back by midnight, maybe sooner," Remo said.

"You never take me anywhere anymore," Chiun called.

"You don't seem to want to go lately."

He closed the door as Chiun continued eating. It was a short walk to his car. The night was cool, but not unpleasant. Remo wore a black cotton T-shirt and matching chinos. Leather loafers completed his ensemble.

Once around the Chrysler, and he quickly satisfied himself that no one had dropped by to tamper with the car. Remo had not expected it—they were in Dogwood, not Chicago or Los Angeles—but you could never be too cautious, dealing with professional killers, even when their methods were a trifle crude.

That afternoon, after some vague remarks about a rich and errant niece, he had asked questions at the diner and the general store, about Ideal Maternity: Where was it? Did the locals get along with tenants of the home and members of the staff? He got a mixed reaction—call it eighty-five percent indifference, seasoned with a pinch of caution—but a quest for information was not Remo's top priority in town. Rather, he was intent on finding out if Dr. Radcliff had a spy or spies in Dogwood, maybe set off an alarm that would provoke some hasty action from his target.

Driving out Highway 11 in the dark, he doused his headlights half a mile before he reached the turn-off for Ideal Maternity. It was a risk, and would have meant at least a traffic ticket if he had met a sheriff's deputy or state patrolman, but he had the highway to himself. Three-quarters of a mile beyond the private driveway, on his right there was a rest stop he had noted earlier, complete with picnic tables and a narrow gravel track that stretched for twenty yards or so, allowing him to hide the Chrysler from the view of anybody passing on the highway.

He climbed out of the car.

There was no traffic on the narrow country road as Remo crossed it, worked his way into the trees for thirty yards or so and started back in the direction of the private driveway that served Ideal Maternity. He took his time, no hurry over unfamiliar ground, his passage silent in a forest where the wind, insects, night birds and scuttling animals provided constant background noise. Ten minutes brought him to the unpaved driveway, and he paused once again, to watch and listen.

If the "home" had posted guards, it stood to reason that at least one of them would be assigned to watch the access road. From where he stood he could not guess how far the driveway extended through the trees, but it made no sense for a guard to let potential enemies get close enough to strike, when he could stop them at the turnoff from the highway. Remo checked the shadows, gave full attention to his Sinanju-trained senses, alert for any sign of human life—and came up empty.

It was getting better all the time.

He didn't actually use the driveway, but struck a course that would run parallel and take him to his destination by what seemed to be the quickest route. In fact, it might be shorter cutting through the woods, but Remo had no plot plan for the property, no other way of homing in directly on his target. This way he was bound to reach the home in minutes.

His next immediate concern was what to do once he arrived.

Ideally Remo meant to nose around the place, examine it from different angles, maybe try to slip inside and see what kind of operation Dr. Radcliff had created for himself. It could be no more than a haven for unwed mothers, as advertised, but Remo didn't think so. Radcliff had invested too much time on his first love, genetic research, to abandon it entirely and revert to nursing teenage mothers through their final days of pregnancy. As for the clinic in Kentucky, what was that about? It seemed a bit ironic that the same man would be dealing with unwanted children, on the one hand, and attempting to increase production on the other, with a clinic aimed at treating infertility. The two facilities would have a vastly different clientele, of course, and yet there was a quantum kind of connection.

Remo had a sneaking hunch that Dr. Radcliff's goals—had never really changed. He had abandoned the Eugenix Corporation when it suffered fatal cash-flow problems...or in an alternative scenario, before the sham of money problems was employed to give him an escape hatch. Once out on his own, with brand-new sponsors, Radcliff would be free to carry on his work.

Which was what?

How did it gel with cookie-cutter hit men snuffing lives around the country and around the world? What value did a dead assassin, gassed with cyanide in 1965, have to a scientist engaged in pure research?

Remo's first glimpse of the maternity home was startling. It reminded him of a big, old-fashioned ski lodge more than any kind of medical facility. The unpaved driveway circled right around the rambling two-story structure, lost to view before it came out on the other side and met itself again. Garage or carport in the back, he thought, examining the structure from a distance, noting lights in several windows.

An easy circuit of the grounds, and Remo would

be ready to approach the building proper, try to get a peek inside. No rush, but he could feel a measure of anticipation building and focused on suppressing it to leave his senses crisp and clear.

He had as much time as he needed to complete his survey of the property. No sign of any guards, and if he met one, it would be the sentry's problem.

Remo had not come this far to be diverted from his goal.

JOY PATTON WAS AFRAID, but her outrage and determination overrode the fear, gave her the nerve to carry out her desperate plan. She didn't know exactly what the staff would do if she was caught—nothing to harm the baby, Joy was fairly certain—but whatever happened, it was worth the risk.

She had to get out now, before it was too late.

A number of the girls had talked about it—slipping out when it was dark, or even using sex to bribe an orderly and make him look the other way—but none had ever followed through, as far as Joy could tell. Not in the seven months of her confinement, anyway.

She gave a toss to her shoulder-length, thick gingery hair. A bunch of fraidy-cats is what they were, intimidated by the matron and the orderlies, much less by the doctor and his bedside manner. Of course, some didn't mind the place that much, and a few actually seemed to enjoy it.

Hate to think where they were coming from, she

told herself as she completed preparations for her flight. It took all kinds.

She wore dark clothing, layered against the slight risk of exposure to a chill, and the athletic shoes she wore the day they checked her in. Joy's feet were often swollen now, but she had loosened up the laces, and they still fit well enough to let her run.

No problem there. She would run barefoot over nails and broken glass, if necessary, to escape her stylish prison in the woods.

There wasn't much in terms of luggage for the getaway. She always traveled light, had checked in with a duffel bag that disappeared somewhere along the way, but that was life. She had the basics in her pockets: toothbrush, comb, her lipstick, and the twenty-seven dollars she had managed to conceal for seven months. Hell, there were thieves and murderers who served less time and had more waiting for them when they hit the streets again.

Everything would be all right, she told herself, when she was free and clear. The first priority was getting out. Whatever followed the escape itself was secondary; she would take things as they came.

Joy had a semiprivate room all to herself these days, since Karen had her baby and they cleared her place. It was another strong incentive to get cracking, not to wait until they found another girl who might turn out to be a weakling, or worse, a squealer. Each day she waited was another day of freedom lost forever, coming that much closer to the time when she, in turn, would disappear.

The matron said her "graduates" were doing great outside, but Joy would never swallow that, regardless of the phony letters posted in the TV room from time to time. She knew damn well that Sheila and Regine had vowed to blow the whistle when they hit the street again, no matter what inducements the doctor offered in return for silence. They would take his money, clothes, whatever, and report the bastard anyway.

But they had not.

No cops told Joy that neither of her friends had ever made it to the outside world. The sight of Sheila's postcard—from Hawaii, yet—delivered two weeks after she was "graduated," made Joy want to scream, cry, beat her fists against the walls.

It wasn't even Sheila's handwriting, for Christ's sake.

Time to go.

Her door was locked as usual, but Joy had been around a bit before she landed in her present situation, and the lock was no great challenge. Getting all the way outside would be another story—they had noisy "fire alarms" on any door that didn't have an orderly assigned to watch it—but Joy had another exit route in mind.

There was a window in the basement laundry room that looked out onto grass, a worm's-eye view. The window had a set of burglar bars outside, but they were old and the surrounding wooden window frame was even older. It had taken Joy the best part of a month, with stolen moments here and there, when they allowed the girls outside, but she had loosened up the screws enough that one or two good kicks should clear the way and give her room to run.

She faced a whole new set of risks outside. There was the dash across the open lawn, then navigating through the woods in darkness, praying for a car to stop once she was on the highway, but the worst of it was simply getting out. Once she accomplished that, Joy figured she would stand a fairly decent chance.

And if not, this wasn't living anyway, so what the hell.

When she was finished with the lock, she cracked the door a bare half inch, enough to listen for the sound of anyone outside. No footsteps, voices, nothing. It was clear, unless they had somebody waiting just outside the door, prepared to pounce the moment she revealed herself. In that case, Joy was done before she started, and she might as well just forge ahead.

Two inches, and a wedge-shaped section of the corridor was visible. No lurking shadows fell within her line of sight.

She stuck her head out, checked both ways and then ducked back again. Her heart was pounding, and she felt the baby move, as if her own raw desperation was communicated somehow, through the blood.

Hang on.

Seven months, and Joy was barely showing. Slender to a fault, she still had speed on her side, nothing like the nausea and weakness some girls suffered around the clock. Another reason for proceeding now, while she was still in shape to run—or fight, if necessary, to protect herself.

She left the room and closed the door behind her. For the last time, God, please let it be! No noise to tip the others off, if anyone was listening.

Joy moved along the corridor on tiptoes, scarcely breathing, terrified of making any sound that might betray her. The orderlies made scheduled rounds, at least in theory, but you never really knew when one of them would deviate from the routine and double back to give one of the floors a second look. More often, though, the night shift took it easy, kicking back, secure in the knowledge that Ideal Maternity had never suffered an escape.

Until tonight.

She reached the stairs and paused again, ears straining for the sound of voices, footsteps, the rustling of clothing. When Joy was satisfied, she scurried down the staircase, almost tripping in her haste. She caught the banister and saved herself from tumbling down, knowing the baby was well cushioned from simple jolts.

Maternal instinct was a killer, regardless of the

circumstances. This time last year, Joy would have belittled anyone who said she had the instinct locked inside her, waiting to assert itself, but she knew better now. She was escaping for her child as much as for herself.

The ground floor seemed deserted. That was an illusion, but she took advantage of the moment, slipping to her left along a shadowed hallway, past the silent dining room and kitchen to the pantry, where another flight of stairs gave access to the basement. There was no lock on the door, and Joy was grateful for the darkness, even though she had to feel her way downstairs, afraid of falling, breaking something, getting caught.

It seemed to take forever, but she reached the basement's concrete floor and felt her way in the direction of the washer-dryer combo on the eastern wall. She climbed up on the Maytag washer, peered out through the window, praying there would be no guards outside. The empty lawn invited her to take a shot at it.

She slid the window open, gave the burglar bars a solid straight-arm shove and watched them fall away. It was a little awkward, crawling through the window, but she made it, wound up belly-down on damp, cool grass. She pushed off in a flash, broke for the tree line sixty yards away.

She almost made it.

Ten or fifteen paces from the trees and safety a

flashlight blazed in front of her, the white beam blinding, painful.

"Where the hell you think you're going?"

Shit!

Joy recognized the voice. It was Mahoney, probably the worst of the orderlies, a thirty-something lech who liked to catch the girls undressing. Mahoney's conversation ran toward reasons why the girls should "try a real man on for size." What could it hurt, he often asked, since they were pregnant anyway?

"You blew it, babe."

A second voice. It sounded like Gutierrez, but she wasn't sure. What difference did it make? They had her. She was busted. Any chance she had of getting out was dead and gone.

"You know we'll have to write this up for Matron," said Mahoney. "No harm done, but rules is rules. Unless..."

"Forget it, asshole."

"Suit yourself, bitch. Let's go see what Matron has to say about your little moonlight stroll."

REMO THOUGHT his eyes were playing tricks on him at first, the basement window opening, a pale arm punching out the burglar bars. He stood and watched as a young woman crawled through the window, scrambled to her feet and ran across the lawn, apparently intent on getting to the woods. And she was almost close enough to taste it when a light flashed in her face and two men stepped out of the shadows to intercept her.

Remo was moving as the woman stood her ground, the two men separating, flanking her. They both wore khaki uniforms that could have worked as well for rent-a-cops or janitors. The flashlight seemed to be their only weapon, but they shouldn't need one to control a girl this age, this size.

Remo assumed she must be pregnant, though her bulky clothes concealed the fact. He could be wrong, of course, but it wasn't important. All that counted for the moment was that he had found an inmate who was apparently intent on getting out.

"You know we'll have to write this up for Matron," said the taller sentry. "No harm done, but rules is rules. Unless..."

"Forget it, asshole." There was spunk there, and defiance.

"Suit yourself, bitch. Let's go see what Matron has to say about your little moonlight stroll."

The woman bolted, running straight toward Remo, even though she had no way of knowing he was there. The surprised guards were after her a heartbeat later, cursing bitterly.

"You little bitch, I'm gonna kick your ass!"

All three of them stopped short as Remo stepped out of the dark. Defeat was written on the woman's face until the taller of the sentries spoke from behind her.

"Who the fuck are you?"

Her look changed, then. Not hopeful, but alert and watchful.

"The Sandman," Remo told him. "Time for you to say good-night."

"You think so, smart-ass?"

Remo drifted to his left, and the two goons shifted with him, losing focus on the woman. She was free to run now if she wanted to, but something kept her rooted where she stood.

"This here is private property," the short Latino said. "You're trespassing."

"You'd better make a citizen's arrest," said Remo.

"Think we can't?"

"I don't think you can find your dick without a road map," Remo told him, putting on a grin.

The woman laughed at that, a high-pitched sound, almost hysterical. The taller of the goons shot her a warning glance and shook a fist in her direction.

"Watch it, bitch!" he snapped. "This prick a friend of yours?"

"I'm new in town," said Remo, forcing both of them to focus on himself. "You guys could use some manners, if you want to keep on working for the welcome committee."

"Fuck you, buddy! Way I see it, you've got just two choices. You can split or you can get your ass kicked."

"There's a third choice," Remo said.

"Oh, yeah?"

"You go bye-bye for good—last exit, no return, pain guaranteed."

"That's it!" the taller of the goons declared. "That's fucking all she wrote!"

He charged at Remo, swung his heavy flashlight like a club, with all his weight behind the blow. It slashed through empty air, his target having side-stepped at the final instant, fading to the big man's right.

It was a simple thing to grab his wrist and use the momentum of his rush against him. Remo heard the arm snap one, two, three times, at the shoulder, elbow, wrist. He kept the pressure on, ignored the slugger's scream and caught him with a jab behind the ear that turned his adversary's brain to jelly, leaving Remo with a lifeless body at his feet, the dead man's flashlight in his hand.

"Your turn," he told the short Latino.

"Hey, man, fuck it! What's the big deal anyway? You wanna go out walking in the woods, man, that's your business."

"Wrong. I'm trespassing."

"Hey, I don't give a shit, okay?"

"You've got a job to do," said Remo, circling around the second goon to cut off his retreat.

"You're pushin' it," the khaki watchdog warned him.

"That's exactly right."

"Okay, man." Reaching in a pocket of his slacks, the sentry drew a folding knife and flicked it open.

From the way he held it, Remo understood that he had gone this route before, on more than one occasion. He was probably one of the toughest hombres in whatever bar he chose to frequent, but there was a world of difference between that kind of brawling and the fine points of Sinanju.

"Are you gonna move or what?"

"Or what," said Remo, waiting.

There was no wild-assed rush this time. The young Latino took his time, advancing slowly, feinting with the five-inch blade and waggling his free hand in an effort to distract his adversary. Remo watched him going through the motions, stood his ground and waited.

When the lunge came, it was telegraphed by the expression on the young man's face, a kind of grimace, lips drawn back to bare his small white teeth. The blade was aimed at Remo's stomach, but it never got there. Remo parried with a left-hand sweep across his body, clasped the young man's wrist and yanked him forward, so the open-handed killing blow didn't have far to travel. Remo barely felt the impact in his palm and wrist; he heard and saw the young man's head jerk backward, with the left side of his face imploding, while the force of impact snapped his neck.

The girl was trembling when he turned to face her, trying to decide if she should wait and try to talk with him or simply run away. Her fists were clenched, pressed tight against her thighs, and he

could see the shiny tracks of fresh tears on her
cheeks.

"Are you all right?"

She almost jumped as Remo spoke, but she recovered quickly. "Yeah," she said. "I mean, I
guess so. Who are you?"

"Hang on a second while I get these jokers out
of sight."

There is a trick to carrying outlandish weights,
and it does not involve a lifetime wasted pumping
iron. The trick is leverage and motion, never letting
deadweight drag you down by hanging in one place.
It seemed entirely natural, therefore, when Remo
picked the corpses up, their belts employed as han-
dles, and walked off into the trees, the bodies swing-
ing in his grasp like empty suitcases.

He dumped them several yards inside the forest,
partly hidden by a stand of ferns. He half expected
the young woman to be gone when he returned, but
she was waiting for him, dabbing at her eyes with
one hand, staring at him with a mixture of suspicion
and respect.

"We haven't got much time," he said. "You
wanted out of here, I take it?"

"Right."

"I'll trade a lift for information," Remo said.

"Who are you?" she repeated.

"Right now, the only friend you have."

She sniffed and smiled at that and said, "What
are we waiting for?"

11

Once upon a time, the Master of Sinanju had compiled a list of all that he found pleasing in America. The list was short and read as follows:

1. It isn't China.

2. It isn't Japan.

3. It isn't Vietnam.

4. It isn't Thailand.

5. It isn't France.

He did not mention television, though TV seemed to occupy much of his time. In fact, it would be no exaggeration to describe him as a TV addict.

Which is not to say that all of television's offerings met with Chiun's approval. In fact, almost none of them did. However, when Remo asked him on occasion why it was he watched so much TV, Chiun explained that he was monitoring the decline of so-called Western civilization.

That night, cooped up inside his squalid quarters at the Dogwood Inn, Chiun had found yet another example of something Remo called an infomercial. He had been watching these programs on and off lately, preferring those that dealt with psychic and astrological themes.

The one on television that night was not one of his favorites. He had seen it dozens of times. A fat man in a ridiculous wig and puffy white shirt was revealing the secrets of the universe to a bubbly ex-MTV veejay. She grinned vapidly, nodding in appreciation at every lisping observation the man made. It was truly awful.

Still, Chiun watched, for there was nothing else to do. He had already scanned the local newspaper, found nothing to amuse him in the drab reports of nearby goings-on. The county high school had elected cheerleaders. The ladies of the Hidden Valley Church had turned a profit on their bake sale, with the proceeds bound for charity. Three local teens had been arrested for defacing rural mailboxes.

All drivel.

Chiun reached out to Remo with his mind and wondered how the mission was proceeding. Obviously he was not concerned for Remo's safety. So far, the enemies he faced on this assignment for Mad Emperor Smith had been no challenge for the next Master of Sinanju. Still, if their targets could truly

raise the dead, they might have tricks in store that
would take Remo by surprise.

Chiun wondered how the local newsmen would
describe events unfolding at Ideal Maternity. There
was a tendency among most men to cover up their
own mistakes and oversights, he realized. It would
be too much to expect the unadulterated truth from
any branch of the American news media, but they
would find it difficult to totally ignore the matter, if
some version of the truth spilled out. There would
certainly be corpses to explain, but that wasn't
Chiun's concern.

He was enduring the last fifteen minutes of his
infomercial when the enemy arrived. A flash of
headlights first, across the flimsy curtains, as the car
pulled up outside. It was too soon for Remo to return, and two doors slamming meant at least that
many passengers emerging from the vehicle. Chiun
counted footsteps and revised his estimate to three.
Male voices were jabbering, when any skilled assassin would have held his tongue.

Chiun did not rise to greet them, leaving them to
do the work. It was sufficient inconvenience that
they chose to interrupt his watching television, even
if it was a program he did not really enjoy.

For a moment, Chiun imagined his assailants were
so stupid they would pass right by his door. They
did, in fact, go several steps too far, as if proceeding
toward the motel office, but then one of them barked
at the others to come back.

Between them, they made noise enough to wake the dead.

The talk was bad enough, a fatal error in itself for a would-be assassin when his trade demanded stealth, but Chiun could also hear them draw their weapons, cocking pistols as they stood outside his door, for all the world to see.

Such fools.

Chiun sat and waited while they worked their courage up. The effete star of his program-length commercial was now on a boat. His MTV friend had been joined by two other shrill females. The three of them flounced around the boat and the wig-wearing seer with equal amounts of awe and insipidity.

It was truly horrible.

Even so, Chiun watched.

By the time the program ended, Chiun knew his enemies as Ernie, Jack and Dave. They were such idiots that they used names when speaking to each other, certainly too stupid to have chosen false names in advance. Chiun might have pitied them if they had not brought such dishonor on his own profession with their negligence.

They were deserving of no mercy, and would get none from the Master of Sinanju. It was not his job to teach them what they should have learned in nursery school.

He did have lessons for them, though. It was a

pity they would not survive to share his boundless wisdom with their friends.

On second thought, Chiun reckoned it unlikely that such fools had any friends.

The world would miss them not at all.

IT WAS SUPPOSED TO BE an easy touch-and-go, the way it was described to Ernie Becker. Two guys at the Dogwood Inn, who had been asking questions out of turn. He was supposed to brace them, find out what they wanted, who they worked for and eliminate the problem.

Simple.

Getting stuck with Jack and Dave was something else, though.

Becker didn't mind them normally, when all he had to do was sit around and shoot the shit, throw back some beers and talk about how tough they were—that kind of thing. They were all right for breaking legs, collecting debts, a minor rubout now and then, okay. No sweat.

He had some doubts, though, when it came to matching Jack and Dave against professionals.

Of course, he didn't know these jokers at the Dogwood Inn from Adam. They could both be stumble-bums for all he knew, real losers, but he didn't walk in taking anything for granted.

That was how you got your ass shot off.

Another prime example—how they'd almost bitched it, running off to find the motel manager instead of simply going in and getting down to business. It was downright unprofessional, a show of ignorance and weakness, wasting time and energy.

Their orders were specific. On the telephone that evening, Garrick Tilton had allowed no room for argument or improvising. Grab the nosy bastards, squeeze them dry and dump them somewhere inconspicuous, so it wouldn't reflect on Tilton's moneymen.

The motel manager had called it in apparently, and he had given up the number of the room. It was miraculous what bribes could do in terms of nailing down security. A few bucks here and there at key positions in some pissant little town, and you had spies prepared to give their mother up if she got out of line. It wasn't Ernie Becker's place to ask what Tilton was protecting here in Dogshit, Indiana, and he didn't care. As long as he was working, getting paid to do what he loved best, then everything was cool.

He pulled his .45—a knockoff on the old Colt classic manufactured by the Springfield Armory—and thumbed the hammer back, then waited while his two companions drew their automatics, jacking shells into the firing chambers.

Ready.

Becker figured there were two ways they could do it: either knock and hope for a polite response, or walk right in and take their chances. He had been told the Dogwood Inn was empty at the moment, all except for his targets and the managers—a man-and-wife team who were smart enough, presumably, to keep their heads down and remain invisible until the smoke cleared.

As they pulled in off the highway, Becker wondered why there were no vehicles in evidence. The old sedan down by the office didn't count; he figured it belonged to the proprietors. He almost decided to hide somewhere and wait awhile, but there were lights in number 17, all flickery like television on the blinds, and Becker reckoned someone must be home.

He had another brainstorm, standing on the sidewalk with the pistol in his hand. Suppose one of the snoops was out, and he returned to find a strange car parked outside his door. There went surprise, and it could ruin everything.

"Hang on a second," he told his colleagues.

"What's the matter?" Jack demanded, looking nervous in the semidarkness.

Becker took the car keys from his pocket, handing them to Dave. "Go stash the car around in back," he said.

"What for?"

"Because I said so, dammit! Jesus, do I have to get an argument from you on every fucking thing?"

"Hey, man, relax!"

"Just move the car, all right?"

"I'm going! Shit, man."

As Becker stood and waited, he felt Jack watching

him like he was something just descended from a UFO. To hell with explanations, he decided. If the two of them weren't smart enough to figure out the simple things without a damn diagram, he didn't have the time to wise them up.

Five nervous minutes later, Dave came strolling back like he had nowhere to go and all night to get there. Becker felt like decking him, but resisted with an effort as his so-called helper joined them.

"What took you so long?" he demanded.

"Had to take a leak," Dave said, and shrugged like it was nothing, hauling out his piece.

Becker gritted his teeth. "Okay," he said at last. "On three."

And started counting.

"One."

"You mean we go on three, or after three?" Dave asked.

Becker clenched his teeth, ignored the stupid bastard.

"Two."

"'Cause I don't wanna fuck it up, you know, and—"

"Three!"

He gave the door a solid kick, no serious resistance from the cheap pot-metal lock. Across the threshold with his pistol leading, Ernie Becker swept the room and stood there blinking, while the others blundered into him and almost knocked him down.

"Back off! And check the toilet!"

There was no one in the bathroom, just a little old man sitting on the floor and watching television, like he didn't notice three armed men had just kicked in his door. A gook, at that, if things weren't weird enough already. Maybe deaf, the way he sat there, staring at the tube, oblivious to Becker and his boys.

"You never said he was a Jap," Dave muttered.

"Shit," Jack said, "he's older than my grandma."

Ernie Becker felt himself relaxing just a little, even as he wondered what the hell was going on. There was an outside chance that Tilton had been led astray by his informants, but that wasn't Becker's problem. He did what he was paid to do, and if he had to come back later, maybe punish someone for misleading Tilton in the first place— well, that simply meant **he** got paid twice.

And what was wrong with that?

One ancient Jap who hadn't even faced them yet...but where was number two? Forget it. They could wrap the old fart up before his buddy came back with their take-out meal, whatever, and it would be easier that way.

First, though, he had to try and talk to the old man. And that meant getting his attention.

Ernie stepped between the old Jap and the television set that had him captivated, reaching backward with his free hand, switching off the sound.

"Hey, Pops," he said, "we need to talk."

THE PSYCHIC INFOMERCIAL had faded into another of the insipid programs. In this one, a woman with factory-molded teeth and a stomach flatter than a crepe extolled the virtues of a thirty-cent piece of plastic that was supposed to be the next exercise breakthrough. It was shaped like a potato chip and cost eighty dollars, plus tax. Terrible. Still, it was better than the various insipid comedies or bland newsmagazines stacked up as competition on the other channels.

Chiun would suffer the idiot woman and her stupid device with his usual good grace...if only the barbarians would let him watch in peace.

It was an insult when they broke his door instead of knocking—though in truth, it would be difficult to make the room look worse than it already did. The motel manager would clearly not attempt to bill Chiun for the damages, unless he had grown tired of life in Dogwood and was anxious to pursue another incarnation. Either way, it was a trifling matter to the Master of Sinanju.

There was a question of respect, though, which he could not, in good conscience, overlook. Barbarians didn't offend him, in their proper place—a social station that included drudge work in the fields and mines—but Chiun didn't appreciate them being forced upon him otherwise. The loathsome situation was exacerbated by the ignorance and rudeness of the three inept killers.

"You never said he was a Jap," one of them told the others.

"Shit," a second one replied, "he's older than my grandma."

Chiun considered whether he should kill them swiftly and be done with it, or make them suffer for their insults. Three barbarians were hardly worth his time, but there was still a principle to be upheld.

The Master of Sinanju did not suffer insults lightly.

He was meditating on the problem—quick and clean, or slow and painful—when the seeming leader of the three stepped in to block his view of the old TV and turned the sound off on the set.

"Hey, Pops," the stranger said, "we need to talk."

Chiun examined him the way a butcher might regard a cow or hog, deciding where the first cut should be made. He didn't speak, returned the killer's gaze without a hint of trepidation.

"You speak English, man?" the door-breaker asked.

Chiun nodded, still not speaking. As a mental exercise, he found the thug's carotid artery and spent a moment counting heartbeats. This one did not want his friends to know he was afraid.

"Say something, then," the young barbarian demanded.

Chiun obliged him. "You should step aside," he said, "and turn the sound back on."

The man blinked, incredulous. "I don't believe this shit," he told his friends, and forced a smile to make himself appear at ease. He turned back to Chiun. "You got more problems than a fucking TV show, old man."

"It is poor quality, of course," Chiun allowed, "but better than 'Roseanne.'"

One of the others giggled nervously, a woman's sound. Chiun had his position marked, without the need of facing him.

The young barbarian was glaring at him now. "Forget about 'Roseanne', all right?"

"It is my pleasure," Chiun conceded.

"So, where's your buddy?"

"Who?"

"You've got somebody staying with you. Where is he?"

"Gone," said Chiun.

"Gone where, old man?"

Chiun offered the suggestion of a shrug, his shoulders barely moving. "Who can say?"

"You'd better say. We haven't got all night."

"Then you should not waste precious time with foolish questions."

"What?" The young man turned to his companions. "You believe the fucking nerve on this old Nip?"

"I can't believe it," one replied.

"Fuckin' nerve," the other echoed, without conviction.

The young man aimed his pistol at Chiun, its muzzle hovering six inches from the Master's face. "You know what this is, Grandpa?" he demanded.

"I believe it is a boom device."

"Bet your skinny ass it is! You gonna make me use it?"

"No man is compelled to prove himself at the expense of reason," Chiun replied.

"Say what?"

"Do what you have to do," Chiun translated.

"You heard him, Ernie," one of the companions chimed in from the sidelines. "Fuck 'im up."

"He's makin' fun of you," the other said.

"That right? You making fun of me, old man?"

"I am not Mother Nature," Chiun informed him, reasonably. "I am not responsible for your deficiencies."

Another high-pitched giggle from the shortest of the three. Chiun wondered if the young man was retarded or just easily amused.

"You gonna take that shit?" the other asked.

"Fuck no!" the one called Ernie answered, stepping closer, drawing back his arm to strike Chiun with the gun.

He never made the swing.

It would have been a challenge for the quickest eye to follow Chiun as he reached out to grab the young man's genitals, his razor-sharp nails incising and separating a critical area. That brought the young man to his knees and instantly negated any risk of future generations being sullied by his evident genetic defects. By the time the gunman found his voice to scream, the rigid fingers of Chiun's left hand had crushed his larynx, canceling the sound and cutting off his flow of precious oxygen. He would be dead in seconds flat, but Chiun didn't wait to observe the process.

He had other work to do.

The two survivors gaped at him in shock as Chiun leaped from the floor and closed the gap between them to convenient striking distance. Both men raised their guns and fired at once, but hastily. In truth, a fleeting pause to aim would not have saved their lives, but reckless haste made Chiun's work that much easier.

His movements hardly visible to the eye as he ducked and twisted slightly to his left, the bullets whining past like insects, shattering an ugly lamp and drilling through the wall behind him. Wasted effort. He was on the giggler in a flash, the Master's hands a blur as he struck two, three, four blows in the time required to blink an eyelid. Bones snapped with the sound of green twigs breaking underfoot, and Chiun's unworthy adversary toppled over backward, dead before his body hit the threadbare carpet.

That left one, and he was breaking for the door as Chiun stepped up to intercept him. It was child's play, stretching out a foot to trip the clumsy killer, watching as he vaulted forward, skull colliding with the wooden door frame.

He was barely conscious when the Master picked him up one-handed, holding him at arm's length like a half-drowned cat. The application of a bony fingertip revived him, and he was gasping at the sudden pain.

"Who sent you here?" Chiun inquired.

"Hey, man, I just go where I'm told, okay?"

Another probe, and this time it produced a breathless scream.

"Hey, Jesus! I don't know who let the contract out, awright? We got a call from Ernie, he says let's go roust these guys outa the Dogwood Inn. That's all I know, I swear to God."

"Who told him to come here?"

"Aw, shit...the manager, I think. That's what he said. Why don't you let me go, huh? I won't tell a soul, I promise."

"I believe you," Chiun replied, and snapped his neck.

The narrow bathtub had not been designed for three, but it would serve for now. Reluctantly Chiun switched the television off and straightened his kimono. There was one more small job to complete before he could attempt to find another worthy program.

Humming to himself, he went to find the owners of the Dogwood Inn.

12

"So, have you ever seen these guys before?"

Joy Patton, standing in the bathroom doorway, blinked at Remo, then went back to staring at the bodies in the bathtub. She was looking slightly green around the gills, but Remo thought she handled it all right, considering the circumstances.

"Maybe that one," Joy said, pointing to the one on top. "It's hard to say for sure. He looks familiar in a way, but then again, I haven't seen that many purple faces lately."

There was nothing he could do about the color, after Chiun had smashed the shooter's larynx, cutting off the flow of oxygen and leaving him to strangle.

"You'd have seen him at the home?" he prodded.

"Right. One time, I think—if it was even him. I couldn't swear."

"Okay, forget it."

"Are they dead?" she asked.

"I hope so."

The ID wasn't important, anyway. From Chiun, he knew the three goons had been summoned on the basis of a call from the motel proprietor. That meant five bodies to get rid of in a hurry, but at least Chiun had switched the feeble neon sign out front to read No Vacancy. From what Remo had seen already, they weren't exactly in the midst of tourist season, but the sign should fend off any late-night travelers who happened by while he was cleaning up.

He could expect no help from Chiun in that regard, of course. The Master of Sinanju didn't mind a workout every now and then, if he couldn't avoid it, but he drew the line at housekeeping. He had already found another program on the tube—some goofy show about a group of friends who shared a large apartment and spent all their on-screen time discussing sex—and Remo had already given up on rousing him to help.

"My nerves," Chiun muttered vaguely in response to Remo's first and last entreaty for a helping hand.

It was a hopeless case.

"You may as well relax awhile and watch TV," he said to Joy.

"Relax? Is that supposed to be a joke? You've got three dead men in your bathtub!"

"Not for long. They're checking out."

"I don't believe this."

"It gets easier," he told her, stepping out to look for someplace where the bodies would be safe.

And found the motel's ice machine.

It had a spacious bin—enough for several hundred

pounds of ice cubes, Remo estimated—but the unit was unplugged. No point in wasting power, if you had no guests in residence—or none that you expected to survive the night. He found the socket, snapped the three-pronged plug in place and went back to his room to fetch the meat.

It took three trips, because he didn't want an extra body stretched out on the pavement, just in case an unexpected visitor should pull in from the highway. Two more trips for Raynard and Matilda, wedging them inside the bin before he closed the metal trap. The first few ice cubes had already tumbled into place, on top of them, as Remo finished up his chore.

Chiun had managed to extract a name and number from Raynard, the proprietor, along with the admission that he had received a hundred dollars monthly for the past five years, with no requirement other than a warning if suspicious strangers stopped at the motel and asked about Ideal Maternity.

In the beginning, it had probably seemed like a good idea. And it was too late to reconsider now.

The name was Garton, almost certainly an alias. The number was long-distance, somewhere in the neighborhood of Louisville, Kentucky. Remo dialed it from the motel office, after taking care of Raynard and Matilda, just in case there was an automatic tracer on the other end.

The distant telephone rang half a dozen times before a man's voice answered. "Yes?"

"Put Garton on."

"Who's calling?"

Remo hesitated, listening to tension crackle on the line. He stretched it out, deliberately not answering.

"Who is this? How'd you get this number?"

Remo smiled and cradled the receiver. It was petty, almost childish, but he pictured someone sweating in Kentucky, wondering what kind of damage they had suffered to their cover without even knowing it. The number could be changed in no time flat, but Smith could trace it anyway, despite a disconnect. And in the meantime, Remo still had work to do.

"We're getting out of here," he said, as he reentered their room.

"Thank God." The mere announcement brought some color back to Joy's young face.

"My program," Chiun protested, eyes still fastened on the TV screen.

"You'll have to catch the reruns, Little Father," Remo said. "We can't afford to stay here any longer."

"Stay, go," muttered Chiun. "Is there no respite for the aged and infirm?"

"I'll ask them if we meet some," Remo said. "We have to go now."

Running well does not mean running far, in every case. New Albany was only fifteen miles away, but it was in a different county, large enough to offer Remo a selection of motels. With distance, change of jurisdiction and potential lag time on discovery of corpses at the Dogwood Inn, he reckoned they should have the best part of a day, at least, before the heat came down.

By that time, Remo hoped, his work in Indiana would be done.

He stopped once, on the way, to use a public telephone in Lanesville. Smith picked up on the first ring. He promised to investigate the Garton alias and see what he could learn about the phone number in Louisville. The casualties in Dogwood were of no concern to Smith, a strictly local problem that would not reflect on CURE. Three minutes saw the briefing done, and Remo drove until he found a motel called the Singing Pines.

Joy Patton joined him while he checked in—to make it look more natural. She was a trifle pale, but the old man behind the registration counter didn't seem to mind. His eyes were locked on to her sweater like a smart bomb's sensors homing on their target, even when he spoke. It was the first time Remo could remember watching someone have a conversation with a woman's breasts.

"Old creep!" Joy muttered as they left the motel office. "Did you see him staring at me?"

Remo shrugged. "At least he's got good taste."

She broke into an unexpected smile. "You think so?"

"What I think," he told her, "is we need to talk."

Their conversation had been brief and rudimentary as Remo drove her from Ideal Maternity back to the Dogwood Inn, and after cleaning up that mess, he had been busy watching out for stalkers on the drive from Dogwood to New Albany. At this point, Remo knew the lady's name, together with the fact that she was willing to risk life and limb in an escape from Dr. Radcliff's "home." The rest of it was still a blank, but Remo knew she must have more to say. The strange behavior he had witnessed at Ideal Maternity, along with Joy's determination to escape, told him it was no ordinary home for unwed mothers.

The room had HBO, and Chiun soon found an action film with Arnold Schwarzenegger. He was sitting on the floor and arguing with someone on the TV screen when Remo sat Joy down and started to debrief her.

"Look," she said before he got a fair start on the questions, "I am really whipped, okay? It's been the strangest day I can remember, and I need some rest."

"Some answers, first," he said. "I have to know what's going on in Dogwood, at the home."

"You mean the baby bunker?" Joy surprised him with her vehemence. "Call that a home, I guess you'd think San Quentin was a theme park."

"How old are you?"

"Eighteen," she said, then added, "in November."

"Seventeen," said Remo. "You're from California?"

"How'd you know? My accent?"

Remo smiled and shook his head. "Most people, when they want to name a prison, mention Leavenworth or Attica. Old-timers go for Alcatraz. A California girl would know about San Quentin."

"So, I guess you're Sherlock Holmes."

"Not quite. I try to pay attention."

"I see that."

"So, fill me in about the baby bunker."

"Look," she said, a grim expression on her face, "I'd rather just forget about the whole damn thing, if that's all right."

"Too late for that, I'd say."

"You mean the kid?" She hesitated, and a trace of color came back to her face. "It really isn't mine, you know."

"How's that?" he asked.

"You really don't know what they're up to, do you?"

Remo frowned. "I understood it was an unwed-mothers home."

Joy laughed at that, another sharp note verging on hysteria, reminding Remo of the way she acted in the woods as he was squaring off against the khaki goons.

"I guess that's true," she said. "None of the girls were married. Doctor wouldn't go for that."

"Doctor?"

"The honcho," Joy informed him. "Dr. Radcliff. Mr. Big."

"He chose the girls himself?"

"Recruited us, would be more like it. There were physicals and tests, the whole nine yards, for anyone who passed inspection. Answering the ad just meant an interview. From there, you had to sell yourself—and that's exactly what I mean."

"What ad?" He was confused, as if the girl had veered off into subject matter foreign to their conversation. Remo felt as if he were a Yankee tourist, getting street directions in Chinese.

"What ad? Oh, man, where have you been?"

"Behind," he told her, "but I'm catching up."

"Okay. He runs this ad, you know? In different papers, freebies from the underground, that kind of thing. It's like, some university or hospital will advertise for human guinea pigs to test a new vaccine, whatever. You've seen those, I bet."

He nodded. They were on the television now and then, requests for patients suffering from allergies, arthritis, hypertension—any variety of ailments—to earn some extra money taking new, untested medication under rigid medical controls.

"Go on," he urged.

"Well, it was just like that... except it wasn't medicine, exactly. They were interested in single women—though I found out it wasn't hard to lie about your age—who would agree to serve as surrogates for families who couldn't make a baby on their own."

Remo felt as if he had received a stinging slap across the face. "So, you weren't...?"

"Pregnant when I joined the program? Uh-uh," Joy replied. "No way."

It was a twist that he had not considered. "Who's the father?" Remo asked.

"I wouldn't know."

"Can we go back and start from the beginning, Joy?"

She rolled her eyes but said, "Okay. I saw this ad in the *Free Press*. Los Angeles, you know? I don't recall exactly what it said, but there was money mentioned—no specific details—for some kind of personal service. They listed a toll-free number at the bottom, and I made the call."

"Sounds like a come-on from an escort service," Remo said.

"Well," Joy responded, "I was working at the time, same kind of thing, but L.A.'s dangerous, you know? I didn't mind relocating, if there was better money to be made."

"So, you were—"

"Hooking. You can say it."

"Right. What happened when you made the call?"

"This grandma-sounding woman picks it up and asks some general questions—age, health, this and that. She says they're doing interviews for something special, but she can't spill any details on the telephone. I'll have to talk to Doctor if I want the scoop.'' She read the question in his eyes and said, ''They always call him 'Doctor,' like he was the only one. Like God, you know?''

''And that was Radcliff.''

''Yeah, turns out it was. First thing, I asked the woman where they're doing interviews, and she says Bloomington. Big college town, up north of here.''

''I've heard of it,'' said Remo. ''Bobby Knight, whatever.''

''Yeah, they're crazy over basketball. I figured, later on, they set it up that way so it would seem legitimate, like maybe they were tied in with the university somehow.''

''Could be,'' said Remo, thinking to himself that it would also point investigators in the wrong direction—north, away from Radcliff's clinic in Kentucky—if security broke down. ''Go on,'' he urged.

''Okay. I told the lady she could put me on the 'maybe' list. I figured at the very worst, I'd get myself a free vacation, see some countryside. They wouldn't spring for plane fare, but they put me on a Greyhound from L.A. to Bloomington. I never did much riding on a bus before, since I got out of school. It gives you time to snooze.''

''I guess that's right,'' said Remo.

''Anyway, we get to Bloomington on Friday, and they've booked a room for me at this hotel down by the depot. Doctor comes and takes me out to dinner

Friday night, which struck me as a little odd, but who am I to bitch about free food? Red Lobster's where we went. It wasn't bad.''

She hesitated, glanced down at the nervous fingers twining in her lap. ''You wouldn't have a smoke, by any chance?''

''I'm sorry, no.''

''No sweat. I'm not supposed to, anyway. The kid, you know? I haven't had a cigarette for nearly seven months. I guess that means I quit.''

''Sounds like it.''

''Anyway, we just made small talk over dinner, then he drives me back to the hotel. It crossed my mind that Doctor may have been a lech, but nothing happened after all. He just explained the program, like, to fill me in.''

''Which was?''

''Was what?''

''The program,'' Remo said.

''Oh, right. He said he was a baby doctor—and he worked with couples who were having difficulty in the reproductive area. No matter what they tried, the women couldn't get knocked up, so they were hiring surrogates. I have to tell you, I was floored at first. The thought of being pregnant, first of all, then carrying a kid around for nine months and it's gone, like that.''

''What made you go for it?'' asked Remo.

''Money, and the way he laid it out all scientific sounding. I never had to meet the couple—that was one thing. It was artificial all the way, no hassles. Once I passed the physical and all, I would be artificially inseminated, spend the next nine months at Doctor's place—Ideal Maternity, no less—and once the baby was delivered, I'd have fifty grand to get me started someplace fresh. A whole new life, you know?''

"They offered fifty thousand dollars?"

"Right. No money down, of course, but that was cool, since I'd have no expenses of my own. It seemed all right."

"You mentioned physicals."

"Oh, yeah. I had to take all kinds of tests—for HIV, fertility, a bunch of stuff I didn't even understand. They've got all kinds of laboratory gear back at the so-called home. Technicians come and go with Doctor all the time."

"I see."

"They had about a dozen girls already there, when I moved in. All pregnant, due at different times. I never knew what Doctor and the staff were getting paid, but if the girls were getting fifty grand apiece, I figured he and Matron must be taking in a pretty penny."

"Matron?"

Joy made a disgusted face. "Althea Bliss," she said. "House mother, chief bad-ass, you name it. Doctor owns the place, but Matron runs the show, with assholes like the two you met tonight."

"They were security?" asked Remo.

"Matron calls them 'orderlies,' like any decent hospital would let them through the door. Fact is, they do a little bit of everything, from cleaning up around the place to making sure the girls stay put."

"Did many try to run away?"

Joy shook her head. "A couple, in the time I spent there. I'm the only one who ever made it out, and that was thanks to you."

"Forget it."

"That'll be the day."

"I need to hear the rest of it," he said.

"Okay. They do the dirty deed, all nice and sterile like, in the infirmary. Next thing you know, I'm pregnant. Thing is, by that time, I've had a chance to ask some questions, get to know some of the other girls. It's coming to me that Ideal Maternity's not so ideal. You get my drift?"

"Not quite."

"First thing, we never get to leave the grounds—and I mean never. They've got TV, VCR, all kinds of games and hobby shit, but no one can go shopping, take a walk out in the woods without a chaperone—forget it. Right away I figure Doctor's covering his ass, 'cause selling babies is illegal, and he doesn't want some yokel putting two and two together, 'kay?"

"Makes sense," said Remo.

"Right. Except it's more than that. The seven months I spent there, half a dozen girls delivered, got their payoff checks and split. A couple of them,

you could say were pretty tight. They were supposed
to write and stay in touch, you know?''

"But never did?" asked Remo.

"Oh, they did, all right...except it wasn't them."

"You lost me, Joy."

"Okay, take Karen, for example. I got notes from
her, all right, but they were typed, even the signature. But neatly. Karen couldn't type a sentence
without spelling half the words wrong if her life
depended on it."

Joy chewed her lip for a minute nervously, then
went on. "There's more. A couple of the girls were
pissed off in a major way before they left. The orderlies had tried to fool around with them, that kind
of shit. Their names were Sheila and Regine. They
left about three weeks apart, and both of them swore
they would blow the whistle on Ideal as soon as they
had cashed their checks and banked the money
someplace safe."

"But nothing happened?"

"Zip. A few weeks later, there's a postcard from
Hawaii, supposed to be from Sheila."

"And it wasn't?" Remo asked.

"No way. The handwriting was off, and all she
talked about was how she felt such gratitude for
Doctor and the others helping her to get a brand-
new start on life."

"And what do you think happened to the other
girls?"

Joy shrugged, a nervous twitch. "I couldn't say,

but nothing would surprise me. If a girl lips off, gets out of line around the home, there's discipline, you know? Like slaps across the face or whippings with a belt. They don't do anything to hurt the babies, but the rooms are locked at night—and in the daytime, too, if Matron puts you on restriction. Ever see the movie *Cool Hand Luke?*"

"Long time ago."

"It's like that, in a way. No guns, I mean—at least, I never saw any—but they've got tons of rules. All for the baby's sake, they tell you, but it comes down to a lot of grunt work in the house, and childish shit like making sure you clean your plate at every meal. Mess up a time or two, and Matron lectures you, but it gets tougher after that. The baby bunker, like I said."

"You think the so-called graduates were harmed somehow?"

"Hey, I don't know! I mean, where are they? Did they ever cash their checks? Things happen, right? A bullet don't cost fifty grand."

"So you decided not to wait and take the chance."

"Would you?"

He shook his head. "Do you have family in L.A.?"

"None that I'd care to see again."

"I know how this must sound, but—"

"You feel like protecting me," she said. "Is that about the size of it?"

"Not quite. I have a friend who runs a sanitarium. That's like—"

"I'm not a dummy, mister. I know what it is."

"Right, sorry. Anyway, he's got connections, and I'm sure he'd put you up while you're, uh, waiting for the, uh…"

"Delivery?"

"And keep you safe," said Remo.

"So what's his angle?" Joy inquired.

"Just someone I used to know years ago," Remo lied. Smith would go berserk if he let the girl know too much.

"You're after Doctor, right?" she said suddenly.

"Could be."

"And when you find him?"

"That depends."

"You'll do him like Mahoney and Gutierrez?"

"Who are they?"

"Those two jerks at the home," she said.

"Hey, don't worry your head about things. If there's something off, I'll fix it so no more girls end up in your spot."

Joy thought about it for a moment, finally said, "You know, I'd hate to wind up chilling in a hotel ice machine."

"No chance," said Remo. "You're a friend."

"You make friends, just like that?"

"I try."

She thought some more. "Where is this sanitarium?"

"Sorry. That's a secret."

"I've had enough bus rides," she warned.

He smiled. "I thought we'd try an airplane. How about first-class?"

"You'll have to call, I guess, and check it out."

"That's right."

The smile lit up her face. "What are you waiting for?"

13

The sun had been up for an hour by the time he started driving west again, on Highway 62. This time Remo picked up Highway 11 south from Edwardsville, down through Elizabeth, and came in toward Ideal Maternity from the reverse of his original approach. He pushed the Chrysler well beyond the posted limit, watching out for cops along the way, aware that precious time was slipping through his hands.

Two guards and one young woman missing. Even if they didn't find the bodies, it was bound to cause a flap with staffers at the "home." It was impossible for him to guess how they would take it, how they would react, but Remo had a nasty feeling in his gut.

If Dr. Radcliff and his flunkies started cutting losses, the young women might be first to go.

He had enjoyed the second wake-up call to Smith at Folcroft. Smith listened carefully while Remo ran the problem down, and though he cleared his throat from time to time, as if about to speak, he managed not to interrupt. When Remo finished, Smith agreed to everything, albeit reluctantly. There was a place for Joy at Folcroft Sanitarium. An open first-class ticket would be waiting for her, in the name of Alice Jones, when she checked in at the Louisville airport. A car and driver would be waiting for her when her flight touched down at White Plains.

"One thing," Smith said before he severed the connection. "Does the girl have any useful information?"

"Nothing on the look-alikes," said Remo. He had shown her Thomas Hardy's mug shot, but it drew a total blank. "If you were setting up a charge of false imprisonment or baby-selling, she could make your case."

"Too bad," Smith said. "I do not see this one going to a jury."

"No."

So, he was driving through the woods in early-morning sunlight, wondering what he would find on this, his second visit to Ideal Maternity. He was prepared to bluff or tough it out, whichever method seemed the more appropriate once he was on the scene.

Joy's explanation of the Radcliff scam made sense, or course. With the adoption crisis in America, disabled children and minorities were stacked up on the waiting list for parents, while your average childless couple was Caucasian, set on bringing home a healthy infant who resembled them in all respects. It was a seller's market, nationwide, and the restrictions placed on baby-brokering by state and federal laws did little to prevent black-market sales. As far as Remo knew, the Radcliff operation might be absolutely legal, up until the point when pregnant women were confined against their will or made to disappear once they had given birth.

A baby-selling racket was despicable, the more so if it had incorporated homicide to cut its overhead, but Remo still saw no connection with the carbon-copy hit men wearing Thomas Hardy's face and fingerprints. There must be more, a link back to Eugenix Corporation somehow, but each time he thought he had it, the solution skittered out of reach and found a hiding place in his subconscious.

Experience told Remo that he would get nowhere agonizing over the elusive problem. Rather, if he put it on a mental shelf and concentrated on the task at hand, let his unconscious mind deal with the riddle for a while, he stood a better chance of coming up with a solution.

Or, he thought, if all else fails, I just may need to have a chat with Doctor, find out what he has to say.

The prospect made him smile.

He motored past the private driveway once more, no special reason, just to check it out, but what he saw made him brake his Chrysler in the middle of the road. The heavy chain was down and puddled in the grass to one side of the driveway, its warning sign forgotten. There was nothing to prevent his driving in.

Was it a trap...or had something bad gone down here?

He thought about retreating, going overland on foot, as he had done the night before, but Remo didn't want to waste the time. He had a sickly feeling in his stomach—formless apprehension mingled with a premonition of disaster—but it did not translate into fear. He thought about the girls—young women—who would be the only living witnesses against their captors if the game went sour, wondering exactly how far Dr. Radcliff and his staff would go to save themselves.

He turned into the driveway, checking out the trees on either side. He kept one hand on the door latch and the other on the steering wheel, prepared to bail or ram with equal speed if he was ambushed. As it was, he had an uneventful drive up to the building.

He circled once around the brooding structure, watching windows, picking up no signs of movement behind the glass. There were no cars in evidence, and Remo saw the back door standing open, just an inch or two, as if the last one out had more-important things to think about and didn't care much if the building was secured or not.

He recognized the signs of an emergency evacuation, but he parked out front and blew the Chrysler's horn regardless just to see if any stragglers might reveal themselves. The flicker of a curtain at an upstairs window, anything at all.

But there was nothing.

Remo was too late.

He left the car, not bothering to lock it, walked up to the front door and tried the knob.

It opened at his touch.

He lingered on the threshold, sniffing at the air for any scent of blood or death. Instead, he picked up Lemon Pledge and Lysol. They were keeping clean, whatever else transpired inside these walls.

He stepped into the foyer, listened, heard no sounds that would suggest a living presence in the house. Immediately on his right was a parlor with chairs and couches arranged around a Sony console television with a VCR on top. The coffee table held a spread of magazines that ran toward *Seventeen* and *Tiger Beat,* in keeping with the average age of inmates at the home. The room was spotless, nothing to suggest a whirlwind had ripped through it hours earlier.

He checked the dining room, found nothing, moved on to the kitchen. Twin refrigerators were well stocked with food, milk, lean meat but there would be no breakfast served this morning. Pots, pans and utensils had been washed up after supper, neatly put away in readiness for morning, but the staff and inmates had evacuated prior to feeding time.

From Joy's description of the place, he knew the laundry room would be downstairs, with storage in the basement. Past the kitchen pantry with its loaded shelves, the office lately occupied by Matron, or Althea Bliss, revealed the first clear evidence of a departure staged in haste. The desk had been swept clean, drawers dumped and scattered. In the corner, two green filing cabinets stood with empty drawers pulled open. Nothing in the closet but a metal hanger lying on the floor.

Whatever paperwork might have existed to detail the operation of the home for unwed mothers, it was gone. A watercolor painting of a meadow bright with poppies hung askew beside the office door, forgotten in the rush to get away.

He checked the next four rooms downstairs, staff quarters by the look of them, and found no clothes, no personal effects of any kind. Each room had beds for two, one pair still neatly made, not slept in, while the others were in disarray.

The maid would not be coming in today.

The last room on the ground floor would have been what Joy had called the lab, complete with vinyl floor and cabinets that reminded Remo of a medical-examination room. The operating table Joy described was missing, though, marks on the floor remaining where it had been bolted down. The other furnishings were also gone, including the track lighting overhead, and someone had cleaned out the cabinets, left nothing but a paper-towel dispenser on the wall above a sink constructed out of stainless steel.

The kind of heavy-duty gear you found in operating rooms wouldn't fit in a normal car, which meant Bliss and her people had been stepping lively for their getaway. One truck, at least, called in from somewhere, probably with extra muscle to complete the move in record time. Wall sockets, scuff marks and assorted other signs told Remo they had also taken out a large refrigerator, plus some countertop appliances. The air was sharp with disinfectant, even now, and while he couldn't prove that Joy's report was accurate in all particulars, he was prepared to take her word.

He left the operating room and went upstairs, still listening for any sound that would betray a lurker in the house, to search the rooms once occupied by the young mothers of Ideal Maternity. Ten rooms, again with two beds each, though three rooms apparently had been unoccupied before the hasty exodus, beds stripped of linen, drawers and closets undisturbed. A fourth room had one bed made up for sleeping and the other bare, exactly as Joy Patton had described the room she occupied alone.

And that left six. Twelve pregnant girls, all missing now. Their dresser drawers and closets had been emptied out in haste, but no private items were left behind. There was a common bathroom at the far end of the hall, some of the hanging towels still damp, but nothing in the way of makeup, medicine, perfume—in short, no other trace of habitation by a living soul.

Forensics experts could have torn the place apart, thought Remo, and come up with clothing fibers, fingerprints, perhaps hairs clinging to a bar of soap—but what would be the point? It was no crime to occupy a room or take a shower, and his work was not geared toward a trial, in any case.

As for Thomas Allen Hardy and his doppelgängers, Remo knew no more for having toured Ideal Maternity than when he took the case from Smith. He had a sense of precious time escaping, slipping through his fingers. Where would it end? And how?

One thing he knew for certain: if the place had been evacuated overnight, then Dr. Radcliff must be on alert. Would he attempt to flee, abandon home and clinic in Kentucky, or would he assume that he was safe, his anonymity preserved by the preemptive strike in Dogwood, Indiana?

Remo didn't know, and there was only one way to proceed. He had to find the man, or try to. Face him one-on-one and wring the secrets of his operation out of Radcliff, one way or another.

At the moment, he was hoping the doctor would resist, give him a reason to inflict some pain.

The ghost was waiting for him when he stepped out of the common bathroom, standing twenty feet away, holding a semiautomatic pistol. Remo recognized the face immediately.

He had smashed it several days earlier, in Florida.

The walking dead man smiled at Remo, raised his pistol in a firm two-handed grip and fixed the sights on Remo's chest.

"Come here," he said.

"Okay."

It was a serious miscalculation, bringing Remo closer, but the stranger had no way of knowing that. He held the pistol steady, keeping both eyes open, just the way they taught it at the FBI Academy. At this range, anyone not educated in the fine points of Sinanju should have been dead meat, but Remo wasn't worried.

As Remo closed the gap, his adversary started backing toward the stairs, kept roughly fifteen feet between them all the way. He knew exactly where the staircase was, without a backward glance, and wedged himself into the nearest corner, giving Remo ample room to pass.

"Downstairs," he said.

Up close, it was a simple move. Assume you couldn't stop the first shot, dodge the bullet as you closed to striking range, disarm the goon and finish it at leisure. Remo hesitated long enough to glance downstairs—and saw two more Hardy doppelgängers. They were even dressed alike, in denim jeans and jackets, though their shirts were different colors: red and green.

Both men had pistols aimed at Remo's face.

That complicated matters somewhat, but it was only a matter of strategy. If they simply wanted Remo dead, he guessed, all three would probably have come upstairs and opened fire the moment that he showed himself. If they were taking prisoners, it meant whoever sent them must have questions. That, in turn, gave Remo time and space to plan his move.

If they were any good at all, they wouldn't try to shoot him on the stairs, where any rounds that missed or passed completely through his body would endanger friendly troops. A cross fire in cramped quarters was the worst way to prepare a trap, and they would know that going in.

For now, it was best to play along and assume they knew what they were doing.

"I'm going," Remo told the nearest of the triplets. "Don't get nervous."

"Shut your face and move it!"

"Yassuh, boss."

He started down the stairs, heard the assassin behind him, hanging back a little so that Remo could not turn and try to grab his weapon. Down below, the other two goons were backing up and separating, to triangulate their fire if anything went wrong.

From Remo's point of view, it couldn't hurt to shake them up a little. If they got rattled in the process, it could only help his cause.

"I don't know what the trouble is," he said to no one in particular, "but maybe one of you could introduce me to the man in charge. I've got this cousin with a problem, see, and I—"

"Shut up!" one of the ground-floor goons commanded.

"What I heard in town, a certain Dr. Radcliff was

the man to see, but I can talk to someone else, if he's tied up.''

"Shut up!" the other one downstairs growled, taking one step forward as he spoke, for emphasis.

"Okay, no problem."

Remo reached the bottom of the staircase, heard the first man coming down behind him, while the others held their ground. They had him boxed, now, but the cross-fire problem had not been resolved. He still did not believe they meant to kill him outright, while they had a chance to question him. Their sponsor would be desperate for answers by this time, when everything appeared to be unraveling.

"Who sent you here?" the man behind him asked.

Remo half turned to face him as he answered. "Like I said, my cousin—"

"Cut the shit! We want the truth."

"Okay, you got me, pal. She's not my cousin. Are you happy now? I don't know what you people charge to handle the delivery and adoption, but I've got some money put away. You don't need guns, for Christ's sake! It's a business deal."

"Who sent you?" the first man repeated, stepping closer, till his gun was almost touching Remo's chest.

It was the break he had been waiting for.

The timing had to be precise, but Remo had it covered. Reach out with the left hand for his adversary's wrist and clasp it tightly, while his right palm pushed the automatic's muzzle out of line. The gun was a Baretta, double-action, with the hammer down, but Remo kept his enemy from firing with a sharp twist of the captive hand and arm.

The goon cried out in pain and furious surprise, but he had been disarmed by that time. Remo swung him like a weightless dummy, lifting him completely off his feet, boots slamming hard into the ribs of the second assassin.

The third man saw it coming, squeezed off two quick shots in self-defense. The hollowpoints struck Remo's human shield, mushroomed on impact, ripping into lungs and liver while his body was still airborne, flying.

Remo let him go, saw the surprise and anger fade to nothing as he died. Momentum slammed him into the gunman, and they went down together in a heap, the dead man's weight encumbering his sidekick.

The second thug was down on one knee, groping for the pistol he had dropped, about to reach it when a shadow fell across his face, and he glanced up to find Death watching him with dark, impassive eyes.

"Did Radcliff send you?"

"Fuck yourself!"

"Wrong answer," Remo said, and kicked him hard enough to dislocate his left shoulder, flip him over on his back, the fallen pistol hopelessly beyond his reach.

A backward glance showed the third gunner about to wriggle out from underneath the body of his comrade. He had also lost his weapon, but he wasted no time looking for it, rather grabbing for a knife sheathed on his belt. The blade was six or seven inches long and double edged, black tinted, with a long groove down the center that allowed a straight-on puncture wound to bleed without obstruction, even if the knife was not withdrawn.

It was a killer's weapon, forged for one specific purpose, but a blade's utility is measured by the man who wields it. This man, under other circumstances, would have been a deadly adversary, but he didn't understand whom he was facing. With a snarl of anger, throwing caution to the wind, he came at Remo, leading with the blade, and thereby sealed his fate.

Remo sidestepped the thrust, allowed the blade to pass him by, and struck out with a vicious backhand to the assassin's ribs. He heard bones crack and felt the ribs implode, curved lances shearing into lung, spleen, diaphragm. A strangled cry of pain erupted from the hit man's throat, immediately followed by a rush of blood as bright as poster paint.

The man collapsed, not dead but dying, slumped on hands and knees, the knife forgotten now as he surrendered to the waves of mortal pain. His arms were trembling, barely able to support him. Remo crouched beside him, tangled fingers in his hair and gave the head a twist, examining the too familiar face.

"Who sent you?" Remo asked.

"Fu-fuck you!"

He broke the doppelgänger's neck and shoved the body over on its side. The sole survivor of the hit team was watching him and clutching at his injured shoulder, looking for a way out of the trap as Remo turned to face him.

"You're a little short of help right now," he said. "Why don't you make it easy on yourself?"

"No, thanks."

"I don't mind doing it the hard way," Remo told him, "but it seems like such a waste."

"You don't scare me," the doppelgänger said. "I'm not afraid of dying."

"Death's no threat," said Remo. "It's the quick way out."

"Do what you want," the wounded hit man sneered. "You're dead already, but you're just too dumb to know it."

"Suit yourself."

He was advancing on the prostrate form when the gunner jack-knifed, brought one knee to his chest and drew a stubby derringer from its concealment in an ankle holster. Remo was prepared to dodge the bullets, knowing that the small gun only held two shots, but he misjudged his captive's plan. Instead of trying for a kill from six or seven paces, the hit man reversed the derringer, shoved it into his mouth and fired.

Despite its size, the little gun was loud—perhaps a .44. The power of a bullet fired into the skull at skin-touch range puffed out the dead man's cheeks. His eyes bulged in their sockets, streaked with crimson, and his head slammed back against the floor. The bullet did not exit, telling Remo that it must have been another deadly hollow-point.

"Well, that just beats all," Remo complained.

In other circumstances, Remo would have tidied up the battleground, but he would leave it to the cops this time, in case some trace of evidence remained to haunt the owners of Ideal Maternity. He could imagine local uniforms, attempting to dissect the triplet act and getting nowhere fast, besieged by federal agents once they put it on the wire.

He spent the next five minutes looking for a telephone and came up empty. Almost every room had wall jacks, but the instruments themselves had been removed when Matron and her crew were cleaning house.

No matter. He would find a public phone somewhere along the highway on the drive back.

He took a final look around the place, saw nothing he had missed the first time and went back outside. His rented Chrysler was the only vehicle in sight, and Remo guessed his three late adversaries must have hiked in through the woods, or else been left behind deliberately, to deal with any problems that arose.

He found a pay phone in Elizabeth, outside a supermarket and made the call collect to Smith. The head of CURE's voice was crisp, alert.

"Report," he said, in place of salutation.

He briefed Smith on the outcome of his latest visit to Ideal Maternity and waited for a moment while the older man thought it over. When he spoke again, Smith's voice was grim. "There does not seem to be much choice," he said.

"No choice at all."

"You may as well proceed, in that case."

"Right. I'll be in touch from Louisville, before I make the move. We'll send that package off to you, and in the meantime, I've got several names you need to check. Find out if they're available for interviews."

"Who am I looking for?" Smith asked.

"Some former tenants of Ideal Maternity," said Remo. "Word is they were graduated, so to speak. I'd like to know what happened to them—and their children, if it's possible."

"All things are possible," said Smith, "if you know where to look and who to ask."

14

Dr. Quentin Radcliff took pride in his self-control. No matter what went wrong or how he seethed with anger inwardly, he cultivated an ability to put the best face on the worst of situations, show subordinates that he was always in control. It was another mark of the superiority that set him apart from common men. As the commercials frequently advised, he never let them see him sweat.

Not even when his life's work had been jeopardized by idiots.

He stared across his spacious desk, regarding his unwelcome visitor with thinly veiled contempt. Althea Bliss was silent, knowing anything she volunteered could easily be turned against her, used to make her seem incompetent, a liability. She shot a furtive glance at Warren Oxley, seated to the left and slightly behind her, but otherwise she sat and waited for the other shoe to drop.

"You've disappointed me, Althea," Radcliff told her, swallowing an urge to grab a paperweight and fling it at her pale, round face.

"I understand."

"You do? I wonder."

"What I meant to say—"

Dr. Radcliff interrupted her. "Do you recall what you were doing when I found you?"

"Yes, sir."

"You had about run out of luck, as I remember, at the women's prison down in Talladega. Three distinct and separate charges of brutality before that ugly business with the eighteen-year-old girl."

The woman's doughy face showed color for the first time Radcliff could remember, anger and embarrassment combining to suffuse her cheeks with crimson.

"Those were lies," she said defiantly. "No case was ever filed. I'm innocent."

"On paper, anyway," said Radcliff, giving her no respite from his glare. "Your resignation kept the state from filing charges, I believe."

"I'm innocent," Bliss insisted, but there was conviction in her voice.

"Aren't we all?"

In better times, the former prison guard could be a grim, imposing figure. Five foot seven in her stocking feet, she tipped the scales around 190 pounds, some of it muscle. Any softness in her face was strictly flab. Her eyes resembled flakes of granite, set above a nose that always put Radcliff in mind of dorsal fins. She overcompensated for her thin slash of a mouth by using too much lipstick, but it didn't help. Her knuckles bore the scars of punches thrown in fits of rage.

"It's not my fault," she told him, sounding desperate. "You have to see that."

"What I see," he answered, "is that we have lost our primary facility—a quarter-million dollars for the land and renovations when we moved in, seven years ago—and risked exposure that could cost us everything. If I've missed anything, Althea, please be good enough to fill me in."

"I've never lost a girl before," she said, as if that somehow mitigated the disaster.

"No, I'll grant you that." Radcliff believed he was a reasonable man. "You had a perfect record up until last night."

"It's not my fault!"

"Please, please, Althea. Don't be tiresome."

"But Mahoney and Gutierrez—"

"Are no longer with us," he reminded her. "At least they saved me severance pay, whereas the girl—what was her name again?"

"Joy Patton, sir."

"Whereas the girl has simply vanished. Gone. Kaput."

"She didn't kill those two gorillas by herself," Bliss said.

"Is that supposed to reassure me? Knowing she has allies is supposed to put my mind at ease?"

"I only meant—"

''The background check was very thorough. Mr. Oxley?''

Oxley cleared his throat, referring to a slim manila folder. ''Surviving family of Joy Patton consists of a stepmother and half brother, out in Bakersfield. The brother started trying to molest her at age twelve, apparently succeeded on the day she turned fourteen. Stepmother took his side when Joy complained. Girl headed for Los Angeles and hit the streets. If she has any friends worth mentioning, we couldn't find them.''

''So.'' The tone of Radcliff's voice was neutral now, dispassionate. ''Who could have followed her halfway across the continent and met her in the middle of the night, just when she needed help to get away?''

Althea Bliss could only shrug. ''If I knew that—''

''Then you would have some value,'' Dr. Radcliff finished for her. ''As it is...''

''You can't blame me for this!''

''The home was your responsibility. You've let me down, Althea.''

''No. No, sir!''

''You censor correspondence, I believe.''

''Damn right. Girl writes a letter, we get rid of it and tell her it was mailed. No answer comes, she figures it's a brush-off.''

''Did the Patton girl write any letters?''

''Not a one.''

''You're positive?''

"Yes, sir."

"She could have smuggled something out, presumably."

"Nobody ever has."

"That you know of," said Dr. Radcliff.

"Well…"

"I mean, the orderlies were in and out. There were occasional deliveries. Young women can be most persuasive when they're motivated."

"No, sir, you can put your mind at ease on that score. Everyone on staff, I had a private chat the day they joined the program. We were crystal clear about the rules, and what would happen if they didn't toe the line."

"You trusted them?"

"Let's say I had them covered. On deliveries, we always had them scheduled in advance and kept the girls away from any strangers. There's no way Joy passed any notes to a deliveryman, no sir."

"To recap the event, she slipped out of her room—"

"The locks were no great shakes," Althea told him, interrupting. "You'll remember we discussed that, and you said it was enough to put the fire alarms on outside doors."

"Which brings us to her manner of escaping from the house," said Radcliff.

"Basement window, like I told you. One way or another, she got through the burglar bars and made her way outside."

"Where we assume she met the orderlies?"

"Mahoney and Gutierrez, right. Joy had the early kitchen shift, like I explained, and when she turned up missing, I sent everybody I could spare to check the grounds. The bodies were a hundred yards east of the buildings, give or take. No sign of Joy. That's when I called you to report."

The doctor turned to Warren Oxley with a frown. "Mahoney and Gutierrez. Do we know how they were killed?"

"No hard specifics," Oxley told him, "but it looks like they were beaten."

"Is there any way to tell—"

"How many people were involved? We haven't got a clue."

"All right."

It wouldn't have been the police; that much was obvious. The law arrived with badges, warrants, fanfare. Sound bites on the evening news. It was conceivable that one or more policemen might have helped the girl escape, in hopes of making her a witness, but they wouldn't beat two men to death and leave their bodies in the forest.

No. It must be someone else.

But who?

The FBI had started asking questions several days ago, about Eugenix and the Thomas Hardy deal...if it had been them. Dr. Radcliff knew how cheaply false credentials could be had. These days, with the desktop technology available, a high-school freshman could present himself as King Farouk, complete with sterling credit references, passport—the works.

But if the Feds were not his enemies, who was?

Someone had questioned the mortician in Nevada, interrupted Jasper Frayne's assassination down in Florida and turned up just in time to help one of his subjects vanish from Ideal Maternity. It added up to major trouble, and the less he knew about his enemy, the more Radcliff was bound to worry.

Calm down, he told himself. You have to keep your wits about you.

"Have the girls begun to settle in?" he asked Bliss.

"More or less," she said. "There's not much room, you understand."

"It's temporary. We should have a larger place available within a day or two."

"All right."

"I'm sending someone out to help you with security. You understand, of course."

The matron's voice was stiff, but she did not resist. "Of course."

"That's all."

Dismissed, Althea Bliss rose and left the room. She had a plowman's walk, whatever femininity she once possessed eradicated by her years in uniform. She was a plodder, but efficient in her way—until last night.

"Shall I get rid of her?" asked Warren Oxley.

"No. Not yet. Let's wait and see the final damage estimate."

"She could have been involved," said Oxley.

Radcliff frowned, considered it, then shook his head. "She doesn't have the nerve or the imagination," he replied. "Much less the sympathy. What could a girl like this one offer that would make Althea risk her life?"

"You never know."

Oxley was thinking of the fourth complaint in Talladega, with its allegations that Althea Bliss had used her office as a prison matron to coerce one of her female charges into sex. Radcliff assumed the charge was true, and he had warned Bliss on the day of her employment that any misbehavior endangering Project Lazarus would be severely punished. She had known exactly what he meant and didn't argue. For the kind of money Radcliff paid, she could restrain herself—or find some method to indulge her twisted passion that did not affect the project.

"She's not that stupid," Radcliff told his chief lieutenant. "She'd be cutting off her nose to spite her face."

"And what a nose, at that."

In other circumstances, Radcliff might have smiled at Oxley's joke, but he had lost his sense of humor when he got the news about Ideal Maternity. There was no time for joking, not when his life's work was at stake.

"We need to find out who's behind this," he told

Oxley. "Cutting out potential leaks is no damn good if they've already tracked us down."

"I'm working on it, Quentin."

"So, work harder, Warren. And remember what's at stake, for all of us."

"As if I could forget."

"See that you don't," said Radcliff. "If Lazarus goes down, we go down with it. I mean everybody."

"Understood."

"In that case, you have work to do."

"I'm on my way," said Oxley, sounding chastened.

Radcliff watched him go and wished he felt more confident about his aide's ability to sort the problem out. A part of him, however, feared things might have gone too far already—that they might have passed the point of no return.

To hell with that. He couldn't give up.

The best part of his life had been devoted to the dream he labeled Project Lazarus. Not only had he managed to succeed beyond his wildest dreams, make fools of those who mocked him back in school, but it had paid off well enough to leave him set for life, whatever happened next. Those who had failed to recognize his genius would eventually see the light. They would come crawling to him on their hands and knees, to beg for immortality.

The trick in being set for life, though, Dr. Radcliff knew, was managing to stay alive.

From this point on, survival had to be his top priority.

No matter what the cost.

JOY PATTON CAUGHT the ten-fifteen from Louisville, on Northwest Airlines, bound for JFK. She said goodbye to Remo at the gate and surprised him by standing on tiptoe for a parting kiss.

Before the 727 lifted off, Remo was halfway to the parking, intent on getting back to the motel. Chiun was staring out the window watching the passing cars when Remo came in. He wore a bored expression on his parchment face.

"Smith is waiting for your call," Chiun told him, eyes locked on a red Buick.

"How long ago?" asked Remo.

"Eight minivans."

He lifted the receiver, entered the special CURE code and got an answer midway through the first ring.

"What's the word?"

"I ran the names you gave me, with the information from your source. It is not encouraging."

"Go on."

"Regine Miskele, age nineteen, from Kansas City—the Missouri side. She has been arrested twice, for shoplifting and drug possession. Marijuana, I believe. A chronic runaway, dropped out of high school in her sophomore year. There is nothing to suggest how she made contact with Ideal Maternity, but no one in her family has heard from her in thirteen months.''

''She left the home nine weeks ago,'' said Remo.

''Altogether possible,'' Smith said, ''but I cannot trace her. If she has a bank account or driver's license in the States today, she used another name.''

''That's one.''

''On Karen Woodruff, I confirmed her age as seventeen, born in Muskegon, Michigan. Another dropout—there appears to be a pattern here—but no arrests on record. It has been eleven months since she touched base with any friends or relatives. She has vanished, too.''

''Are you sure?''

''As sure as can be,'' Smith said. ''The closest match, age-wise, turned out to be a black girl in Miami.''

''Two for two,'' said Remo.

''Make that three,'' Smith told him. ''Sheila Stroud is on the record in Seattle, as reported. Turns nineteen next weekend.''

''If she's still alive,'' said Remo.

''This one almost graduated, but her parents split in January of her senior year and she unraveled. Got in trouble with a boyfriend and dropped out to have the baby, then miscarried. One way or another, she decided no one wanted her around.''

''What is it with these parents?'' Remo asked.

''I do not know. In any case, she left home about

a year ago. The family says she kept in touch the first few weeks, then nothing.''

"That would be when she hooked up with Radcliff's people," Remo said.

"Presumably. The CURE mainframes flagged three Sheila Strouds, but none of them match up. Two women over forty, and a six-year-old in Birmingham.''

"Adoption records?" Remo prodded.

"Nothing. I can tell you Dr. Radcliff and Ideal Maternity have no official link with any recognized adoption agency in the United States or Canada. Data on the black market is not definitive, of course—it changes every day—and Radcliff could be operating independently. His clinic there in Brandenburg, for instance, could provide him with a hard-core clientele, and word of mouth would do the rest. For all we know, infant adoptions could be written off as births, with Radcliff altering the paperwork. I will need his patient files to check that angle out.''

"Good luck."

"Precisely."

"What about Althea Bliss?"

"One scrap of good news." Smith replied. "I found her right away."

"So, tell me."

"Althea Delaney Bliss, was born in 1946 in Dothan, Alabama. Her father was a member of the KKK, but he got drunk one night and set himself on fire while he was lighting up a cross outside a synagogue. He was unemployable from that point on, and drank himself to death. He apparently lived long enough to pass his racist attitudes on to his teenage girls. Althea was youngest of the three. She graduated high school with a D+ average. She spent one year in business school, but did not do well. As soon as she turned twenty-one, she found a civil-service job—as a matron at the Talladega women's prison."

"Sounds about right," Remo said blandly.

"As you might guess, she had some trouble on the job. There were a number of complaints about excessive force, though none were finally sustained. An eighteen-year-old inmate charged that Bliss co-erced her into, er, 'unwilling and unnatural relations' in the laundry room. That case was pending when she finally decided to quit. She turned in her resig-nation and disappeared."

"And showed up managing Ideal Maternity for Dr. Radcliff."

"Apparently so."

"Instead of getting canned and sent to jail, she winds up with her own house full of living dolls."

"It is still no proof of murder," Smith reminded him, "but I am inclined to agree with you. I will be watching out for Bliss and company if they resurface in the neighborhood."

"Twelve pregnant girls and all that staff, they can't just disappear," said Remo, but he knew they could and maybe had. If nothing else, he knew that Dr. Radcliff and his cohorts planned ahead.

"I am working on it," Smith replied. "It may take time."

"I can't see any way around a face-to-face with Radcliff," Remo said.

"What is the approach?"

"I've overdone the Bureau angle," Remo said. "Let's try a freelance journalist, reporting on advances in fertility research."

"Sounds good," Smith agreed. "At least to get you in with a minimum of fuss."

"I can do a little snooping this way."

"You are still going with the soft approach?"

"As far as possible. I don't expect Radcliff to break down and confess."

"Too much to hope for, I suppose. You will keep me posted?"

"Don't I always?"

"Well." Harold Smith seemed uncomfortable, at a loss for words. He settled for a brusque "Good luck" and severed the connection.

Remo glanced at the Master of Sinanju who was still at the window and told him, "I'm going out again."

"Of course. To meet with Smith's amazing doctor who makes dead men walk again."

"See if he's home, at least."

"Does he use sorcery, this man?"

"I doubt it very much," said Remo.

"Does Smith the insane think so?"

"No I think it's scientific, Little Father."

"In another time, before my youth, the scientists were sorcerers. It is all the same. They play with Nature and attempt to change the way men live."

"Is that so bad?" asked Remo.

"It depends," Chiun told him, "on the method and the goal. Why should an old man in a coma be connected to machines that do what his own flesh cannot? Is he so great that we must keep him with us always? Or are men so afraid of what may follow death that they delay its call, regardless of the cost?"

"This life is all we have," said Remo.

"Then by all means, live it!" Chiun replied. "If you spend all your days evading death, where is the time for life?"

"What is this? Today's freaking inspirational sermon?"

"I am bored. You continually stuff me away in hotel rooms like some deranged spinster aunt. I must do something to while away the time. Are you going to kill Smith's doctor?"

"Most probably."

"It is for the best," Chiun said. "We can end this wild-duck chase and go home." He turned back to the window.

It's for the best.

Could be, but Remo had to find his target first, and make some sense of what was going on. A simple hit on Dr. Radcliff would not end the story if important questions still remained unanswered. Remo had to know what he was up against before he could destroy it.

So get on with it, he thought.

And closed the door behind him, moving swiftly toward his car.

15

Remo followed Highway 60 south from Louisville to Muldraugh, several miles above the Fort Knox gold depository, where he branched off to the west toward Brandenburg.

It was a gamble, dropping in on Radcliff uninvited, but he had a feeling that the doctor would be shunning interviews today, if he was given any choice. Remo was interested in seeing how his adversary dealt with unexpected visitors the morning after losing one of his facilities.

Of course, there was a chance he might not get to see the doctor, after all. Radcliff could be in hiding, or he might refuse to meet with Remo. Stranger things had happened to reporters, but whichever way it went, he would be able to examine part of Radcliff's clinic.

Whatever happened in the next few hours, he would get a feeling for the man.

The Family Service Clinic had a wholesome ring to it. A passing motorist would have to stop and read the fine print on a sign no more than three feet square to realize the clinic dealt exclusively with

Family Planning and Fertility. At that, the clinic proper was concealed by ivy-covered walls and weeping willows, but the wrought-iron gate was open, waiting for him.

Remo took the bait and drove inside.

Ideal Maternity had been an older building, modernized and renovated, while the clinic was a relatively new addition to the landscape, cunningly designed to look antique—at least from the outside. There was a blacktop parking lot on the west side, with spaces for a dozen cars marked off in yellow paint. The spacious lawn was neatly trimmed and bordered, with a flagstone path that led him from the parking lot to the front door.

Inside, a blond receptionist who could have modeled swimsuits for a living greeted Remo with a dazzling smile. "How may I help you, sir?"

Women had not been pursuing Remo relentlessly since his shark-eating episodes, and his interest in them had been revived. Now he checked an urge to tell her how she could help and replied, "I'm hoping for a chance to speak with Dr. Radcliff."

"Ah. Is he expecting you?"

"Unfortunately, no, but I was in the neighborhood and thought I'd take a chance."

The smile took on a hint of frost. "And you are...?"

"Remo Washington, reporter. I'm with *Newstime,* working on a feature piece for next week's issue.

Infertility, its causes, new treatments—that type of thing."

"I'll have to see if Doctor is available," she said. "We normally require appointments."

"Understood," he told her. "I appreciate your help."

"No promises," she said, and put some warmth back in her smile.

He wandered over to the nearest picture window while she buzzed the intercom, picked up her telephone receiver and conversed in muted tones with someone Remo couldn't see. Outside, the grounds resembled snapshots of a well-kept park, except they were deserted. Where a park would have had children running, shouting, lovers strolling hand in hand, the clinic grounds had been monopolized by two fat squirrels who chased each other up and down the trunks of old, established trees. The whole place had a sterile feel about it, as if Radcliff had constructed his ideal oasis underneath a dome that let the sunlight in but kept the world at bay.

Long moments passed before he heard the click of heels on vinyl, turned to see a sleek brunette approaching. She was tall—five eight or nine—with thick, dark hair that framed an oval face: full lips, a perfect nose, green eyes that could be warm, he guessed, when they were not on full alert. A stylish three-piece suit could not disguise the luscious body underneath. Even without a smile, she bumped the blond receptionist back to the second string.

"Good morning, Mr. Washington, is it?"

"Remo Washington." He palmed a business card to verify the lie. "I write for—"

"*Newstime.* So I understand. You asked to see my father?"

Remo blinked at that one, honestly surprised. "I'm hoping for a word with Dr. Radcliff," he replied.

"I'm Chelsea Radcliff," the brunette informed him, still without a smile. "We weren't expecting you."

"And I apologize for that. The truth is," Remo told her, offering the phrase that was so often preface to a lie, "I spent the last two days in Indianapolis, with Dr. Kirk and Dr. Russell. They suggested that a visit to your father's clinic might add something to my story."

"Really? Kirk and Russell?"

"As I live and breathe."

"You could have called ahead."

"They didn't bring it up until last night," said Remo. "Anyway, you know the freelance writer's rule of thumb—it's easier to get forgiveness than permission. What if I had called ahead and Dr. Radcliff still refused to see me?"

"Mr. Washington—"

"Please, call me Remo."

"Mr. Washington, my father is a very busy man."

"I understand, of course."

"You do? And yet you never heard of him before last night."

"By reputation, certainly," he told her, scrambling desperately to salvage credibility, "but I had no idea where he was working."

"We do not invite publicity."

"What could it hurt?" asked Remo.

"Mr. Washington, my father's work is not confined to pure research. His patients have included many wealthy, influential families. They aren't celebrities, of course, and we intend to keep it that way. Infertility is still considered an embarrassment in certain quarters. Confidentiality is critical, not only from a legal aspect, but in terms of simple trust."

"I understand," said Remo. "If your father would agree to speak with me in general terms, about his research, some of the advances he has made, I'm sure it would be good for business."

Chelsea Radcliff stiffened, as if Remo's breath offended her.

"We're less concerned with profit here than service to our clients, Mr. Washington. I don't believe—"

"No insult was intended, Miss Radcliff."

"That's 'Dr. Radcliff,' Mr. Washington." She noted his expression, adding, "Ph.D."

"What field, if I may ask?"

"Psychology."

"I'll bet that comes in handy, with the cases you get here."

"I really don't have time—"

"How's this for an idea," he said. "Why don't you ask your father if he wants to talk to me. If he says no, I'm out of here, and no hard feelings. On the other hand..."

"*I* screen the visitors who show up unannounced," she told him.

"And I'm sure you do a bang-up job," said Remo, "but I have a hunch your father can decide this kind of question for himself."

A hint of color tinged her cheeks. Her full lips tightened with annoyance.

She looked at him frostily, then seemed to relent a little.

"Wait here, please."

Remo tracked her with his eyes, appreciating the unconscious sway of Chelsea Radcliff's walk. Was it unconscious, though, or simply one more way to put him in his place? Take that, you snotty bastard. What you see is what you can't get.

Remo smiled. He felt a bit of a challenge there, but at the moment, his mind was focused on the job at hand. And it looked likely that she was in agreement with the enemy.

She was back within five minutes, same determined stride, but with a new expression on her face. It fell short of concern, but there was something else that had not been present in their first encounter, moments earlier. Confusion, maybe?

"My father has agreed to see you," she told Remo. "I'll show you the way."

"With pleasure." Smiling just enough that Chelsea couldn't miss it as she turned away and led him past the blonde, along a spacious, antiseptic corridor.

"It's quite a layout you have here," said Remo.

"All the latest methods, with a touch of down-home comfort," she informed him. Was she warming up a little, albeit reluctantly, or was the tone a standard part of guided tours?

She led him past a dozen doors—due north, in the direction of the river, Remo thought—before they reached the last door on the left. Its simple label—Private—could have served a broom closet as well as Dr. Radcliff's inner sanctum. Chelsea knocked, three short, decisive taps, and waited.

"Come!"

The single syllable told Remo much about the man before he crossed the threshold and beheld his quarry in the flesh. Whatever else he was, whatever he aspired to, Quentin Radcliff had an ego on him that demanded deference, a visible distinction from his various subordinates. And those subordinates, apparently, included daughter Chelsea—in the public eye, if nowhere else.

She led the way into a stylish office, furnished with a desk, settee and heavy chairs that may have been antiques or just expensive knockoffs. Remo couldn't tell, nor did he care.

The man who came around the desk to meet him was a stocky five foot seven, shorter than his daughter, but his attitude made up the difference. Quentin Radcliff had a shock of snow-white hair, receding slightly in the front, which he combed back stiffly from his squarish face. His nose was thick and broad, above a narrow mouth, but Remo focused on his eyes. They looked like amethysts, just short of violet, shaded by his spiky, bristling brows. The tan was probably a sun-lamp special, since it did not seem to reach his large, blunt-fingered hands.

"Good morning, Mr....?"

"Washington," said Remo, knowing the display of ignorance was part of Radcliff's act. He would have heard the name from Chelsea moments earlier, but he appeared far too busy and important to remember it for any length of time.

"From *Newsweek*, I believe you said?"

"*Newstime*," Remo corrected him.

"Is that the tabloid?"

"Well..."

"No matter. Please, sit down." He gestured toward one of the vacant chairs, and Remo sat, a bit surprised when Chelsea settled in another, to his left. "What brings you all the way to Brandenburg?"

"As I told your daughter, sir, I'm working on a piece for next week's issue that will deal with human infertility from several angles—common causes of the problem and the latest medical solutions, psychological effects of infertility on married couples in today's society...the whole nine yards.''

"If you'll forgive the observation, Mr. Washington, your premise won't exactly break new ground."

"No, sir, that's true. Some topics never lose their impact, though, and that includes most subjects where the family and children are involved. Times change, as do the expectations and reactions of a childless couple. As for medical advances...well, six months can mean a whole new ball game, so to speak."

"And which concerns you more? The human side or science?"

"I would hope to find the two are integrated, Doctor."

"Ah. Of course. You spoke to Dr. Kirk and Dr. Russell, I believe?"

"That's right."

In fact, the names had come from Smith. Remo had no idea what kind of help he could expect if Radcliff telephoned the Indiana clinic to confirm his nonexistent visit.

"I'm surprised they mentioned me at all," said Dr. Radcliff, sounding peevish, "much less recommended that you speak to me in person."

Remo picked up on the tone, deciding he could use it. "Well, it wasn't so much a suggestion, Doctor, as...how should I put it? No offense intended, sir, but Russell seemed to take it as a joke."

"I see." The tight smile on Radcliff's face seemed sculpted out of ice. His daughter glared, the angry flush returning to her cheeks. "Of course, they would attempt to mock my work."

Remo shifted his weight from one foot to the other, as though he felt slightly uncomfortable. "May I be frank, sir?"

"Please do."

"I wasn't that impressed with Doctors Kirk and Russell, if you follow me. I mean, I read up on the subject pretty well before I started doing interviews, and much of what they've done struck me as being, well..."

"Derivative?" Radcliff suggested, leaning forward with his elbows on the polished desk. "Perhaps a trifle unoriginal?"

"Exactly! When they mentioned you in passing, such a denigrating tone, I wondered if there could be something in the nature of jealousy behind it. Medical research is so competitive, I thought perhaps..."

He left the sentence dangling, saw a spark of interest flare in Dr. Radcliff's eyes. Beside him Chelsea had relaxed a bit, but not entirely. She was obviously still prepared to intervene if he impugned her father's work or character in any way.

"You're quite perceptive, Mr. Washington."

"I've done my homework, too," Remo responded, "even though I didn't have much time. Thank God the morgue was open."

"Pardon me?" One of the bristling eyebrows arched into a perfect bow.

"The reference library at *Newstime*," Remo said, translating. "Sorry. Once you're used to newsroom slang—"

"Homework, you said?"

"On you. The background stuff. I hate cold interviews—they always come out sounding lifeless, and we waste time going over things I should already know. Of course, I only had time for the basics."

"Basics."

"Right. Your schooling," Remo said, "the internship and residency. All the years you spent as head of research for Eugenix Corporation."

Radcliff blinked at that. It only took a fraction of a second, eyelids dropping, flicking up again, but Remo seemed to watch it in slow motion, like the action of a camera's lens preserved on time-lapse film. He had a sense that Dr. Radcliff would preserve that moment, when he spoke the unexpected name, and take it out for later study when he was alone.

"Eugenix?"

"Right. In Belding, Michi—"

"Yes, yes, of course. It takes me back to hear—"

"And you recall the CEO?"

"Excuse me?"

"Jasper Frayne?"

"Old Jasper, certainly. I haven't talked to him in years."

"You missed your chance," said Remo. "Someone killed him at his home in Florida, a few days ago."

Radcliff went through the motions of appearing shocked, but Remo focused more on Chelsea, judging her reaction as the real McCoy. She frowned. Was it surprise or something else?

"There's so much crime in Florida, these days," said Dr. Radcliff. "When I finally retire, I plan on Arizona. I have the land already, near Lake Havasu."

"You'll miss him, then?"

"Not really," Radcliff answered bluntly. "We were colleagues, but I never thought of us as friends. Frayne handled cash, you understand—which does make the real work possible but he wasn't a scientist."

"I understand. You spent so much time on genetic research, Doctor, that I can't help thinking there must be some intimate connection with your present work. Has anything from the Eugenix period been useful in your treatment of infertile couples?"

"Well, we draw on what we know, that's only natural," said Radcliff. "Infertility per se is often the result of injury or illness, possibly a birth defect or some environmental factor—anything from choice of clothing to conditions on the job. If a specific difficulty is remediable, then we intervene with the most efficacious, noninvasive means available. If we can modify behavior to achieve results, so much the better. Drugs would be the next line of attack, with surgery reserved for special cases.''

"That includes genetic surgery?'' asked Remo.

Dr. Radcliff smiled, as if the question came from a well-meaning but simpleminded pupil. "You're discussing theory now,'' he said. "Such work has been successful on the lower animals, under controlled conditions, but we have not yet achieved the skill required to work such magic on our own.''

"You've thought about it, though.''

"What scientist has not? I can assure you, Mr. Washington, that childless couples are as much concerned about the quality of offspring they produce—more so, I should imagine—than about the simple act of giving birth. If we had choices, who would not prefer to sire a Beethoven, an Einstein—even a McCartney—than a simple drone who trudges through his life and never truly rises to the challenge? Wouldn't you prefer a child to make you proud, who leaves his mark behind?''

"I never really thought about it,'' Remo said. "I take it, then, that you don't carry on genetic research at the clinic?''

"The specifics of my work are not for publication yet,'' said Dr. Radcliff. "As you pointed out, the field is quite competitive, and some of my esteemed colleagues, unfortunately, have a minimal concern with ethics.''

"But it's safe to say that any research you have done—or may be doing—is distinct and separate from the treatment of your patients here?"

"Indeed. You know as well as I do, Mr. Washington, that most testing on human subjects is confined to government facilities or major universities, where bureaucrats can practice oversight."

The final word was spoken with thinly veiled contempt, as if it left a sour taste in Radcliff's mouth. The doctor checked his watch and frowned.

"I wonder if there's time for me to take a look around the clinic," Remo said. "I'd like to get some pictures—"

"That's impossible."

"Perhaps the place, to give my readers some idea of what the cutting edge feels like."

It was a short step from outrageous flattery, but Quentin Radcliff didn't seem to mind. "A walkthrough should be harmless, I suppose," he said magnanimously. "Sadly I don't have the time right now, but I believe my daughter—"

"Yes, of course," she said before the dictum was completed.

"There you are." The doctor rose, came back around his desk, squeezed Remo's hand in lieu of shaking it. "I'm glad we had this little talk, and I look forward to your article."

"I'll have a copy faxed out in advance," said Remo, "to make sure you're quoted accurately and I have my facts straight."

"Fair enough. Good day."

Dismissed, thought Remo as he followed Chelsea Radcliff back into the corridor.

"We'll have to make this quick," she said. "I do have work."

"Of course. Lead on."

"Examination rooms," she told him, passing by the numbered doors that stood between her father's office and the foyer. Choosing one at random, Chelsea led the way inside. It was, indeed, a standard treatment room, complete with padded table, chairs, a stool on casters, sink and paper-towel dispenser, metal cabinets on the walls, assorted medical equipment on the counters.

"No one stays the night, then?" Remo asked.

"On rare occasions, when there's minor surgery involved, or a reaction to some medication, but we always try to send them home as soon as possible."

"And treatment normally includes a course of counseling?"

"Where indicated," Chelsea said. "Some couples don't require it. Others are distraught and desperate by the time they come to see us. Since emotions may influence both fertility and fetal growth, we treat all aspects of the problem."

Their next stop was an ultramodern lab where sperm and eggs were frozen, thawed and merged in vitro, in the cases where traditional attempts had met with failure. Remo listened, made a show of taking notes, but it was gibberish. So far, he was no closer to an answer for the riddle of a dead assassin and his doppelgängers than he had been yesterday.

The clinic had a fully sterile operating room with all the fixings, plus a spacious lounge of sorts where Chelsea said she met with clients who required her services.

"You must be running short of time right now," he said.

"That's right," she confirmed.

"But I would love to hear some more about your end," he said.

"My end?"

"Of what goes on here."

"I don't see—"

"Unfortunately, Dr. Radcliff, I'm on deadline, and my editor...well, let's just say he makes Saddam Hussein look like a pussycat."

"You ought to find another job," she told him, not quite smiling.

"I've considered it," he said, "but I can't shake the curiosity."

"That killed the cat, you know."

"I've had my shots."

"In any case—"

"And I was thinking," Remo interrupted, "if you're free tonight..."

"Tonight?"

"If I could buy you dinner, talk some more about your work. No names, of course. I understand the ethics problem. But we don't hear much about the mental and emotional impact of infertility.''

She thought about it for a moment, looking Remo up and down before she answered him. ''Where are you staying?''

''Nowhere, yet. I drove from Louisville.''

''You've got a fair wait, until suppertime.''

''I'll manage.''

''Seven-thirty, then,'' she told him, pushing it. A test. ''You passed Antonio's as you were coming into town.''

''Italian place, out on the highway.''

''Right. I'll meet you.''

''I could pick you up,'' he said.

''I doubt that very much,'' said Chelsea Radcliff as she turned away and left him staring after her.

Again the suggestion of a challenge in her tone. Another time, it might have been amusing to find out, but there was too much work left to be done, and it was deadly serious. The Radcliffs needed more investigation before he could decide on what to do.

Two doctors in the family, he thought.

A paradox.

But he was getting closer. He could feel it.

He was on his way.

16

Remo had some time to kill, but he didn't enjoy the thought of driving back to Louisville and sitting in the motel room while Chiun stared sullenly out the window. Instead, to play it safe, he phone from a public booth.

Chiun answered on the second ring. His normally singsong, voice was flat. "Hello."

"It's me," said Remo.

"Me who?"

"Don't start, Chiun. I just called to say I won't be back for supper."

"You are doubtless too busy busting ghosts."

"You know this might go faster if you helped out instead of sulking," Remo said.

"We will never know."

Chiun hung up on him, the dial tone buzzing like a wasp in Remo's ear. Frowning, he slammed the handset in its cradle.

Some things never changed.

The booth was situated near a Monarch filling station, on the edge of town. He crossed the asphalt minidesert to the station, went inside and got directions to the public library. It was a long shot, but with spare time on his hands, he had nothing to lose.

The Brandenburg librarian was in her early forties, ash blond hair pulled back and tied off. Her baggy slacks and sweater tried to hide a body that, in Remo's estimation, would have made most men look twice. He pegged her as a competent, no-nonsense hand when she was on the clock, but guessed she might cut loose and let her hair down after hours.

She directed Remo to the corner where a filing cabinet held back-issues of the local newspaper on microfilm. The reader was a vintage hand-crank model. Precise dates would have narrowed down his search, but none such were available, so he selected rolls of microfilm for 1983 through '85, relieved to find the local paper was a weekly.

Remo scored in April 1984. The paper didn't tell him what his quarry had been doing in the nearly three years since he left Eugenix Corporation, but it trumpeted the plans for Dr. Radcliff's clinic, calling him an "imminent" physician and geneticist. The typo brought a smile to Remo's face. The author of the piece, one Reuben Sprock, would never know how right he was.

The article laid out an overview of Radcliff's plan to build a family-planning clinic in the neighborhood of Brandenburg, with no specific mention of a site. Considering the neighborhood and local politics, friend Sprock had made a point of finding out that no abortions would be offered at the clinic. Three short paragraphs about the doctor's background and the anguish of infertility wrapped up the piece.

They broke ground on the clinic two months later, with an article and photos on page two. Another five months, and the clinic's opening was featured on page one, below the fold.

And that was all.

Reporters came around when buildings were erected, and again when they burned down or were demolished, but between times, it required some newsworthy event to bring them back. A strike or lawsuit, major accidents, a juicy crime committed on the premises, complaints from patients or the staff. In Radcliff's case, there had been nothing of the sort, and he was left alone.

Remo pegged Chelsea somewhere in her early thirties, which meant she was barely out of college—probably still working on her doctorate—when Daddy opened Family Services in Brandenburg. It was a sweet gig, stepping out of grad school into an established job, with no one but a parent supervising. Some of that depended on the parent, though, and Quentin Radcliff didn't seem like anybody's candidate for Father of the Year. That might be totally unfair, of course, based on a fleeting interview, but Remo was a decent judge of character.

He spent the afternoon in Brandenburg, ate rice at a little mom-and-pop café for lunch and introduced himself—complete with phony press credentials—to a dozen downtown merchants who looked old enough to have some detailed memory of Brandenburg before the clinic came. Eleven of the twelve knew the clinic existed, and nine were capable of giving him directions to the site, but only five had any real idea of what went on behind the clinic's walls. Those five agreed unanimously that the clinic was a good thing for the town of Brandenburg. One knew a girl who worked part-time for Radcliff, making decent money, while the others allowed with approval that ''Doctor'' always paid his bills on time.

So much for small-town amateur detective work.

It struck him as the kind of town where nothing much went on. Perhaps a little craziness on Friday night or Saturday, when good ol' boys got liquored up, along with some wife-bashing from time to time, a few wild young ones on occasion and a fair amount of petty theft, but nothing weird. Much like the quiet towns in old B movies, where the aliens or vampires scored an easy victory with simple, sometimes simpleminded, folk. The kind of town he might have picked to hide in if he had a secret to conceal.

And what of Chelsea Radcliff? Was the lady Ph.D. a conscious part of Daddy's machinations— whatever they were? She would have been an infant when Eugenix Corporation purchased Thomas Hardy's corpse, but that did not exempt her from suspicion in more recent incidents.

Slow down.

It was entirely natural—well, at least not unnatural—for children to pursue a parent's line of work, to some degree. The fact that Chelsea Radcliff went to work in the family business, so to speak, did not necessarily incriminate her, in and of itself. She was protective of her father and the clinic, obviously, but that didn't mean a damn thing, either.

Not unless he found a way to play connect-the-dots and link her to the contract murders Smith had sent him to investigate.

He went to check Antonio's a full two hours before his date with Chelsea, drank a Coca-Cola at the bar and used the men's room, casually checking out entrances and exits.

He could always dazzle them with footwork if it came to that, but he didn't believe that Chelsea Radcliff would be bringing guns to dinner. Rather, he imagined she would want to feel him out—his mind and motives, anyway—to see if he was leaning toward a straight report on the Family Services Clinic, or angling for a hatchet job.

For Remo, it would be an opportunity to do some feeling of his own.

He wore the same maroon T-shirt and tan chinos he had worn out to the clinic. A quarter hour early on his second visit to Antonio's, he waited in his car until a black Infiniti G20 pulled into the parking lot, with Chelsea Radcliff at the wheel. She parked nose-in against the west side of the building and was

climbing out with keys in hand before she noticed
Remo standing close beside her.

"God!" She jumped and dropped her keys.
"Don't do that!"

"What?"

"Sneak up on people, dammit!" When she bent
down to retrieve the keys, her skirt rode up and offered him a glimpse of golden thigh.

"I'm sorry."

"Where'd you learn that, in reporter school?"

"The orphanage," he said. "Stealth was useful,
sometimes."

Chelsea stared at him. "You grew up in an orphanage?"

"Let's say I came of age."

"I never actually met someone who— Never
mind. I'm sorry."

"Ancient history," he told her, meaning it.
"Shall we go in?"

"They don't have car hops."

"Ah, a sense of humor."

Chelsea watched him closely as he held the door
to let her pass. "You sound surprised."

"I never know what to expect," he said. "New
people. To be honest with you, the psychologists
I've known were pretty humorless."

"You never met Bob Newhart, then," she answered, smiling.

"Not until he changed his name and opened up
the inn."

"A TV fan."

"My father's hooked. I get it by osmosis."

"Father? But you said—"

"Adopted," Remo told her. "Late in life, you might say."

"Ah."

A teenage hostess greeted them and showed them to a small booth in Antonio's nonsmoking section. Checkered tablecloth, red vinyl on the seats, a stubby candle in some kind of goblet with a plastic net around it, like a fishing buoy. They held the conversation in abeyance while a forty-something waitress took their order—for Remo, some water, and for Chelsea some Chianti—before leaving them to scan the menu.

"I can recommend the veal," said Chelsea.

Remo frowned. Even the thought of eating beef in any stage of development repulsed him. And he certainly wouldn't choose it—not unless he had no choice. One thing, though, with his body so perfectly attuned now, eating the odd unorthodox meal did not seem to harm him. It was a big difference from his early days of the Sinanju life, and he hadn't been certain why his body would be more tolerant. But Chiun had laughed at him when he'd asked why.

"That is the world of difference between the glorious East and the rapacious West," he said, his eyebrows flung high. "Learn a rule, and they never know when to make an exception. Even you, with your smidgen of good blood from Korea.''

When Remo had cocked his head and looked at him askance, the Master of Sinanju held his long-nailed index finger up, like a scolding schoolteacher.

''A superior man, Remo, that is what Sinanju produces, when rightly lived and practiced. But think! How superior is a creature when it can never vary its food? What happens if his environment changes, if the usual foodstuffs become scarce? It dies, Remo, that is what happens. It is not superior, but weak in one aspect.

''So, when you were nearly new to Sinanju your body knew you had to respect the rules—and reminded you when you did not. Now you do it effortlessly, and your body will forgive the occasional lapse because it is not made in wrong-headed error.''

He had looked at Remo, his eyes twinkling, then wagged his finger. ''But no corn!''

Remo suppressed a grin at the memory, then looked across the table at Chelsea, waiting to see what he'd choose. ''I'm more a duck man, myself,'' he said.

''The fetuccini's always good.''

''Duck,'' he said firmly.

Moments later, she had her wine in front of her, he had his water, their orders had been taken and their waitress had retreated to the kitchen.

Remo said, ''I'm glad you came.''

"You thought I'd stand you up?"

"Agreed to come, I mean."

"I'm interested in seeing that the clinic gets a fair shake in your article."

"We aim to please."

"I'm sure." She didn't sound convinced. "It is a tabloid, though, am I correct?"

"Of sorts. We don't run articles about a UFO attacking Moscow or the vampires in Manhattan dropping dead from AIDS."

"But bad news sells."

"Of course," he said. "Just like at NBC, the *New York Times,* and CNN."

"You won't find any scandal at my father's clinic," Chelsea said.

"I'm glad to hear it."

"Really." Skepticism heavy in her voice.

"I don't expect you to believe me," Remo said, "but trashing total strangers isn't half the fun it's advertised to be. I like to tell the truth, from time to time. It helps me sleep at night."

"A newsman with a heart of gold?" she asked.

"No halos here," he said. "But I don't thrive on being sued for libel, either."

"That should be no problem, if you always tell the truth."

"Oh, you can still get sued," he said. "The plaintiff may not win, but it's a hassle, either way."

"You speak from personal experience?"

"I've been around," he said. "Yourself?"

"Lawsuits?" She looked confused as Remo shifted gears.

"Professional experience," he said. "I've tried to guess your age—"

"A lady never tells."

"—and any way I run the numbers, it appears you joined your father's clinic shortly after leaving school."

"That's true. Before you start in with the nepotism thing, though, I should tell you that I'm fully qualified."

"I never doubted it," said Remo.

"Oh?"

"It's not my field, of course," explained Remo, "but you sound a little paranoid."

"Defensive, maybe." Chelsea took another sip of wine, attempting to relax. "Like any other scientist, my father has detractors."

"At the moment, I'm more interested in you," said Remo.

"Why?"

"The subject of our interview, remember?"

"I assumed—"

"That I'd be pumping you for dirt about the clinic?"

"Elegantly put," she said. "But, frankly, yes."

"But you can see, I'm not."

"It's just as well," she said almost defiantly, "because there isn't any dirt. My father is devoted to the work of building families, or giving them a second chance. Besides the clinic, he encourages adoptions through a home for unwed mothers, up in Indiana, and provides his services at no charge to a boys' home several miles from here, at Ekron.''

"Boys' home?" Remo felt the light go on above his head, as if he were a cartoon character.

"That's right. You sound surprised."

He tried to cover with a shrug. "Well, I assumed that he confined his work to treating infertility."

"By no means. He—"

The waitress interrupted Chelsea as she set their plates in front of them. They took a break from talking for the next few minutes, Remo chewing pensively on his duck, watching her as she ate her veal.

"If we could just get back to you," he said at last.

"I'm not that interesting."

"I disagree."

Suspicion lingered in her eyes, but she was warming up a little. Remo spent a moment thinking what it would be like to heat her up a lot, then put the thought behind him.

Stick to business.

"You're in no position to judge me," Chelsea said. "Much less my father or his work."

"I'm a reporter, not a judge," he replied.

"Is there a difference?"

"I should hope so."

"Maybe in a perfect world," she told him, sounding dubious.

"I take it you've had some unpleasant run-ins with the media," he said.

"In my experience, reporters pander to their audience. They crave approval. Give the people what they want—or what they think they want—instead of what they need."

"It's hard to do a fair job from the outside, looking in," he said, "especially when the blinds are drawn."

"My father has his reasons for the secrecy," she responded.

"Such as?"

"You mentioned one yourself. The whole genetics field is frightfully competitive. Some so-called honorable men of science aren't above stealing from a genius and putting their names on his work. Failing that, they will do anything within their power to smear him and misrepresent his work."

"Sounds more like Washington or Hollywood than the frontier of science," Remo said.

"There's precious little difference."

"You've shattered my illusion."

"A reporter shouldn't have illusions, Mr. Washington."

"Touché. Your father must have something pretty special going on to generate that kind of animosity."

"I really can't discuss it any further," Chelsea said.

"Not even off the record?"

"I'm supposed to trust you now? A perfect stranger?"

"No one's perfect," Remo said.

"In any case..."

"I'd think your father would be glad of the publicity. I mean, once his discoveries are down in black and white, it would be much more difficult for anyone to rip him off."

"You are naive," she said.

"Enlighten me."

"My father's work is more than just original," she explained, "It's revolutionary. He—"

She caught herself about to cross the line, and stepped back from the precipice. A slight blush added color to her cheeks.

"I'm sorry," Chelsea said.

"What for?"

She shrugged and forced a smile. "For rambling. I get carried away sometimes."

"There's nothing wrong with passion," Remo told her. "But I have a problem putting it across on paper, if I don't know what I'm talking about."

"I understand," she said. "But after everything my father's been through, he can be a little—"

"Paranoid?" suggested Remo.

Chelsea stiffened, glaring at him. "No! There's nothing wrong with him. He's brilliant. You have no idea how much his work—his dream—has cost him."

"So, enlighten me," Remo prompted.

"What's the point?"

"Assume that my reporter's curiosity won't let me drop the story. If you freeze me out, you've got no input on the final product, nothing in the way of quality control."

"That's blackmail, Mr. Washington."

"Not even close," he said. "I'm interested in truth, and I'll pursue whatever sources I can find. You know I've done my homework on your father's background, as it is. The people who refuse to talk with me have no legitimate complaint when I omit their point of view. I don't read minds."

"And I don't care for threats," she said. "Not even when they're phrased politely."

"I'm not threatening your father, Chelsea. I have no stake in attacking him or making him look foolish. As for confidential details of his work, most of my readers wouldn't understand it, anyway. Some kind of plain-folks summary is all I'm after."

"Something that will sell your magazine," said Chelsea.

"Absolutely. Is there something wrong with that?"

"Depends on how you do it," she replied.

"You're absolutely right. I give celebrities a boost from time to time and I've been known to comment on their shortcomings, but hatchet jobs are not my style."

"So you say."

He shrugged. "You have to trust somebody, sometime."

"Why?"

"You have to ask, I'd say there's more at stake here than your father's academic standing with his peers."

"Psychology's my field, remember? Spare me the analysis."

"I'd like to know where all that bitterness comes from."

"None of your business," Chelsea snapped.

"Okay. Just let me get the check, and we can hit the bricks."

"Hang on," she countered. "I thought they taught persistence in your average journalism school."

"They do," he said, "but beating a dead horse is something else."

"So I'm a horse, now?"

"Chelsea..."

"Listen, this is difficult for me, all right? My father's not the only one who's suffered losses, following his dream."

"I'm listening."

"My mother left him thirteen years ago. She couldn't take the arguments, the isolation, the back-stabbing office politics. She found somebody else, and six months later she was dead. A car wreck. I was still in junior high school."

A car wreck? Remo thought of Mrs. Jasper Frayne, and said, "I'm sorry, Chelsea."

"Not your fault. Nobody's fault, in fact. Stuff happens, right? You need to understand that he's been there for me, no matter what. As for his work...well, dammit, there I go again."

"If you could only give me some idea..."

She shook her head. "I'm sorry, no."

"Try this for size—suppose I got you final editorial approval, put it down in writing. Let your father set his own parameters for any technical discussion. Think you could convince him?"

She thought about it for a moment. "I'll ask, all right? No promises. Don't get your hopes up."

"Fair enough."

They finished up with small talk, over coffee. Remo paid the check and walked her to her car. She offered him a cautious smile before she drove away, and left him standing in the twilight, watching as her taillights disappeared.

It would not qualify as any kind of major breakthrough, nor could Remo even claim to be closer to the truth, but he was certain that the lady and her father had a secret. Now, all he had to do was try to find out what it was.

17

Dr. Quentin Radcliff was a man who didn't panic, even in the worst adversity, but rather kept his wits about him, challenging his colleagues and subordinates to do the same.

He was, in short, a problem-solver.

He had launched the project he called Lazarus to benefit mankind. He might still achieve that goal, if bureaucrats and other meddlers would but leave him to his work. Of course, the termination of his early funding from the government had left him at loose ends, but he had solved that problem in his own inimitable style. Another mark of genius, that was, turning his adversity around and using it to prove his theories were correct. Correct and practical. If he had turned a tidy profit in the bargain, what was wrong with that?

America was built by people looking out for number one. The idiots in Washington should get down on their knees to thank him for his work, instead of treating him like a pariah, some demented modern Frankenstein.

Radcliff had been there, and he knew the truth:

mankind would doggedly resist improvement to the bitter end.

Advances were still possible, of course, but why should any work done on behalf of an ungrateful race be viewed as charity? Drug companies made billions from the treatment of disease, with hospitals and doctors rooting for their own place at the trough. Public officials, pledged to serve the common good, were never shy in voting raises for themselves or lapping up the perks that came with electoral victory. Evangelists begged constantly for cash to help them live in luxury while they were saving souls.

Radcliff had no regrets—except that he had failed to see the latest problem coming. He had been distracted by his work, and left the details of its application in the field to others, lesser intellects, but that was changing now. Henceforth, he would exert a more direct control, the hands-on method, even if it meant more hours on the job.

Perhaps he could have been more cautious in his choice of clients, more selective in the use to which his children had been put, but mercenary soldiers did what they were paid to do, without debating the morality of a specific cause or customer. What good was an assassin with a conscience, after all?

Inevitably they had suffered losses. All the preparation in the world would not make any man invincible. From the beginning, Radcliff knew that losses were unavoidable, but he always hoped they could be minimized, protracted over time and space to keep the law from catching on. Bad luck, or maybe Fate, had intervened, two losses in the past twelve months—and then another four, within a week.

The first two had been unavoidable, perhaps. When news of the arrest in Florida reached Dr. Radcliff, he had waited to be sure his child would go the limit, as programmed, and sacrifice himself to frustrate the authorities. It had gone off like clockwork, perfectly, and Radcliff's clients had been duly satisfied. No comebacks on the operation meant they could proceed with business, rolling up their profits once the problem was resolved.

The mishap in Wisconsin, while regrettable, was likewise an event for which Radcliff had long prepared himself. He didn't have the details, didn't want them, but he understood some negligence had been involved. His man had missed a federal agent, going in, and wound up dead because of the mistake, but he had done the job before he died. His death itself ensured that there would be no grilling by authorities, no test of his resolve.

In theory, one dead soldier should have cleared a list of pending cases in America and Europe, but a second loss, so soon after the first, had obviously touched off an alarm somewhere in Washington. What happened next—the questioning of Yuli Cristobal, Devona Price's disappearance—told Radcliff that he was perilously close to trouble. Once they made the link to Thomas Hardy, only incredulity itself could help save Project Lazarus. The Feds would not, could not, believe, and therein lay the doctor's hope.

He had done everything within his power to cut their losses, reaching out to silence Cristobal and Jasper Frayne. The fact that they had quickly lost another man in Florida disturbed Radcliff, as much for how it happened as for the mere fact itself. Whoever had eliminated Frayne's assassin didn't stick around to file reports or take the credit—which told Radcliff that the person had not been a cop. From what he had been able to discover unobtrusively, from sources near the scene, the mode of death had also been unusual: no guns involved, perhaps a bludgeon, though the medical examiner's preliminary findings leaned toward something in the field of martial arts.

Before Radcliff had managed fully to assimilate that information, he had been confronted with the problem at Ideal Maternity. Two orderlies found dead, one of the breeders missing. There had been no choice but to abandon the facility. Three of his children had been left behind to watch the grounds, report if the police or Feds showed up, and deal with any trespassers who didn't wear a badge. Instead of cleaning up the mess, however, all three had themselves been killed—again with no apparent weapons used, by someone who slipped in and out, left nothing of himself behind.

At least the other breeders were secure, for now.

He would be forced to find more-permanent accommodations, start from scratch on that end of the operation, but luckily the farm was still intact and undisturbed. While that remained, he was in business.

He would have to guarantee that no one found his children while their education was in progress.

Dr. Radcliff sipped his whiskey and prepared a mental list of who would have to die to keep his secret safe and sound.

THE SCOTCH BURNED Chelsea Radcliff's throat, but that was normal. She restricted her intake of whiskey to ''medicinal'' occasions, when she needed something less than Valium but more than transcendental meditation for her nerves.

Like now.

It had been foolish, going out to dinner with the newsman. Even then, she could have salvaged something from the situation, if only she were better at suppressing her emotions where her father was concerned.

It was ironic, Chelsea thought, that despite her training in psychology—a doctorate, no less—she still had problems sometimes, when it came to self-control. If someone pushed the ''daddy'' button, she was off and running, rising to defend him, even when he obviously did not need her help.

When did he really need her, after all? The man was self-sufficient, always had been. Chelsea had no doubt that he appreciated all her work around the clinic, but she knew that any competent psychologist could do the job. Sometimes, despite her self-confidence, she had to ask herself if it was simple nepotism that had prompted him to put her on the staff at the Family Services Clinic, or something else.

Perhaps an understanding that his little girl could keep a secret.

And she had. She didn't understand the technical minutiae of her father's work, but she had seen and heard enough to recognize his genius, realize that he was years—beyond his rivals in the field. He had not come so far by lavishing attention on himself, his family. Her mother should have understood that from the start.

It had been worse than foolish, dredging up the story of her parents' separation when she spoke to Remo Washington. Chelsea had hoped that it would help to soften her father, maybe add the human touch, offset the chill that always seemed to blight his contacts with the press. Now she was worried that it may have been a grave mistake.

Who was this Remo Washington? She hadn't checked him out at *Newstime* yet, though that was still an option. It ran against the grain for her to trust him on such short acquaintance, and she didn't yet. His charm was a facade, as with all men; it didn't move her...much. In other circumstances, possibly...

She caught herself and made a sour face, sipped

at her drink and tried to get her focus back. How could the newsman jeopardize her father's work? He wasn't even in the ballpark yet, much less acquainted with the details. She had come that close to telling him at dinner, maybe dropping hints that he could follow on his own, but Chelsea's sense of honor had restrained her in the end.

She owed her father everything, for hanging in there when her mother left, not sending her to live with relatives as she had feared. Their time together had been limited, of course, considering his work, but that was only natural. She understood and held no grudge. His work was her work now, at least to some extent. They were together, and she would do nothing to betray his trust.

Chelsea considered warning him, but wasn't sure what she would say. A journalist had bought her dinner and requested that she ask permission for a second interview. There was no crime in that, no threat that she could see...but what if she was wrong?

She could report the meeting to her father, tell him everything. She would have to anyway if they were going to discuss the prospect of a *Newstime* article about his work. She had a sneaking hunch how that idea would be received, but asking wouldn't hurt. He might even surprise her and agree to do the piece. It could turn out to be a feather in his cap.

Not that her father cared for public recognition.

There had been a time, admittedly, when he had fumed at criticism from his peers. She knew it still upset him when lesser intellects received huge grants and public honors for achievements Dr. Quentin Radcliff had surpassed a decade earlier. It galled him, watching plagiarists and sycophants presented to the world as innovators of the day, but there was nothing he could do about it, short of going public with his work. And that, as Chelsea knew too well, was something he was not prepared to do.

Sometimes she wondered at the secrecy. She understood the fear that ''colleagues'' might attempt to steal her father's work and claim it for themselves. That risk was real enough in scientific circles, as in industry, the garment trade or any other field where new ideas could make a fortune overnight. Still, there were times when she was moved to wonder if her father didn't take his passion for security to an extreme.

And then she thought, what of it?

Who was she to question him, his motives or his understanding of a situation that was very possibly beyond her grasp? He knew the stakes involved if his discoveries were broadcast prematurely. It was not her place to think on his behalf, perhaps to jeopardize the labors of a lifetime in pursuit of crass publicity.

Still, she would ask...but not tonight. It was a subject that could wait until tomorrow, the journalist's deadline notwithstanding. Chelsea had been taken with him, in a way, but his request was no emergency. He had not even talked the story over with his editor as yet.

Tomorrow was soon enough, she thought. Perhaps next week.

And in the meantime, she had work to do, a stack of files to read. Her normal days were filled with counseling the clients who approached her father for assistance in their efforts to conceive. She helped them deal with issues ranging from the pain of long-term infertility to the adjustments called for by the presence of a new child in their lives. Her father rarely called upon her to examine any of his ''special'' girls, and while she knew about that aspect of his work—some of it, anyway—she understood that they were screened before acceptance to the program, so that nothing would go wrong.

There had been one occasion, going on three years ago, when one—named Jane—apparently attempted suicide with sleeping pills. Chelsea recalled the urgent summons in the middle of the night, her drive up to Ideal Maternity, where lights were burning late. The girl had been sedated when she got there, obviously frightened. Chelsea's father would not leave the two of them alone, insisting that he had to monitor his patient's physical condition.

There was talk of vague anxiety, the kind of thing young women often felt with first-time pregnancies, but nothing Chelsea could detect that should have triggered off a suicidal episode. There was no evidence the baby had been damaged, though you couldn't always tell with chemicals, and Chelsea never saw the girl again. When she had asked her father, once or twice thereafter, he said that Jane was doing fine. She marked her calendar to ask about the birth when it was due, and got her father's reassurance that there were no complications in the case.

Somehow Jane kept haunting her.

She felt a burning pang of guilt, the very thought of questioning her father tantamount to treachery. He was a certified genius, well off the scale on any test you could name, a man who should have had procedures—even hospitals—named after him, by now. The time would come when he was recognized for his achievements, both at home and around the world.

Still, she was troubled by the thought that she should warn him. Remo Washington seemed harmless, but you never really knew about news types, the way their information could be twisted and misused, even the pieces that had started out with good intentions. There was no telling who had sent him here or put him up to all those pointed questions. She should let her father know.

Tomorrow.

There was no point in disturbing him tonight, she thought. His schedule put him at the boys' home in the morning; she could always catch him there and brief him on her conversation with the journalist and let him decide what should be done.

It was the only way to go.

She stripped her clothes off, showered—trying not to think of Remo Washington, his hands and powerful wrists while she was lathering her body—brushed her teeth and took a sedative to calm her nerves before she crawled in bed and killed the lights.

With any luck at all, thought Chelsea Radcliff, she might even get to sleep.

"I UNDERSTAND COMPLETELY," Morgan Lasser said. He listened for another moment, frowning at the mouthpiece of the telephone, but otherwise displaying no emotion whatsoever.

"Yes, of course," he said at last. "I'll see to it myself.... In person, yes, that's right.... We'll pull out all the stops.... I know that, Doctor.... Yes, indeed... I will.... Good night."

He cradled the receiver, fought an urge to slam it down with force enough to crack the plastic. Swiveling his high-backed chair toward Garrick Tilton, Lasser found his number two regarding him with nervous eyes.

"Sounds like he's freaking out," said Tilton.

"Let's say he's understandably concerned."

"That's what I meant to say."

"We haven't done too well for him so far," Lasser stated.

"Morgan, I explained—"

"Of course. The problem with an explanation is,

it always covers failure. If you were successful, if you did your job, no explanations would be necessary. Am I right?''

"I guess so.''

"What?''

"You're right, okay? We blew it.''

"We?''

"Well, hey, the drones. I wasn't even there, you know?''

"Was that the problem, Garrick?''

"What? Hey, no, I didn't mean—''

"Forget it. We've got more-important things to think about right now.''

"Okay.'' Relief was audible in Tilton's voice. Smart bastard thinking he was off the hook.

Not even close.

"Do we have any kind of handle on what happened at Ideal?''

"Not really,'' Tilton said. "The move was nice and clean to start with, and I left three of the drones behind to watch the place, just like you said.''

"Their orders?''

"Were verbatim what you told me,'' Tilton said. "Hang out and keep a low profile. Take off if any Feds or uniforms showed up. If someone else stopped by, they were supposed to find out who he was, pin down his interest in the place.''

"And now they're dead,'' said Lasser.

"Right. I can't explain it, Morgan. I mean, someone took them out, that's obvious, but as to who, your guess would be as good as mine.''

"We don't have any time for guessing games, goddammit! Blowing the Ideal Maternity connection puts us all in danger. Do you understand that, Garrick?''

"Sure."

"When I say all of us, that means you, too.''

"I hear you."

"Relocation may not be enough," Lasser declared. "Radcliff hasn't mentioned anything about the breeders yet, but we already know he lost one before he called us in."

"He can't blame us for that," said Tilton.

"Blame's beside the point, for Christ's sake! It won't mean shit who's guilty if we all go down the tube together."

"Can we fix it?"

"Maybe. You got rid of the two losers they called orderlies, correct?"

"Deep six," said Tilton, with a wary smile. "They're gone for good."

"All right, then. Say the girl finds someone to believe her story and the cops come looking. There's an empty building, with no forwarding address. So far, so good."

"Except for Radcliff."

"Right. He's on the paperwork, and people know about him in the town. It won't take long to trace him back to Brandenburg."

"The clinic's covered, right?"

"Should be. I mean, it's ninety, ninety-five percent legit already, and you'd need a scientist to spot what's cooking in the lab. No way an Indiana sheriff's going to see through it. Even if they bring the FBI along, they'll need a special team and have to know exactly what they're looking for."

"We're covered, then," Tilton concluded, starting to relax.

"Unless they stumble on the farm."

"Aw, shit!"

"'Aw shit' is right," said Lasser. "They won't need a fucking Sherlock Holmes to figure out there's something wrong about that place."

"So, are we moving them? The drones, I mean?"

"Not yet. With things stirred up right now, it's risky, drawing more attention than we have to. Think about it. We don't know for sure this runaway—what was her name?"

"Joy Patton."

"Right. We don't know where she is or who she's talking to—if anyone. She may be satisfied to get away and let it go at that. File says she was a hooker in L.A. before she came on board the project. That's a knock against her credibility, right off the top."

"But, still…"

"We need to take it easy for a while and see if anybody else shows up in Dogpatch."

"That's 'Dogwood.'"

"Whatever. Radcliff still has people on the payroll there, and we can tap into the cop shop if we have to.''

"Jesus, Morgan."

"Jesus, nothing. This one is for all the marbles, Garrick. If you haven't grasped that yet, it's time to give your brain a wake-up call.''

"I hear you. What's the plan?"

"We're staking out the farm ourselves. We leave in twenty minutes."

Tilton blinked. "You're going?"

"What did I just say?"

"Well, hey...that's great."

Lasser could well imagine what his number two was feeling. Disappointment, even anger, tempered with a measure of relief. It was demeaning to be pushed aside and have the boss take over, like a slap across the face, but Tilton also had to realize that full responsibility for any more snafus would fall on Lasser's head. That wasn't quite the safety net that Garrick Tilton would have wished for, but he wasn't about to find himself a better deal.

"Who are we using?" Tilton asked him.

"Drones. They've got eleven trained and ready as it is. The rest of them can treat it as an exercise."

"That's pretty smart," said Tilton, trying on some flattery for size.

"It makes more sense than having independents on the grounds. We've had too many problems lately, as it is."

"I'd better pack."

"Forget about it. They've got everything we need, already."

"Yeah, okay."

"Remember, Garrick, this one is for keeps. Two reasons why we're doing it ourselves. The first is, Radcliff asked me to come out, but more importantly, when I sign off on something, I expect it to go down as planned. No explanations, no excuses, no mistakes."

"I hear you, Morgan."

"Good. Let's roll."

18

"Cloning?" Harold Smith sounded incredulous. "Is that supposed to be a joke?"

"No way," said Remo. "It's the only answer that makes any sense, considering the circumstances."

"But we are years away from cloning human beings. Maybe decades."

"I suppose that all depends on who you mean by 'we,'" said Remo. "I think Radcliff and Eugenix pulled it off."

"With Thomas Hardy?"

"Right."

"But that is—"

"Impossible?" asked Remo. "How else do we manage to explain the faces and the fingerprints? These shooters don't just look like Hardy—they are Hardy."

Smith considered that for several silent moments. When he spoke again, he sounded weary, like a runner in the last mile of a marathon. "So, you imagine that he has found a way to take...material...from Hardy's corpse and use it somehow to impregnate women? That is the angle on Ideal Maternity?"

"It looks that way to me," Remo confirmed. "All the talk about adoptive homes and surrogates was bullshit. Radcliff had his so-called unwed mothers giving birth to Hardy time and time again. He gets rid of the women afterward, and starts the whole thing over with another batch."

"The clones we have seen—if they are clones— were in their twenties, Remo. That would mean—"

"That Radcliff's been producing little monsters since the early 1970s. That's right."

"It will not hold up," Smith said. "There is nothing in the research to suggest that criminal behavior is genetic. Certain types of mental illness, granted, but there is nothing to support a claim that Hardy was insane. Hit men are not born, they are made."

"Which brings us to the doctor's home for boys."

Smith saw where they were headed, and the view did not improve his mood. "Some kind of school for homicidal maniacs," he said. "Is that the theory?"

"Not at all. You can't control a maniac. What Radcliff needs is trained professionals. The kind you get from years of training and emotional conditioning."

"Like boot camp."

"Starting from the cradle up," said Remo.

"The place would need some kind of license," Smith retorted. "There would be inspections and evaluations, gossip by employees and deliverymen.

He could not hide that many clones or pass them off as twins and triplets.''

"First of all, we don't know how many he has," said Remo. "Six, for sure, and no one's saying he produced them all at once. Radcliff had thirteen girls in Dogwood, all at different stages of their pregnancies. Let's say, at peak production, he can count on six or seven clones a year. They're no good to him till they're old enough to pass as adults, and it takes that long to train them, anyway."

"Still—"

"Let me finish. Formal education doesn't start until the age of five or six, and I'd be very much surprised if any supervised facility could get away with taking children much below that age."

"Which means—"

"He's got another place to stash the infants, right," said Remo. "Let them cut their teeth on war toys, watching *Scarface* on the VCR, whatever. I suppose we'll have to try and squeeze someone to find out where it is."

"And when they are old enough—"

"He sends them to the boys' home,' maybe keeps them separate from the other kids, some kind of special classes. I don't know. Inspectors come around, they see the usual. If they run into any little Thomas Hardys, even two together, it could be explained. It wouldn't happen often. Anyway, inspectors come and go. I'd guess that some of them are more agreeable than others."

"What about the regulars?" Smith asked. "The normal boys?"

"There's bound to be a number of legitimate adoptions," Remo speculated. "The rest would be cut loose when they become adults, at age eighteen. Radcliff would need security to keep them separated from the clones, but if a boy got curious and saw too much, it's easy to arrange an accident or have him disappear."

"Another teenage runaway," said Dr. Smith.

"Exactly. With an orphan, my guess is that no one bothers looking very hard. The cops would file some paperwork and then forget about it overnight."

"And Radcliff's operation would be subsidized by income from the state."

"I wouldn't be surprised."

"You will have to prove it, Remo."

"Which is why I'm going in."

In a town the size of Ekron, it had not been difficult to pin the boys' home down. They called it the Fairfield Home for Boys and it was situated on a ninety-acre tract of woodland east of town.

"Do you expect resistance?"

"With the way it's gone so far," said Remo, "I expect most anything."

"I will wait for your report," Smith declared, and cradled the receiver.

"I do not understand this cloning," said Chiun when Remo laid the handset down.

"I'm not sure anybody does completely, Little

Father. If the theory works, it means that you can take a piece of tissue from an animal, or man, extract the DNA and raise a perfect duplicate of whatever or whoever you started with. I understand some labs have had a fair bit of success with sheep and monkeys, that kind of thing.''

''So, there could be another Chiun?''

''In theory,'' Remo said. ''Of course, the body's only part of it. Your clone would not inherit memories or skills. He'd have to go through all the education, training and experience that you've absorbed throughout your life to make a perfect duplicate—and even then, I guess, there could be room for some emotional discrepancy that altered his behavior.''

Chiun was scowling at a distant point in space. ''Why was I not informed of this?'' he asked.

''Nobody really believed it could be done on human beings. Hell, I could still be wrong. Smith thinks I'm crazy.''

Chiun replied, ''The pot is calling the kettle black. Still, that does not mean he is necessarily correct.''

Was that a compliment or Chiun's contrariness? Remo wondered.

''Anyway, I'm out of here. I have to check the so-called boys' home,'' Remo told him, glancing toward the road map that lay open on his bed, with route and destination marked in felt-tipped pen. ''I'll see you.''

Chiun folded his hands inside the sleeves of his

silk kimono. "Come back quickly. I weary of waiting."

"THE LINEUP of infomercials was never less than captivating, but the Master of Sinanju found it difficult to concentrate on the blaring set, even when he switched over to a noxious sitcom. His mind went back to Remo and the riddle of a dead man who would never truly die as long as bits and pieces of himself were frozen in a lab somewhere, available for transmutation into embryos. What marvels could have been achieved if such technology had been available in bygone ages! Why, Master Ung the poet could still be penning verses of sweet perfection. Death would lose all meaning, in effect, and if that meant assassins had to do the same job more than once, what harm was there in being paid to kill the same man two, three, even six or seven times?

Would such a killer who had generations to prepare himself challenge Remo? Chiun didn't think so. But since the guinea pig and scientists were all American, they would attach the usual importance to such implements as guns, grenades and knives, neglecting the refinements of a true assassin's art. It also helped that they were clumsy—Remo had killed four of them so far—but he was no immortal, for all his skills. When he met them next, there could be six or seven times as many, better armed, better prepared.

Would that number of identical men confuse even a full Sinanju Master?

Chiun blinked at the commercial that was playing. On the TV screen, a mother and her daughter—indistinguishable by their ages—occupied a blanket in the middle of a meadow bright with flowers. From the wicker basket and array of home-cooked food, Chiun knew they must be on a picnic.

Eyes downcast, the daughter spoke. "I have to ask you something, Mom…about those special days. I've tried the pads and tampons, but they just don't do the job."

"These will," her mother answered with a smile, and reached into the open picnic basket for a brightly colored box that might have held a dozen cans of beer. "I always keep a few of these around for special days. They're more absorbent, and—"

Chiun switched the television off, disgusted with himself. It was a sign of weakness that he did not have sufficient faith in Remo to complete this particular mission unassisted.

Still, a new threat had manifested itself. These so-called clones. Remo might resent Chiun for interfering if it turned out to be a relatively simple mission. But if it was more than that…

Chiun stood up, went to the closet, where his lone steamer trunk was standing in a corner. He was changed in seconds flat, his green kimono traded for a black one. There was nothing else that he required.

Harold Smith had taken several hours to locate all

the legal paperwork on the facility called Fairfield Home for Boys. Of course, it helped that he had known the town to start with, and there weren't that many orphanages in the neighborhood of Ekron, Kentucky, but Smith was intent on proving Dr. Radcliff's personal connection to the place before he unleashed Remo on the staff.

In fact, the orphanage was owned by Fairfield Mutual, a paper holding company that was itself controlled by something called Security Unlimited. That company, in turn, was owned by Quentech International—a firm created and controlled by Dr. Quentin Radcliff.

It was evidence enough for Smith, more than enough for Chiun and Remo. Quentech owned the Family Services Clinic in Brandenburg, and also held the title to Ideal Maternity.

Case closed.

When he was ready, Chiun paged through the telephone directory and found a number for the taxi company located nearest to his lodging. Thirteen minutes later, he was settled in the back seat of a battered yellow cab, giving directions to a sweaty driver several times his size.

"Ekron!" the driver snorted. "Are you kiddin' me? That's close to thirty miles, one-way, and then I gotta come back empty. There's no way—"

"How much?" the Master of Sinanju asked him.

"Huh?"

"How much?" Chiun enunciated carefully, as if conversing with a mentally retarded child.

"Well, jeez, let's see... A trip like that would run you sixty—more like seventy—and with the tip..."

Chiun reached across the driver's meaty shoulder, dropped a pair of crisp new hundred-dollar bills into the man's lap, and sat back in his seat. It was only paper money after all.

"Step on it, if you please," the Master of Sinanju said. "And do not spare the horses."

"Is everything in place?"

"I guarantee it," Morgan Lasser said. "We're set for damn near anything."

"Damn near?" The tone of Quentin Radcliff's voice was skeptical.

"Well, you know what I mean."

"Enlighten me," Radcliff demanded.

"Right." Annoyance showed in Lasser's face, but he wasn't about to argue with the man who held the purse strings. "Let me see...we've doubled up on personnel and hardware—all discreetly out of sight, of course—and visual surveillance is on-line around the property. Eight monitors and forty cameras on staggered, overlapping, seven-second sweeps. The chance of anybody getting through is...well, you can forget about it, Quentin."

Dr. Radcliff frowned at the familiarity but let it pass. "You're saying it's impossible for anyone to penetrate the compound, then?"

"To penetrate the compound unobserved," Lasser corrected him. "You didn't give us time to throw a wall around the place."

"Are you implying this is my fault, Lasser?"

"No! Hell, no! I meant—"

"Because the only bungling I've observed these past few days has been on your part."

Lasser bristled. "That's not—"

"You've lost seven soldiers so far, I believe, and four of those were on loan from Project Lazarus. So far, we don't have anything at all to show for it."

"You gave me clearance on the drones," said Lasser, angry color showing in his face.

"Because I thought you knew what you were doing," Radcliff countered. "Thus far, it seems I was mistaken."

"Look, the problem is—"

"I've heard the problems," Radcliff interrupted him. "You can't identify the enemy. You don't know where he is or where he comes from, how he manages to kill armed men without a weapon of his own. You don't know what his motives are or how to stop him. It would seem," continued Radcliff, almost sneering, "that you don't know much of anything."

The others turned away from Lasser's fury, Garrick Tilton staring at his wingtip shoes, while Warren Oxley took a sudden interest in the nearby trees.

"That's damn unfair!" said Lasser, fighting to

control his rage. "We've never let you down before."

"How many failures does it take to constitute a pattern, Morgan? Jasper Frayne. Devona Price. The Dogwood Inn. Ideal Maternity."

"We got Frayne, dammit!"

"And you sacrificed one of my children in the process," Radcliff answered. "Which, I have no doubt, has led directly to the present crisis."

Morgan Lasser, as the reigning honcho of Security Unlimited, bore ultimate responsibility for any failures in the field. No matter how he tried to shift the blame around, regardless of the logic shoring up his arguments, he grudgingly admitted to himself that Dr. Radcliff had a point. Somebody had to be responsible, and since he couldn't even name their enemy, that somebody was him.

"You're right," he said at last, and barely recognized his own strained voice. "We've dropped the ball a few times, granted, but we're back on target now. You won't be disappointed this time, Quentin."

Dr. Radcliff stared at Lasser for a long, still moment. Confidence eluded him, but he was certain he had made his point. If there were any more mistakes by Lasser or his cronies, Radcliff was prepared to cut them loose and punish them accordingly. Meanwhile it was to his advantage if Security Unlimited could solve the problem that was threatening to ruin his life's work.

"I want to see the monitors," he said. "Then we can have a look around the grounds."

"Sure thing," said Lasser, putting on a smile devoid of human warmth. "If you'll just follow me..."

They were a small parade, crossing the close-cut lawn, with Lasser leading Dr. Radcliff, Oxley bringing up the rear with Garrick Tilton. Three decades of painstaking research, breaking new ground in genetics, opening the frontiers of established science, and it all came down to this. His life's work—and his very life itself—depended on a pair of thugs who were, from all appearances, stuck in the middle of an epic losing streak. Still, they had served him in the past and might again if they were able to derail his present enemies.

Who were they, dammit? If the FBI was after him, where were the suits and warrants, the United States attorneys with subpoenas for the next grand-jury hearing? Dr. Radcliff was familiar with the law, from years of trying to avoid it, and he knew damn well that no American police force worked this way, attacking in the dead of night—or in broad daylight, for that matter—killing trained hit men without a shot fired at the scene and leaving their remains to be discovered by whoever came along. It smacked of cloak-and-dagger operations from the Cold War days and made him wonder if his rentals overseas had brought some vultures home to roost, but which among the governments he had frustrated in the past could organize such an efficient operation?

None of them, thought Radcliff. They were all inept.

Of course, he had innumerable enemies. They were intimidated and infuriated by his genius, knowing the discoveries he made would put their feeble efforts in the shade for all eternity. It was amazing, Radcliff thought, that he was even still alive. From personal experience, he knew assassins could be found for any job, in every price range, and the jealous bastards who had tried to block him all his adult life would ultimately stop at nothing to destroy him, wreck his plans or claim his monumental breakthroughs as their own.

He did not fear them yet. If anything, he could admire their raw efficiency.

Which left him with a mystery that Radcliff feared might prove insoluble. The way his unknown adversaries operated, here and gone without a witness, only dead men left behind, he could be next to feel the hand of Death upon his shoulder.

He had taken every possible precaution, spent his life preparing for this moment, and he would not be defeated, robbed of all that he had worked for in three decades, by a total stranger. When the chips were down, his children would protect him.

He was sure of it.

They reached a building fabricated out of cinder blocks and separated from the boys' home by a thirty-yard expanse of grass and trees. When state inspectors came to call, at six-month intervals, they were impressed that Dr. Radcliff laid out so much money for security, to keep the children safe from prowlers on the grounds. Of course, they only saw eight cameras in operation, rather than the forty now engaged—a number that would probably have struck the most enlightened social worker as excessive for an orphanage. But then, they never saw the gun room, either, or the backwoods training ground where Radcliff's drill instructors, hired away from the U.S. Marines and Army Rangers, put his children through their paces.

It was just as well. The state would never understand his special ones, or why they needed combat skills in order to survive. The crowd at Health and Human Services would certainly have terminated Radcliff's funding—not to mention calling the police—if they had known what he was up to, how his grand discovery had found a practical and profitable application in the daily world.

Man was a killer, plain and simple, but the fact remained that certain members of the species were too squeamish, or too "cultured," to perform the dirty work themselves. They needed trigger men who were professional, dependable and absolutely guaranteed to keep their mouths shut—even to the point of self-destruction if captured. Quentin Radcliff filled that need, with no apologies to anyone, and if he made a handsome profit at it, who could

say he didn't earn his money? It was another hallmark of his genius, that he saw a need and filled it.
One more in a series of his great gifts to mankind.

Dr. Radcliff had learned to love free enterprise
almost as much as he loved science. Put the two
together, and you had a winning hand. In days to
come, when he was duly recognized as mankind's
savior, he would reap the full reward that he deserved.

"So, here we are."

The bank of television monitors showed bits and
pieces of the grounds—a curious, insectile point of
view when they were taken all together. Morgan
Lasser started tapping buttons, switching cameras,
and Radcliff soon lost interest in the slide show. One
part of the woods looked pretty much the same as
any other, shrunken down and filmed in black-and-
white. He felt a moment's sympathy for anyone assigned to sit and watch the—

"Wait! What's that? Go back!"

Radcliff stabbed a shaky index finger at the second monitor, top row. There had been something—someone?—moving on the screen, a sprint
from one tree to another, furtive, but the scene had
come and gone before he had a chance to focus.

"What? Which one?" asked Lasser, visibly confused.

"That one, you dolt! Go back!"

Two keystrokes, and the camera panned across a
wooded glade, no sign of life apparent.

"But I could have sworn..."

"Let's try a couple of the other cameras," Lasser said. "Remember, we've got interlocking fields of vision."

Two more clicks, and Lasser froze the camera, focused on a man who stood, peered straight into the lens, then ducked his head and kept on going, out of range.

"Who's that?" asked Radcliff.

"I don't have a fucking clue," said Lasser, reaching for a compact walkie-talkie on the desk in front of him. He brought the handset to his lips and pressed the button to transmit.

"All stations, listen up!" he snapped. "We have a male intruder on the grounds, incoming, Sector Five. Proceed to intercept. Detain for questioning, if possible, but terminate if he seems likely to escape. Let's move it, people. This is not a drill!"

IT WAS PERHAPS not the best way to go, Remo thought, but he'd created a situation they would have to deal with now. Otherwise, he was concerned that Radcliff's people would evacuate the so-called orphanage before he had a second chance to look around, and Remo would have lost his last real chance to prove his theory of the Thomas Hardy killer-clones.

They would be waiting for him now, of course, but waiting was not necessarily the same as ready. Three guns had been waiting for him at Ideal Maternity, as well, but he was still alive and they were not. He could expect a stronger, more determined opposition this time, but they weren't Masters of Sinanju.

He stayed alert for any sign of sentries or booby traps as he navigated through the woods. There was another camera up ahead, which he could hear whirring on its pivot, but he got around that one by waiting for the lens to turn in one direction while he scampered in the other.

Simple.

Even knowing he was here and roughly where he was, the other side would have to work their asses off to take him down.

Too bad the woods were sparse on this side of the ground, he thought. There was sufficient undergrowth to cover him if things got hairy, but it would have given him a greater edge if he could leave the ground behind, take to the trees and make like Tarzan for a while, avoiding both the cameras and any foot patrols that came along.

Still, he was on the scene, and the security devices told him he was getting closer to the object of his quest. A wiser man than Dr. Radcliff might have had the orphanage evacuated at the same time he was clearing out Ideal Maternity, but Remo gambled on the supposition that events had overtaken Radcliff in a rush, compelling him to face one aspect of the problem at a time.

He hoped so, anyway.

If Radcliff had been smart and swift enough to clear the boys' home, Remo could be wasting precious time.

And something told him there was little left to spare.

He knew approximately where the major buildings were, from driving past the Fairfield gates on Webster Road, a short mile east of Ekron. Moving on, he had picked out a narrow service road and found a place to hide his car before he started in on foot. Most of the ninety acres would be woodland, and he estimated that the orphanage would be located closer to the nearest road than to the back half of the property.

So far so good, until he saw the camera—and it saw him.

He kept on moving, knew that it would be a grave mistake to hold his ground and wait for trackers to come looking for him. He was conscious of the cameras now, could keep them guessing to a fair degree, but the opposition had to know where he was headed. No one would assume that he was out there for a simple Nature walk.

He saw the orphanage about the same time that the first patrol experienced their fleeting glimpse of him. A shout confirmed their presence after Remo heard them coming through the trees, away to his left front. Four men, the faces identical, except that two seemed slightly older than the others.

Different generations, Remo thought. Death without end.

He was already ducking, moving, when they opened fire with automatic weapons and the bullets started whispering around him, sizzling through the air.

19

"What are they shooting at, for Christ's sake?" Dr. Radcliff felt a sudden surge of panic. He could hear the sharp reports of gunfire even where he stood, inside the blockhouse, with the heavy door closed. "Don't you give them silencers or something?"

"Not on automatic rifles," Lasser told him, almost sneering. "Anyhow, the nearest neighbor is at least a mile away. We'll have the job cleaned up before they even think about complaining."

Radcliff flinched as more gunshots erupted from the grounds. In front of him, the monitors were flickering, scenes changing rapidly, as Lasser tried to find the source of gunfire, give them all a view of what was happening. It took him several tries, and twice the cameras caught a blur of running figures, then he had them. Four of Radcliff's children, armed with military weapons, closing in a semicircle on a clump of tangled shrubbery that grew between two fair-sized oaks.

"Watch this," said Lasser, sounding pleased. "They've got him now."

As if on cue, the four clones opened fire in unison,

bright muzzle-flashes sparking from their rifles.
There was no sound from the monitor, but Radcliff
heard the sound of shots outside. Somehow the echo
sounded out of sync, retarded, like the poorly
dubbed dialogue of a foreign movie.

The concentrated firing only lasted for an instant,
then his children closed the ring, prepared to drag a
riddled body from the bushes.

"Here he comes," Lasser announced, grinning
like a wolf.

And he was right. No sooner had he spoken than
a fifth man joined the others, dropping from above
and landing in a crouch behind the nearest of them,
with his back turned toward the camera. Even so,
there could be no doubt that it was the same man
they had glimpsed short moments earlier.

"Look out!" Lasser warned, leaning toward the
monitor as if he could protect the children somehow,
warn them of their peril.

It was already too late.

As Radcliff watched the shrunken image, horri-
fied, he saw the stranger grab one of his children by
the head and twist, the body going limp, collapsing
like an empty suit of clothes. Before the others could
react to that, he struck out to the right and left with
blows so swift the eye could not even follow them.
Three down, and when the fourth of Radcliff's children raised his weapon, squeezing off a burst of automatic fire, the stranger started dodging bullets,
closing in to finish off his sweep.

Radcliff could never have explained exactly what he saw—the stranger's body ducking, weaving, almost slithering, and yet without a seeming break in stride. It took perhaps two seconds for the man to reach the fourth of Radcliff's children, twist the rifle from his grasp as if it were a toy, and do something one-handed that left the neck lolling at an odd angle.

"He can't do that!" raged Lasser, grabbing for the walkie-talkie. "All sentries!" he snapped. "We have four men down. The subject has an M-16. Forget about detaining him. Just take him down!"

Again, as if in answer to the words he could not hear, the stranger dropped his captured weapon, turned and passed beneath the watching camera empty-handed.

Headed for the orphanage.

"He's coming," Radcliff said.

"No shit." The look on Morgan Lasser's face was six parts anger, four parts fear.

"What can we do?" asked Warren Oxley, looking pale as three grim pairs of eyes were focused on his face. "I mean, how can he do that?"

"Let's go out and ask him," Lasser said. The chairman of Security Unlimited produced an automatic pistol from beneath his jacket as he spoke.

Beside him, Garrick Tilton also palmed a weapon.

"We're not armed," said Oxley, glancing desperately at Radcliff for support.

"You will be," Lasser said, and turned to Tilton.

"Stop off at the gun room," he instructed. "Fix them up."

"But we're not gunmen," Oxley protested.

"No shit," Lasser repeated. "Anyway, it's time you learned."

"Shut up, for Christ's sake, Warren!" Radcliff snapped. "This is a critical emergency."

"You got that right," said Lasser, moving toward the exit. "All hands to their battle stations."

Radcliff fell into step behind the men who were, in fact, subordinates. It was no time to challenge Lasser, when they needed all his expertise and he held all the weapons. Later, after they had cleared this problem up, there would be time enough to deal with Lasser's insubordination, shop around for someone else to fill in as the leader of Security Unlimited. Perhaps the company itself should be dissolved, a new one organized to take its place.

But first they had to stop the man who was intent on ruining a lifetime's work. Find out what he was doing here and who had sent him. Failing that, destroy him utterly and relocate the whole damn operation to a safer place.

Radcliff was thinking now in terms of the Caribbean or South America. The land that sheltered Dr. Josef Mengele for over forty years should be amenable to visitors with plenty in the bank. The world could be his oyster, after all, but he would have to take it one step at a time.

Step one was getting through the next half hour alive.

THE SOUND OF GUNFIRE in the woods was audible before she reached the driveway leading to the boys' home. Chelsea Radcliff hesitated, rolling down her window with a hand that she found trembling unexpectedly.

It sounded like a war in there, beyond her line of sight, and Chelsea played with the idea of turning back. Stop at the first pay phone she found and call the sheriff's office.

She shook her head vehemently in response to that impulse. One lesson that her father had repeatedly drilled into Chelsea's skull: avoid outsiders as much as possible, and shield the family's business from their prying eyes.

Still, this was serious trouble, obviously. People died when guns went off. Her father's very life might be in danger while she sat there on the roadside, pondering his orders. There was still a chance that she could save his life with one quick phone call.

Again she shrugged it off.

The first thing she would do is have a look inside. She might find out the gunfire was no more than target practice, though the very notion seemed ridiculous to Chelsea at the moment. Why would they have guns around the home at all, much less the kind that sounded like machine guns tearing up the woods?

She rolled her window up again to minimize the racket as she turned in from the two-lane highway. Intertwining branches met above her car to block a portion of the sunlight out and place her in a realm of dappled shadow. She accelerated, taking chances with the narrow driveway, knowing that the longer she remained a moving target, the more likely that some gunman in the woods might draw a bead upon her vehicle. The shooters wouldn't recognize her, wouldn't know her car, and it might well be worse for Chelsea if they did.

Suppose that she had blundered into an attempt against her father's life. What could she do about it? How would she respond?

She would defend him, certainly...but how?

A moment later, she could see the building coming at her through the trees. No one was in sight, but it wouldn't surprise her if the boys were hiding in their rooms, with all the shooting going on. She drove around the south side of the building, still braced for the impact of a bullet that would smash through glass or ring against the metal of her car, but no shots came.

She killed the engine, hesitated, wishing that she had some kind of weapon with which to defend herself. Not that it would have helped her much. No one would readily mistake her for a warrior, even in a pinch.

But if she had to fight, no way around it, to protect her father and his work.

Perhaps, thought Chelsea, she might find a weapon in the house. It would be worth a look, at least, since she was bent on looking for her father, come what may.

Reluctantly, still trembling, Chelsea bailed out of her car and started running toward the nearest door.

THE MASTER OF SINANJU left his cab on Webster Road and barely heard the driver asking him if he was sure he had the address right. The cabbie blinked and shook his head in wonder as his wizened passenger appeared to vanish in thin air. One moment he was standing there beside the taxi, and the next he was a flitting shadow, lost among the trees.

The driver took his hundred-dollar tip and split, no longer interested in what the old man wanted on this stretch of rural highway. Cruising past the entrance to the Fairfield Home for Boys, he barely gave the sign a second glance, before he turned around and started back toward Louisville.

By that time, Chiun was deep into the forest, homing on the compound proper with unerring intuition. The reports of distant gunfire made him hesitate, but only for a heartbeat. He corrected his direction slightly, homing on the sharp, staccato sounds.

It would not be that simple for the enemy to murder his adopted son. Chiun had confidence in Remo's skill. However, faced with a confusing situation, even Remo might falter. And that could give an enemy the moment he needed.

Chiun felt a burning rage directed against those who would attempt to slay the future Master of Sinanju. They were idiots, but even the most simpleminded fools got lucky now and then. It seemed unlikely that they could destroy Remo, but if he was wrong, there would be nothing to protect them from the Master's vengeful wrath.

He would destroy them all in such a fashion that they would regret the miserable days when they were born.

Chiun had another hundred yards to go before he reached the source of gunfire, silent now, when he was interrupted by a shout from somewhere on his left.

"Hey, you! That's far enough! Stop where you are and raise your hands!"

Chiun paused, turned toward the voice and saw three men approaching through the trees. All three held automatic weapons, and their faces were the same. Same close-cropped hair. Same cold, unfeeling eyes. Same mouths and noses. The one on the right looked slightly younger than the others, but Chiun could have been mistaken.

These must be the creatures Remo called the clones.

They were the walking dead.

"Let's get those hands up!" barked the gunman on the left.

"Are you addressing me?" the Master of Sinanju asked.

"Who else, you stupid dink?"

The others laughed at that, enjoying his presumed embarrassment. Chiun frowned and asked, "What is this 'dink'?"

"It's like a gook," the young one answered, smiling. "Chink, Jap, slope—you know?"

More laughter from the walking dead.

"You are mistaken," said Chiun.

"Oh, yeah?" the gunman in the middle said. "You sure look like a dink to me."

"Your eyes deceive you," Chiun replied. "It is a common failing of the mentally deficient."

"Don't push your luck, old man!" one of them snapped. "And get your fucking hands up!"

Chiun complied, the sleeves of his kimono fanning out like bat's wings. When he turned and ran in the direction of a nearby maple tree, the gunmen spent a precious second gaping after him, then opened fire as one, their bullets fanning through the air behind him. They were astounded, gaping, as he ran directly up the tree trunk, then reversed directions like a squirrel and sprinted out along a limb that pointed in their general direction. When he leaped off into space, the shooters tried to track him with their weapons, but they had already lost their only chance.

Chiun fell upon them in a kind of cartwheel, slashing with his feet and open hands. The three men fell as if they had been cut down with a scythe, their bodies twitching on the grass as life fled from their battered flesh and broken bones. He left the useless weapons where they fell and turned away, moved on to find his son.

Those three had not faced Remo; he was sure of it, since they were still alive when they discovered Chiun. The first shots he had heard came from a greater distance, farther to the west, in the direction where he knew the so-called orphanage must stand. Remo had come directly to the site, with something like a twenty-minute lead, but it appeared that he had taken time to scout the property before he ventured into contact with the guards.

So much the better, then. They could complete the work in unison.

The Master of Sinanju did not run, but rather he seemed to glide across the forest floor. A fox or rabbit would not have heard him passing by; an eagle could not have glimpsed him dodging through the shadows. As for the men he hunted, they would neither see nor hear Death coming for them from the east.

Remo would see to that, distracting them, monopolizing their attention as they tried to rub him out. Chiun only hoped his son would leave a few more of the enemy alive for him to play with.

It would be a shame, he thought, to travel all this way and only send three zombies to their graves.

THE FIRST FOUR had been easy. They were quick enough, and fairly accurate with firearms, but they had too much faith in automatic weapons. Push enough lead through a given space, the theory said, and you were bound to score a kill. Assuming, always, that your target waited for the bullets to arrive.

But Remo had not waited, scrambling up the nearest tree while they were wasting countless rounds on earthbound shadows, tearing up the landscape. Moments later, when the firing ceased and they were all below him, it was simple to jump down and take them out.

He saw the camera afterward and didn't care. The firing would have given him away, in any case, and he was in the middle of it now, where strength and speed meant more than stealth. The home and several outbuildings were visible between the trees from where he stood, and Remo moved in that direction, conscious that the enemy was waiting for him, armed and ready for the kill.

How many?

He would have to wait and see.

The sudden burst of gunfire from behind him, several hundred yards away, took Remo by surprise. He hesitated, turned in that direction, but he saw no point in going back to find out what the guards were shooting at. Most likely they were spooked by shadows or some forest creature that had blundered into range. As long as they were wasting ammunition somewhere else, Remo was glad to leave them unmolested, thereby spreading more confusion in the hostile ranks.

If there was someone covering the security monitors—and logic said there must be—then they would have seen the four clones drop like rag dolls, massacred despite the weapons they were carrying. It couldn't hurt to let his adversaries sweat a little, wondering how Remo pulled it off, what he would do to them if he got close enough.

When he got close enough.

Because of children on the grounds, presumably both clones and normal kids, they had not gone all-out with booby traps. There were no trip wires fitted to grenades, no Claymore mines, not even simple snares. The enemy had put his faith in cameras and men with guns to follow up on any images of strangers wandering the grounds. The necessary lapse gave Remo greater freedom, let him move with more haste than he could have in a military free-fire zone.

He thought again about the numbers he would have to face. Close to a dozen of the Hardy clones were dead now that he knew of, but the gunmen at the Dogwood Inn were proof that Dr. Radcliff's force was not confined to home-grown soldiers. Even so, it seemed unlikely that the doctor would expose his most secure facility to strangers if he had a viable alternative.

Send in the clones, thought Remo, with a smile.

He smelled the enemy before he saw them, sweat and gun oil mingling on the breeze. Most humans would have missed it, nostrils jaded by their diet and environment, but Remo caught a whiff from twenty yards, in time to save himself.

Before the guns went off, he bolted to his left, fell prone behind a rotted log and wriggled several more yards on his belly to the cover of a venerable elm. The ambush party—only two men, by the sound of it—was busy tearing up the landscape where they saw him go to ground, apparently believing he would be incapable of movement once he left the trail.

The firing slacked off moments later, like a passing squall, and Remo heard his adversaries stirring from their hideout, moving cautiously into the open. Any second now. It would be foolish to delay his move and wait for reinforcements to arrive, attracted by the sound of shots.

He watched them, braced himself, hung back until he verified that there were only two, both doppelgängers, armed with submachine guns, moving toward the spot where they presumed his lifeless body would be found. He rose and moved into the clear behind them, silently approached the nearest of the two until an arm's length separated them.

"Right here," he told the gunner, almost whispering.

His adversary whipped around, his weapon coming with him, but he wasn't quick enough. The punch that Remo threw was not flamboyant or dramatic, but it did the job, connecting with the shooter's chin and lifting him completely off his feet as vertebrae were separated at the point where skull and spinal column meet.

He caught the dead man falling, spun him with an easy maneuver that made the body look like one of those inflatable "companions" sold in shops that advertise their stock as "educational material" or "marital aids." The flaccid, still-warm body made a shield for Remo as the second gunner spun and opened fire, his bullets flattening against the Kevlar vest his late companion wore.

It would have been a relatively simple thing to duck and fire between the corpse's dangling legs, at Remo's feet, but such a move requires coherent thought, perhaps rehearsal—in the mind, at least—before the actual event. Right here, right now, the second gunner found himself strung out between the two extremes of rage and panic, firing in a kind of automatic reflex.

Remo tossed the body at him, closing in behind it as the shooter lost his balance, stumbled, going down with his dead clone on top of him. The submachine gun stuttered half a dozen futile rounds before the shooter lost it, grappling with the corpse in an attempt to rise.

He never made it.

Remo was beside him in a heartbeat, one hand cupped beneath his chin, the other on his crown. A simple twist, mere leverage, and Remo felt the spinal column separate, the skull twist backward with a realism Linda Blair and Hollywood could never duplicate.

Six down, and Remo was unscathed—so far. Luck was a part of that, he understood, but only part. The plain fact was that his opponents, so far, had been no match for the powers of Sinanju. If they were going to be saved by luck, it would require a great deal more than they had shown yet.

He left the dead where they had fallen and proceeded to his target like a guided missile, homing on ground zero.

MORGAN LASSER squinted in the sudden glare of sunlight as they left the bunker, muttering a curse as he remembered that his shades were in the car. Screw comfort, then, as long as he could see to aim and pull the trigger when their adversary showed himself.

Assuming he survived that long.

More firing came from the woods, a little closer than the last round. This had only been one weapon, and it sounded like a submachine gun. Lasser didn't know which clones had drawn what weapons, and he couldn't tell the creepy pricks apart in any case. What did it matter, anyway? If one of them got lucky with the stranger, he would hear about it soon enough. Meanwhile he had to be prepared for the worst-case scenario.

They had the normal kids—whom Lasser always thought of as the "regulars"—penned up inside their dormitory, closely watched, with orders not to poke their heads outside or even crack a window blind until they got the word. He didn't know what story Radcliff had concocted to explain the shooting, and he didn't care. The little bastards did as they were told, or else. If one of them complained to someone weeks or months from now, who would believe him? There would be no evidence of any paramilitary action, nothing but the nearby target-practice range to help account for gunshots amplified by an hysterical imagination.

If it went beyond that point, he thought, the little shit could always have an accident, or simply run away from home. Without a witness, the authorities would have no case.

He checked the others with a glance, saw Oxley and their fearless leader holding guns as if they were afraid the weapons might explode and tear them limb from limb at any moment. Damn amateurs were worse than useless in a killing situation, but it felt to Lasser like a moment when he needed every man on tap, regardless of their marginal abilities.

He had considered using the trainees, decided

they would only mix things up, get in the way. Still, it would be a fallback option if his first line of defense broke down. And judging from the slaughter he had witnessed on the monitor inside, the drones he had on the perimeter still had a lot to learn about defense.

He wondered how many of them would live to profit from the lesson they were getting here today.

And if they all went down, but he and Dr. Radcliff managed to survive, what then? It would be eighteen months at least before the oldest drone in training was prepared to solo in the field, and they had orders stacked up to the rafters—from the syndicate, assorted right- and left-wing paramilitary groups, a certain Middle Eastern government. None of their clients was renowned for patience or forgiveness when a plan fell through. The very least they would expect was compensation, possibly with interest, and a couple of the psycho fringe groups might suspect betrayal, possibly come looking for revenge.

But he could think about the irate customers tomorrow, if tomorrow ever came. The business end was Radcliff's job, in any case, with Lasser handling operations from behind the cover of Security Unlimited. If things went sour, he could always disappear, pull up one of the several alternate identities he kept on tap for such emergencies and spend the next few years in Switzerland or the Bahamas, where the bulk of Lasser's money was secure in numbered bank accounts. A total bailout meant that he would have to deal with Radcliff, silence him for good, but he could live with that.

It might even be fun.

Right now he had to think about some kind of a defense when he had two drones, Garrick Tilton and a pair of amateurs to back him up. Lasser regretted not importing extra guns to help out with security. So far, they only seemed to be confronting one invader, but he was no ordinary man. If he could stroll through automatic gunfire, kill four men barehanded, he deserved respect. Not fear—at least not yet—but something more than casual disdain.

He wished the place were fortified, but that would be impossible for anybody to explain when the inspectors came around from Health and Human Services. It was hard enough to cover Radcliff's cloning operation with the orphanage facade, pass off the obstacle course and other training facilities as part of a well-balanced program for physical fitness, without trying to explain barbed wire and booby traps. One hint of paramilitary training, and they would have everybody from the Feds to private watchdog agencies and cult busters breathing down their necks.

So he would have to do with what he had. They could not move inside the dormitory block without attracting even more attention from the regulars whom Lasser had already sought to neutralize. The blockhouse was secure enough, if you liked being locked inside a vault, but that would leave their adversary free to roam the grounds at will, while they were forced to sit and watch him on the monitors.

It came down to a confrontation in the open, and he was relieved that some unknown landscaper had contrived to push the forest back in all directions, clearing out a broad expanse of lawn around the buildings. That way, if they were positioned properly, they had the compound covered. Short of beaming in like an escapee from the 'Star Trek' series, their antagonist couldn't approach the dorms or blockhouse without giving someone ample time to blow his ass away.

Unless, of course, they stalled too long before selecting their positions.

"Quickly, now, we have to separate," said Lasser. Turning to the drones, he told them, "You two take the north side of the dorm, both corners. Anybody you don't recognize, he's dog meat."

"Right."

"Yes, sir."

They went like soldiers, no dumb questions or delays, and Lasser wished them well. He turned to Garrick, saying, "Take the west side of the blockhouse. Now!"

"Okay."

So far, so good.

That still left Radcliff and his weasel, Oxley. Neither one of them had ever shot a man before, but they would have a chance today.

"You're on the south end of the dorms," said

Lasser, both of them included in the order. "Any unfamiliar faces, do your best to drop them. Shoot first, save the questions for another day. If you can't bring the target down, at least make noise. I'll try to help you out."

"And where will you be?" Radcliff asked. The hallmark of an amateur with more ego than common sense.

"I'm covering the east side," Lasser said. "You'll know if anybody comes at us from that direction. Are you ready?"

Warren Oxley said, "I've never killed a man before."

"Consider this your lucky day. Now, move it!"

Lasser didn't wait to see if they obeyed him, but set off in the direction of the watch point he had chosen for himself. Thus far, the gunfire had come mainly from the east, in the direction of the road that ran past Radcliff's Fairfield Home for Boys, and Lasser knew that any threat was most likely to come from that direction, also. If the stranger held his course, depicted on the monitors so far, he would come out in Lasser's sector and find death there waiting for him.

Perfect.

Lasser was scanning for a point of adequate concealment to improve his odds. The best that he could manage was a shaded doorway, nothing much, but it would offer him a clear view of the lawn and trees beyond.

He ducked into the alcove, didn't even bother checking it and stiffened as he heard the voice that issued from behind him. Barely audible the whisper was in his ear.

"Surprise!"

THE HOUSE WAS deathly quiet, not at all what she was used to with so many boys around. Where were they? Where was everybody? From the sound of it, the staff must all be out, around the grounds somewhere, unloading with the kind of hardware that was normally restricted to the Army and Marines. It all made Chelsea anxious for her father's safety, but she was not giving up.

A weapon.

The continual shooting outside, though slackened to some slight degree, reminded Chelsea that she might be called on to defend herself at any moment. Stopping by the kitchen, she spent several moments checking out the cutlery. She was about to choose a cleaver, but it seemed too heavy, too obscenely brutal, and she finally opted for a twelve-inch chef's knife.

Chelsea held the knife in front of her as she departed from the kitchen and continued with her search. It would be little use against a gun, she realized, but if she managed to surprise an enemy...

It startled her to realize that she was actually considering the means of stabbing someone, snuffing out another human life by force, but then she thought about her father once again, and knew she would do anything required to help him, save him.

But she had to find him first.

She thought of calling out, then stopped herself, afraid of drawing the attention of her father's unknown enemies. Far better, for the moment, if she searched in silence, kept a low profile and drew no more attention to herself.

Where should she start?

Her father's office. He wouldn't be there, of course, but it was something. There might even be a clue of some kind, something to direct her.

She was wasting time.

Without another moment's hesitation, Chelsea Radcliff hurried off along the corridor.

HE OWED THE BREAK to sluggish adversaries, spread thin on the grounds. They should have had the tree line covered right away, but Remo made it to the building in a rush, feet barely touching down as he took off across the close-cropped grass. Mere seconds after he was wedged into the doorway, thinking what his next move ought to be, he heard the shooter coming. No attempt to mask his progress, taking it for granted that a gun would handle any problems he encountered on the way. The guy was dumb enough to back in, checking out the lawn. He almost jumped out of his skin when Remo spoke to him.

"Surprise!"

The shooter was not one of Radcliff's clones, but

he was quick once he got motivated. Pivoting on one heel, snarling like an animal, he swung a pistol into line with Remo's face—or would have if the gun had still been in his hand.

Disarming him was no great challenge, just a grab and twist, then Remo had the automatic in his hand, the shooter so surprised that he still crooked his index finger, trying to squeeze a nonexistent trigger.

"Shit!"

"You got that right," said Remo, striking out with his fingers in a deadly jab that left the shooter without a heartbeat. The dead man's eyes crossed as he tried to focus, then he slumped over backward, sprawling on the flagstone walk.

Remo decided not to force the door just yet, moved on in search of other prey. He circled to his right, or south. Before he reached the corner, he heard voices, two of them, and recognized the deeper one as Quentin Radcliff's.

"This is a mistake," said someone he had never met. "I'm not cut out for this."

"Shut up, for God's sake, Warren!" Radcliff ordered. "You've been hunting, surely."

"Not since I was ten years old."

"Same principle," said Radcliff. "You can think of this as self-defense, if that will help. Remember not to jerk the trigger when you fire."

"That's good advice," said Remo, coming into view around the corner, as if strolling in the shadow of the bogus orphanage was a routine event.

"My God!" the stranger blurted as he raised a pistol gripped in shaky hands.

Not quick enough. The floater strike sailed past his weapon, found his face and ended it. The straw man vaulted backward, struck the wall with force enough to tear his scalp and leave a bloody smear behind him as he slithered to the ground.

And that left Dr. Quentin Radcliff, standing frozen, with his pistol pressed against his thigh.

"The newsman," Radcliff said.

"Not quite."

"I gathered that. Who are you?"

"I'm from quality control," Remo announced, keeping one eye on the gun. "Your little monsters didn't pass."

"I don't expect you'd understand," said Radcliff.

"On the contrary."

"You're not a scientist."

"Well, that makes two of us."

"You can't kill me," the doctor said.

"I must have missed that rule."

"But my discovery! Think of it! Who'll take over my research?"

"With any luck," said Remo, "no one will."

"You'd throw it all away?"

"I'd flush it down the toilet, if I thought they'd fit."

The doctor winced at that. "But what about...the others?"

Remo followed Radcliff's glance in the direction

of the building, wondering how many clones-in-progress they would find inside.

"That isn't up to me," he said.

"I can't—"

"How many are there?" Remo asked him, interrupting.

"What? Oh, twelve, thirteen, I think." Radcliff's precision memory was failing under stress. "The youngest one is only seven. Will you kill him, too?"

"And what about the women from Ideal Maternity?" asked Remo, pointedly ignoring Radcliff's question.

"Safe," the doctor said. "I have an old house south of here, near Irvington. Althea's with them. She's in charge."

"Not anymore."

"I can't just let you ruin all my work. I won't!"

"So, take your—"

"No!"

The shriek, a woman's voice, came from behind him. Remo cursed himself for letting Radcliff so distract him that another enemy could come so close, unnoticed.

Remo spun, found Chelsea coming at him with some kind of kitchen knife poised overhead, the long blade flashing with reflected sunlight. Everything about her posture and technique was wrong. A punchy boxer could have blocked the swing and decked her.

Remo caught her arm as it descended, used the

least force he could manage in a rush and heard the small bones in her wrist give way. Then she was airborne, gasping through a forward somersault and landing on her back with force enough to drive the air out of her lungs.

He threw the knife away and turned back toward her father. "Your turn."

Dr. Radcliff did his best, all things considered. If he'd had another year or so to practice, maybe Radcliff could have pulled it off.

Or maybe not.

The gun was rising past his hip when Remo stepped in close and drove the stiffened fingers of his right hand under Radcliff's sternum, rupturing his heart. His eyes blinked once, behind the spectacles, and then he sagged, a mounted specimen with all the stuffing leaking out.

The final parting had been overdue, thought Remo. This one had been soul dead for at least three decades.

Remo recognized Chiun's footsteps by the fact they made no sound. One moment he was standing in the bright Kentucky sunshine with a pair of corpses at his feet; the next moment a flicker at the corner of his eye told him the Master of Sinanju had arrived.

"You're not sitting moping in a hotel room, Little Father."

"Do not remind me. There were two clowns watching on the north end of the building."

"Clones," said Remo.

"I speak perfect English," Chiun informed him. "These were clowns. They tried to kill the Master of Sinanju with their puny weapons! Fools!" he spit in disgust.

"Too bad I missed it," Remo said.

Chiun glanced at Radcliff. "Is this the evil one?"

"He'll do until the real thing comes along."

"Where are the rest?" asked Chiun.

"Inside. I was about to go and have a look."

"I will accompany you," Chiun announced imperiously.

"I wish you would."

Together Remo and the Master of Sinanju found the nearest door and went inside to meet the children of a nightmare come to life.

20

"Sixteen," said Dr. Harold Smith. "It is hard to fathom, even now."

Three infant clones had been recovered when the FBI swept down on Dr. Radcliff's house in Irvington, Kentucky, to arrest Althea Bliss and take one dozen unwed mothers into something like protective custody. If all of them delivered healthy children, it would soon be twenty-eight.

"You've seen it for yourself," said Remo from the other side of Smith's desk in his office at Folcroft Sanitarium.

"Yes, unfortunately." Smith had all the animation of a vegetarian confronted with a heap of uncooked beef and pork. "The FBI is sorting through the papers found at Radcliff's clinic, but it is still too early to predict if they will find anything."

"He had to have some kind of scientific staff around the place," said Remo. "His age, I'd bet money Radcliff didn't do it all himself."

"I have some payroll records," Smith informed him, "and I am checking out the names. "At least three known employees of the clinic have already disappeared.''

"The daughter?" Remo asked.

"The FBI is talking to her," Smith replied. "So far, she is still denying any knowledge of her father's covert work. She says she was coming out to visit him and drove into the middle of a war zone. She was simply trying to protect him when she came at you."

"It may be true."

Smith's frown was frankly skeptical. "Perhaps," he said. "It is evident from clinic records that there were some normal patients being treated there, for infertility. The authorities will have to check them all, of course, and make sure Radcliff did not do anything unwholesome to them when their backs were turned."

"He wouldn't leave a Hardy clone with normal parents," Remo said. "You need the proper background to produce a sure-fire killer."

"Possibly." Smith sounded dubious once more. "With Radcliff's penchant for bizarre experiments on humans, though, it is best not to take any chances."

He was right, of course. With thirty years of work behind him, all that blood money to keep him going, Radcliff could have easily conceived some grand new project that would see him through his golden years.

Another shot at immortality, perhaps?

Forget it, Remo thought. They could sit back and

theorize for fifty years and never know what kind
of crazy mischief had been generated by Quentin
Radcliff's brain. How many false starts had there
been, before he got it right with Thomas Allen
Hardy, back in '65? Admittedly the doctor wasn't
that long out of training when he signed on with
Eugenix, but that kind of fascination didn't turn up
overnight, the product of a restless dream. Radcliff
had obviously thought about it for a while—perhaps
for years—before he found a vehicle to make his
fantasies reality.

"The normal kids?" asked Remo, taking first
things first.

"Thirty-three were collected," said Smith. "They
have been distributed to state facilities or foster care
until they can be placed in the adoption system."

Remo knew what that meant, from his own experience in childhood. Most of those penned up at
Fairfield were from nine to fifteen years of age, with
half a dozen younger. Even so, the youngest "normal" boy they'd found was six years old, which
placed him well beyond the normal cut-off age dic-
tated by childless couples seeking pretty infants they
could raise. With thirty-three on hand, he guessed
that it would be a miracle if half a dozen of the
children found adoptive homes.

Still, Remo told himself, a foster home or honest
orphanage was hardly worse than being held as prisoners and cover for a madman who was breeding
monsters in the basement, more or less.

"I wouldn't be surprised if some of them need

counseling, with what they've been through," Remo said.

"They will get it," Dr. Smith replied firmly.

It sounded as if Smith planned to plunder the CURE operating budget, if necessary. An unusual surge of generosity coming from a man noted for his parsimonious nature.

"And the others?"

They were getting to the nitty-gritty now, the Hardy clones whom Radcliff and his people had been training for their future work as hired assassins going to the highest bidder. There was one thing Remo had to say for Radcliff: he had seemingly divorced his work from any taint of politics, religious ideology or racial bigotry. If you could meet his price, the troops were yours, no matter if you served the KKK, Black Liberation Army, Mafia, Hebrew Defense Association or the PLO. In theory, if a husband had the right connections and sufficient income, he could hire a clone from Radcliff to eliminate his wife.

Remo believed the adult clones were all dead now. He couldn't prove it absolutely, but his backup theory said that any troops still in the field would finally reveal themselves or self-destruct when they found out their lifeline to Kentucky had been severed. And if he was wrong, at least they would be stripped of paying clients, no more dangerous than any other psycho rolling in to hit a liquor store on Friday night.

Not much.

"I cannot be sure yet," Smith replied. "They are going to require evaluation, and it takes some time. Of thirteen clones, there are four in their teens who have completed major segments of their training. Frankly, Remo, I am not certain they can ever be deprogrammed. They may be dangerous for life, like pit bulls raised to fight."

"What happens then?"

"Other agencies are involved now," Smith replied. "It is no longer my decision."

Remo knew what that meant. Any subject deemed incorrigible had to be forever isolated from society. The only question would be whether they survived—presumably confined in some secure facility that catered to the criminally insane—or if they would be liquidated in the interest of expediency.

"Damn."

"I know exactly how you feel," Smith said, and Remo knew he meant it.

"What about the younger ones?"

"It looks a little brighter there," Smith told him. "Nine boys, aged six to twelve—the older one is marginal, I grant you—who may still be salvageable. Of course, that is no guarantee."

"I understand," said Remo.

"With the proper counseling and education, maybe medication, some or all of them may come around."

"No suicidal acting-out?" asked Remo.

"None so far. My guess would be their keepers left that for the later stages of the training program, once they had the basics down and were approaching readiness for action in the field. It would not take that long to plant the seed with drugs and post-hypnotic suggestion, especially working with people conditioned from birth to obey without question.''

''What's the long-range forecast?''

''Hazy,'' Dr. Smith replied, a frown etched on his lemon face. ''There is still a world of difference, understand, between deprogramming these kids and making them productive members of society. The younger ones—I am talking six to nine years old, now—may be street safe by the time they hit their teens, but that is a guess. On the older ones, a quiet life in some nice home may be the best we've got to hope for.''

''Jesus. What about the infants?''

''Ah.'' Smith grudgingly allowed himself the bare suggestion of a smile. ''Now, there is some good news. Based on what the matron told us—what's her name again?''

''Althea Bliss,'' said Remo.

''Yes. If we can trust her statements—and FBI pediatric experts suggest we can—the infants range from three months to eleven months in age. Tests are being run to see if Radcliff's people shot them up with anything, but they are too young for any kind of operant conditioning to really stick. He could have taken steps to break the bonding cy-cle—that is apparently one of the keys to breeding psychopaths—or shown them gangster movies day and night, but it is a case of wait-and-see. Meanwhile they are being well cared for, and no one will be teaching them to load a gun before they learn to write their names.''

"The mothers?"

"Well," said Smith, "the twelve who were evacuated from Ideal Maternity are all safe and sound."

"That's a blessing anyway, I suppose."

"Apparently," Smith said, "a couple of the girls saw nothing wrong with what went on inside the home. God knows what they were used to in their families or on the street. I hate to think about it."

Remo nodded, once again surprised by the gentility apparent in this man who daily ordered death the way most people order coffee with dessert.

"Those two will unquestionably be forced to put their children up for adoption. Mentally unstable teenagers with no support or families, raising Radcliff's clones—I shudder to think of what their grown offspring would be like."

"And the others?"

"They will be giving up the babies for adoption as well, just as planned—except they will be adopted by the government. More tests on the genetic end, and toxicology, that sort of thing. We may hang on to them awhile, as a control group. It is difficult to say for certain."

"You can't just place them for adoption?"

"Not until it is determined that it is safe," Smith explained. "You are probably familiar with the great debate on criminal behavior—nature versus nurture. Did abuse make Jeffrey Dahmer what he was, or is 'the bad seed' a reality? We cannot take any chances on a deal like this, until we know exactly what it was that Radcliff did and how it pays off down the line. I am not unleashing any new psychopaths on an unsuspecting world, if I can help it.''

"All those wasted lives," said Remo.

"Maybe not. It is still an open question," Smith reminded him. "Things may work out, for some of them, at least."

"I hate to ask about the process," Remo said.

"Well, now, that is good news, from my perspective. Looking through the files, I have not found a thing so far that details Radcliff's work. For all we know, it may be lost."

"Or maybe not."

Smith shrugged again. "It is never really possible to prove a negative, of course. We cannot rule out the possibility that someone else has Radcliff's paperwork—the daughter, maybe, I do not know. She has not satisfied me of her innocence, by any means, but realistically..."

He let the statement trail away, unfinished. Remo saw where Smith was headed with it, and he didn't like the view.

"Somebody else could start the whole thing over, right? That's what you're saying."

"Theoretically. To start from scratch and follow Radcliff's method, with the breeders, I suppose we are looking at another twenty years or so before the finished product would be ready. In the meantime, we can try to scrounge around, dig up more information on his work, find out if there is a way to nip it in the bud.''

"Is anybody else left from the old Eugenix crowd?" asked Remo.

"There were several lab assistants and another doctor with the company," said Smith. "The doctor is dead, unfortunately. He died in a car crash, back in 1986. Too late for us to say if it was really accidental, but the point is moot, anyway. We are looking for the others, but you should not get your hopes up, after thirty years."

I never do, thought Remo. And he said, "I won't."

"Anyway," Smith said, "it is our game now. We will try to make the most of it. Congratulations on another job well done."

"I don't feel much like celebrating," Remo told him.

"No, of course not. But it could be worse, you know. If someone at the Bureau had not checked those fingerprints against the dead file, we would have no idea what Radcliff was pursuing, even now. He would still be out there, breeding new assassins."

"Right. The good news."

"Absolutely. In this business," Smith reminded him, "we sometimes have to take what we can get and hope for the best."

"You still believe in wishes?" Remo asked.

"Not for us," Smith answered truthfully. "We do what we do so that others may wish."

"Like smoking Radcliff."

"Absolutely. If there is a monster in this mess, I would say he qualifies."

That much was true, at least, and there was one less monster in the world today, because of CURE and Remo's efforts. That was something, anyway.

"I'm out of here," he said, already on his feet and moving toward the office door. "One thing—if you can find a way to keep me posted on the kids, how they make out..."

"I will see what I can do," Smith said.

By his tone of voice, Remo could tell that the CURE director would be keeping track of the progress of Radcliff's experimental children.

Quietly Remo left the office.

CHIUN HAD the television on when Remo got back to the condominium they shared. Some kind of odorless broth was on the stove, just simmering. Chiun knew how long the average meeting took with Smith, and lunch was almost ready now. It would be timed to coincide with the end of the local news and the beginning of another infomercial.

Remo stirred the broth and waited for the editorial segment of the news to begin. Chiun never watched that part of the broadcast. When the editorial started, Chiun got up to join him, fetching bowls and silverware.

"How fares Mad Harold?"

"He's well," said Remo, "and he sends felicitations, Little Father."

Chiun allowed himself a narrow smile. It always pleased him when the men of power and influence acknowledged their indebtedness to him and to Sinanju. All the more so when they paid in gold.

"What is to be done with all the children?"

This was a question he had hoped Chiun would not ask. Children were considered sacred in the tiny village of Sinanju. Untouchable. At least to the Master.

"Nobody knows, for sure," said Remo. "Some of them might be too far gone. The rest may make it. Who knows?"

"You are troubled for them," said Chiun.

"Not really," Remo was lying now, and badly.

"You must bear in mind that they were never meant to be," the Master of Sinanju said. "The very fact of their existence insults Nature. They are products of an evil man's demented fantasy."

"They're children," Remo said.

"Created in a laboratory, with a single purpose," Chiun insisted.

"Like me, you mean."

The Master of Sinanju stared at Remo for a moment, thoughtfully. When next he spoke, his voice had lost its edge.

"Pah! You are not a product of some demented medical experiment," Chiun spit. "Although you have a purpose, it is a great one. You are heir to Sinanju."

"Is what I do so different, Little Father?"

"You compare a blacksmith with a surgeon and

ask me to tell the difference?'' Chiun allowed himself a small expression of annoyance. ''Remo, you sometimes wallow in self-pity as if it were fragrant oil.''

''You've got a point. But since we were speaking of 'demented' to describe some humans, where's Grandmother Mulberry these days? Though she is more like a rattler's grandmother with me.''

''She, ah, had family problems back home,'' Chiun said, ''of uncertain outcome yet.''

''And I'm future Reigning Master. Although sometimes I think I still have much to learn.''

''Acknowledging your ignorance is proof of embryonic wisdom,'' Chiun replied. ''Now, hush! We must eat in front of the television. 'The Amazing Contraption of Dr. Juice-Matic' is about to begin.''

''Turn up the volume, will you? Remo asked. ''I wouldn't miss it for the world.''

**A violent struggle for survival
in a post-holocaust world**

JAMES AXLER
DEATH
LANDS ®

Freedom Lost

Following up rumors of trouble on his old home ground, Ryan and
his band seek shelter inside the walls of what was once the largest
shopping mall in the Carolinas. The baron of the fortress gives them
no choice but to join his security detail. As outside invaders step up
their raids on the mall, Ryan must battle both sides for a chance to
save their lives.

**The Stony Man commandos deliver hard justice
to a dispenser of death**

STONY MAN™ 33

PUNITIVE MEASURES

The Eliminator—a cheaply made yet effective handgun
that's being mass-produced and distributed underground—
is turning up in the hands of street gangs and criminals
throughout the world. As the grisly death toll rises, the
Stony Man teams mount an international dragnet against a
mastermind who knows that death is cheap. Now he's
about to discover that Stony Man gives retribution
away—free.

Available in February 1998 at your favorite retail outlet.

Bolan severs a mob-Chinese alliance
exporting terror...

DON PENDLETON's

MACK BOLAN®

Rage FOR JUSTICE

Bootleg electronic goods are manufactured by slave labor in
a remote part of China, then imported by a Houston-based
mob family and sold below market prices. This unholy
alliance is making huge profits off U.S. consumers and the
misery of the oppressed Chinese. A CIA probe goes sour,
killing one agent and forcing another on the run, calling on
Mack Bolan in the name of old friendship.

But even as Bolan revs into high gear, angered by ruthless
greed, he knows that the stakes are high and the odds
increasingly tough to call.

Available in January 1998 at your favorite retail outlet.

James Axler

OUTLANDERS™

OMEGA PATH

A dark and unfathomable power governs
post-nuclear America. As a former warrior of
the secretive regime, Kane races to expose the
blueprint of a power that's immeasurably evil,
with the aid of fellow outcasts Brigid Baptiste
and Grant. In a pre-apocalyptic New York City,
hope lies in their ability to reach one young
man who can perhaps alter the future....

Nothing is as it seems. Not even the
invincible past....

Available February 1998,
wherever Gold Eagle books are sold.

Taking Fiction to Another Dimension!

Deathlands

#62535	BITTER FRUIT	$5.50 U.S.	☐
		$6.50 CAN.	☐
#62536	SKYDARK	$5.50 U.S.	☐
		$6.50 CAN.	☐
#62537	DEMONS OF EDEN	$5.50 U.S.	☐
		$6.50 CAN.	☐

The Destroyer

#63220	SCORCHED EARTH	$5.50 U.S.	☐
		$6.50 CAN.	☐
#63221	WHITE WATER	$5.50 U.S.	☐
		$6.50 CAN.	☐
#63222	FEAST OR FAMINE	$5.50 U.S.	☐
		$6.50 CAN.	☐

Outlanders

| #63814 | EXILE TO HELL | $5.50 U.S. | ☐ |
| | | $6.50 CAN. | ☐ |

(limited quantities available on certain titles)

TOTAL AMOUNT	$
POSTAGE & HANDLING	$
($1.00 for one book, 50¢ for each additional)	
APPLICABLE TAXES*	$ _____
TOTAL PAYABLE	$ _____
(check or money order—please do not send cash)	

To order, complete this form and send it, along with a check or money order for the total above, payable to Gold Eagle Books, to: **In the U.S.:** 3010 Walden Avenue, P.O. Box 9077, Buffalo, NY 14269-9077; **In Canada:** P.O. Box 636, Fort Erie, Ontario, L2A 5X3.

Name: _____

Address: _____ City: _____

State/Prov.: _____ Zip/Postal Code: _____

*New York residents remit applicable sales taxes.
 Canadian residents remit applicable GST and provincial taxes.

GOLD EAGLE ®

GEBACK20A